WHEN A *Boss* LOVES YOU

Pharaoh & Paige

A NOVEL BY

NOLA JEWELS

Just a note . . .

This book is a re-release. This story was special for me because it was my very first published work. The perfect book to start my writing journey. It was released originally as a series. However, I've decided to combine the series and make it one complete novel. A complete novel with a beautiful new cover. (Thank you, Designsbyaja). Welcome to Pharaoh and Paige's world. I hope you love them as much as I loved creating and sharing them.

-Nola

Acknowledgements

The love of God is both humbling and inspiring. I thank Him for being the leader in my life. His plans are always bigger and then I can imagine. I'm so glad they are. Frank, thank you for allowing me to pursue my passion without question. Also, for allowing the laptop light to shine bright in the middle of the night. Jaelin, Jaiela, Malcolm and Malik, my hearts, thank you for understanding when I locked myself in my room. Also, for all your encouraging words. I am honored to have my family support me as hard as they do. Jessica, thank you for reading my first pages and screaming with excitement with me every step of the way. Thank you to everyone that has been a guiding light to me on this journey. I appreciate all the support, text messages and love I have received. This is the first of many, many great works to come. I look forward to learning and growing on this journey. I plan on riding until the wheels fall off. ***Laissez les bons temps rouler***.

Synopsis

Atlanta's perfect power couple Paige and Kane have it all from the outside looking in. However, looks can be deceiving. Kane desires power and money, and he will do anything to get it. Paige wants love and security. She changed herself hoping to get that love, only to find that Kane's love and loyalty to her wasn't what she thought. Feeling lost and alone and not sure of who she is anymore, she calls upon the one person who she knows will help get her back on track. Synplicity 'City', steps up immediately to help her cousin Paige. Together again, they help each other through their relationship problems.

City has been running from a commitment with Hakeem. The thought of giving up on her career just to settle down in one place with one person scares the hell out of her. Hakeem 'King' Mann was growing sick of waiting on City to love him and give him a real relationship. There on again and off again non-committed relationship was driving him crazy. He was a boss in the streets, but he couldn't manage to boss or control her. She wanted to keep globe-trotting, and he wanted her there with him. He knew what she was hiding and was ready to confront her about it when a secret he's been keeping comes out of hiding. Will his secret tear them apart forever?

While Paige is trying to fix her future, she runs into her past. Ace 'Pharaoh' Mann, the person who showered her will love but created the moment painful in her life. Ace is a boss in the street, but he loves Paige and is willing to give it all up for her. Pharaoh sees another opportunity to right his wrong. He wants nothing more than to love and protect her the way she deserves. Paige is forced to make one of the biggest decisions of her life. She must choose between her past, or her present.

What happens when the perfect life you've created turns into a nightmare? When faced with secrets, can you live with the pain they will bring? Can love out weight the hurt? What's the point of a relationship when it's breaking you. Paige and City's worlds are about to crumble and they're about to find out what happens *when a boss loves you*.

The Dream

A Storm is Coming

My soul cried for you. It begged for your presence in the midst of my pain. It craved your kisses like summer craved rain. My body called for your touch. The tears flowed like rain, with each drop yelling and screaming your name.

She usually pissed excellence. But today, she only brought drama. Her world is cloudy, and it is raining pain and hurt. She needs to move pass it but the steps, the process isn't moving in the right direction. After all, you can't outrun a storm. She needs encouragement. She needs help. She needs love. Hell, she needs fairy dust and a magic wand, but she would settle for happiness. Her requirement isn't much and it doesn't cost a thing. Or does it? Yet, it is the only thing that escapes her grasp. Moments like this are rare but when they come, she hides under the covers and screams silently. But today she is screaming out loud, hoping he hears. All she needs is him. He will bring the happiness she needs.

The moment she is there she can't remember how she arrived. She can't remember the drive over or pressing the elevator button. Yet, there she stands. In that moment she is unsure of everything in her life. This isn't her. She doesn't do these things. Buts she needs this thing, whatever it is. She needs to escape all the things that are hurting her. All the pain. All the thoughts raced in her mind. But it isn't just her mind racing; her heat is also racing. For just a moment, she turns to glace back down the hallway. She can leave right now. She could run. But run to what? She needed this. She needed to feel something more than pain. She raises her hand to press the doorbell. She hears footsteps and realizes it is too late to turn back.

The door opens, and he stands there with those eyes and a smile she knows so well. He pulls her in for a hug. The warmth of his body is intoxicating. It is welcoming to her, and she feels her stress disappear. His cologne is inviting, and she doesn't want to let him go. As if he senses how she feels, he pulls her tighter and squeezes. When they separate, no words are spoken as he takes her hand into his and leads her into his home. They walk down a hallway to his bedroom and then into his bathroom. He fills the tub with water and sits on the edge of the tub and pulls her in front of him. He slowly unbuttons her blouse and removes it from her body. Next, he unzips her skirt and as it falls to the floor, she hears a gasp. She covers herself, feeling embarrassed as his eyes roam over every inch of her body. He begins to tell her, 'you look beautiful and so does your body.' He stands to place kisses on her cheeks and then her neck, as he removes her bra and panties. He helps her into the tub and washes her slowly. She is amazed how good it feels to be taken care of for just a moment. She's always the one taking care of everyone else. But to lay back and get pampered is amazing.

Once he's done, he helps her out the tub and dries her off. He walks her to the bed and says, 'lay down on your stomach, let me take care of you.' No shame, no hiding her scars or fat this time. Besides, he's seen all of her and has not turned away yet. He begins to massage lotion and oils on her body. She doesn't know how he knows vanilla is her favorite scent. But the warm and inviting scent relaxes her even more. He starts at her neck, then goes down to her back. As he approaches her ass, she tenses up. But he skips it and goes to her feet. She is so glad she got a pedicure last weekend. His hands are so huge they almost make her small feet disappear. As his hands begin to travel upward again toward her thighs, he begins to separate her legs. His huge, strong hands are caressing her ass, and she feels the moisture between her legs. And she craves—no needs—him to touch her there. But she can't speak, only soft moans are coming out. Suddenly, he kisses her right butt cheek, then as not to make the left one jealous, he does the same to it. His hands are still rubbing the middle part of her thighs, continuing to make their way up. But his kisses, those soft kisses are driving her crazy. It's more than moisture now; she has a river starting to flow.

He leans to whisper in her ear, 'may I?' And she feels his hardness against her. She responds by begging, 'please.' His fingers are at her opening, rubbing and caressing. She feels his fingers enter her, and hears him say, 'you're so wet; she missed me.' His breath on her back is driving her crazy. What kind of oils did he use? She is burning up. She feels like she is melting but coming alive at the same time. Before she can compose herself, he spreads her legs open wider and she feels his tongue enter her. He is licking and sucking and biting her like she is his last meal. She can taste the blood in her mouth from biting down on her bottom lip so hard. She arches her back and before she can bend her knees, she can feel an orgasm coming so strong she almost screams from the pleasure. But before she reaches it, he flips her over and whispers, 'I want to see your face when you cum.' As he wraps her legs around his waist, she feels his dick at her entrance, and she smiles. Before he enters her, he says, 'tell me you missed me.' And she says, 'I did.' He says, 'oh, you want to be bad?' And slaps her ass. The burn from the slap makes her even wetter and turns her on even more. 'Tell me you missed me so I can come inside.' She closes her eyes; afraid he will see into her soul. And whispers in what could almost be mistaken as begging, 'please, I missed you so much.' He enters and says, 'open your damn eyes, look at me, feel me.' She screams yes, as he fills her up with all of him and begins to stroke slowly and then starts to speed up as they are staring at each other eye to eye. His hands are lifting and pressing her left leg, damn near splitting her body into two, and he dives deeper and deeper into her. He stares directly into her eyes and it's so damn sexy, she can't contain herself from smiling and enjoying this feeling. Her head starts to swim, and she can't move, and her orgasm is right there, and she screams, but she opens her eyes and the room is dark. She is no longer at his home. She is in her bed dripping wet and sweating. It was just a dream. A dream about him again. She gets out of bed and checks the clock; it's 3 am. She walks to the bathroom to take a shower. This is one night she is glad her husband isn't home. She clearly remembers calling out a name in her dream. But what a damn dream. Or was it just a dream?

Chapter One

Fairytales and Promises
Paige Turner Daniels

I promise to love you forever and a day but the day after I will give my love to me because the fairytale will have ended, and I will be free.

I awake to the smell of coffee. That only means he just got here. And I know that because I was up until 5 in morning trying to get back to sleep. I went to the bathroom to handle my hygiene, and my mind was filled with visions from my dream. I smiled to myself, replaying everything in my mind. I could still feel his hands, his mouth and body on me. But it was only a dream, and I had to face reality. Walking into the kitchen seeing the back of his nappy ass head has me hot. And not the "I want him" hot, no, the 38 hot that makes a woman snap. Look at him sitting there with not a worry in the world. I swear this man right here.

"Good morning. Kane, was your trip good?" I ask. "It was good. But I missed you," he responds.

Sure, you missed me. You missed me so much you made sure all my calls went straight to voicemail each time I tried to call you. I'm so sick of him lying to me. I bet he says, *oh you know my phone needed charging.* "I called you a few times. But I didn't get an answer."

"I left my phone charger in my suitcase at the hotel. So, when I was done with the conference my phone was dead. I plugged it in but forgot to turn it back on. Plus, I was exhausted. My conversation would have been nothing but snores," he says with a chuckle.

But I am not fooled. I can see the lies swimming around like a fish out of water. And I can also hear it in his tone. Then he has the nerve to chuckle. I know bullshit when I hear it. He really thinks I can't see through his lies. And if I call him on it, I know he will come up with another excuse. Then, we'll be in here fussing. And I'm just not for it. Besides, I think he gets off on defending himself. I guess that's why he's one of the top defense lawyers in Atlanta.

"Well, I guess." I force a smile. "The important thing is you're here now. Do you want me to fix anything in particular for dinner?"

"No, whatever you make is fine. Perhaps, I'll stop by your office for lunch," he says moving toward me, grabbing me by the waist. Taking his finger, he traces the very top of my breast that must be enticing him through the white button-up blouse I'm wearing. "Then, I could make up for the time I was gone. Show you how much I missed you."

He slides his hand down my knee-length pencil skirt with all intentions on lifting it and getting in a quickie before I leave. But I block and curve him. This man used to be so fine to me. Kane stands at 6'1 and his light skin reminds me of Boris Kodjoe, but his body isn't the same. He is slim, but he has muscles everywhere. He works out 3 or 4 days a week to keep in shape. I loved feeling on his six-pack and the comfort I felt when he wrapped his arms around me. But right now, I just feel… well, I feel sick.

"I have a meeting bright and early. I can't be late today. And I'm not available for lunch either. I'll be picking you up a charger. That way, maybe you can call your wife, check on her or see if she is dead or alive. Two days of nothing. You really expect me to believe for two days you, the person who is glued in his phone, who happens to have his phone in his hand right now, didn't realize it wasn't charged or powered on? You got some damn nerve.

Nah, go back to whatever hoe you just climbed up out of and see if she is available for lunch. You got me fucked up with your bullshit. Thought I would let it slide. You're lucky I'm dressed to impress, or I would take these red bottoms   off and bust you all upside your head."

"Come on Paige don't start this shit today. I just told you what happened."

"Yeah, yeah, and you think I'm boo, boo the fool."

"I don't want to fuss with your ghetto ass. It's too damn early for you to be nagging me. You know I hate to be bugged when I'm away anyway. I told you, you're too damn clingy," he says and walks right out the kitchen.

"Oh, so now I'm ghetto and clingy?" I scream, following him to the other room.

"Yes, Paige, like right now you are walking around here screaming and shit. All you had to do was greet me with some good morning head like any good wife would. But no, I get met with all this neck swinging and not neck work. You should be grateful I work this hard providing for us. In fact, you are lucky I blessed you with my presence. I could have gone straight to work."

"Blessed me! Really Kane! I blessed you by still being here. Like a dumb ass, waiting on you. Hoping you would walk in the door and apologize or even show some remorse for not calling me or answering my calls. Show a little glimpse of the man I married. The man who vowed to love me and promised to never hurt me. But you've done everything to me except love me. What have I done to deserve this treatment?"

"You do this! This nagging, this fussing, this right here. Look, go to work. I'll see you later," he says, turning away from me, walking toward the bathroom and slamming the door.

I stood there staring at the door for a minute in disbelief. *Don't let him keep doing this shit to you. Get it together Paige. I should break down that damn door and go upside his head.* The more I think about it the more I hate he brings out those emotions in me. I am not this person who's loud and angry. But I'm fed up with him acting like it's my fault.

I'm fed up with being hurt. This doesn't feel like love, and it doesn't feel like the fairytales I read about as a child. And it damn sure isn't what he promised on our wedding day. Walking out, *I just feel so defeated.*

Chapter Two

The Need For Perfection

Kane Daniels

I can be yours, within reason. I can give you all you need, but don't need it all. I can accept imperfect, but not your flaws. I can love you, but when and how I want.

Letting the water run over my body in the shower, I think about Paige. Watching her walk into the kitchen this morning, I saw the look on her face. The best thing about being an attorney is being able to read body language. I read her right away; she was mad as hell. She looked good in the pencil skirt she was wearing; it showed her curves perfectly. Paige Turner-Daniels is a golden-brown beauty, that has a body that won't quit. She's 5'7 with a small waist and hips, ass, and thick thighs that go on forever. She is just the right amount of thick. She is the shape women pay Dr. Miami to give them, but hers is all natural. Her hair was up in a messy bun showing the pure beauty in her face. She wore no make-up, just some lip gloss. And that was enough to have my dick jumping at attention looking at her perfect lips. But the more she talked, the more she turned me off. Yes, she is beautiful, but I want her submissive. And that she isn't. In fact, she is intelligent and smart, not at all what I expected when we first met. She isn't my usual and now I feel like it is coming back to bite me in the ass.

Her being smart was cool at first. Her money management skills were amazing. In less than a year her suggestion on investments had my account overflowing. I was already doing good, but who's turning down extra money? She helped me advance my career and she looked good while doing it. But she was head strong. She had this wild side that drove me crazy. Sometimes I would come home, and she would be listening to some bounce music, and I would be embarrassed to look my neighbors in the eye the next day. Image is everything. I've attempted to tame her. Well, mold her into the perfect wife. The wife my colleagues brag about, that doesn't question them on what they do. That only opens their legs when needed. They are homemakers and not working a 9- 5 still trying to climb the ladder to success.

Paige is the opposite of those things. She loves working. And because she is good at what she does, she is a top accountant at her firm. She questions me on everything I do. She wants to know everything all the time. Every convention she wants to be there and every engagement she makes sure she attends. Until a couple of months ago. We were at the client's engagement in their home in Alpharetta. About an hour into the party, I saw Leslie on the other side of the room. Leslie and I have been sleeping with each other for the past 3 years. She was fine with me never committing to her and I loved how she let me just be a man. She knew and she accepted my marriage with Paige along with the other woman in my life. I sent her a text to let her know she looked beautiful, and I watched her blush. When I turned around and saw that Paige was chatting away with someone's wife, I told Leslie to meet me in one of the bedrooms. Before I could turn and make sure Paige was not paying attention, I saw Leslie heading toward the stairs. I adored her willingness to not question me and just do whatever I asked. I found her in one of the bedrooms and allowed her to do what she does best.

She told me she was nervous because Paige was downstairs. I told her that only got me harder knowing I'm with the person I wanted, with the person I didn't want right downstairs. She was on her knees and pulling at my zipper before I could plant my feet good.

She wasn't the brightest, but I swear she studied head. She gives the best head I've ever had in my life. She almost sucked the soul out of me and swallowed my dick. When I walked back downstairs with Leslie walking right in front of me, Paige was standing at the bottom of the stairs watching us. I just knew she would ask but she didn't say a thing. I was starting to finally think she was getting in line with being a good wife. But this morning proves she's still not ready to be controlled.

After showering and getting dressed, I walk over to my safe and open it. I need to make sure the files I need are still safe and secure. I made sure when we got this apartment, I installed his and her safes. She thought it was cute and that I was doing it out of love. Really, I installed it that way to keep her prying ass away from all the things I was involved in. I place the documents I received this weekend inside the safe and close it. I am one of the top defense attorneys in Atlanta, and I didn't get to the top by just doing an excellent job. I work hard at making sure I have something on everyone, to get and keep me at the top. I just need to make my plan with Paige work correctly. If it does, I won't have to cover my ass anymore. I will be set for life. I just need to deal with her disobedient ass a little while longer. I'll stop by and bring her flowers or one of those fruit baskets for lunch and offer to take her to her favorite place for dinner and promise to spend more time with her. She'll eat that up and be just fine. She's easy. In the meantime, let me text Leslie. Just thinking about her has me wanting to get my dick sucked right now. Since Paige isn't willing to do it, someone will.

Chapter Three

Paige Turner-Daniels

I show the world pieces of me. It can't handle all of me. I smile with grace, careful not to leave a trace of my need for its warm embrace. I am empty inside, but I refuse to ever show that side. So, I stand still, feeling invisible, while the world continue to turns around me.

"Good morning Danielle," I speak, walking past my assistant. She smiles and hands me a package while still talking on the phone. I walk into my office prepared for the day. Although I am mentally exhausted; I can't let it show. I am a professional and I don't want these people all up in my business. I can't believe how Kane has changed. Total opposite of the man I met three years ago. I remember when he walked up to me at the Whole Foods and assumed I worked there because I had on green that day. I should've known then he was an asshole. But turning around to correct him, all I saw was this fine, light-skinned man. He was perfect, almost a twin to Boris Kodjoe, except his face was hairless. He smiled and that was it. We dated for a year, and I fell in love with him. We moved too quickly, everyone said, but I knew time couldn't tell you how to love someone. It only improved on the love. Or so I believed back then. I still had hope in love. I should have listened when my cousin told me she had reservations about us being together. And saying reservations was putting it mildly. She basically told me not to trust him, or as she put it, *his bitch-ass*! She flat out cursed him out on several occasions and even threatened to stab him if he didn't start treating me right. I should have listened to her. I wanted to call her and tell her how right she was, but it's been almost two years since we have spoken to each other. I let my relationship with Kane come between us. No, I didn't pick him over her because I loved her too much. But I was sick of all the fussing, so I just stopped calling her as much and I stopped going to her events. But I still support her. She is this great photographer and looking at her website right now, I can still see the world through her eyes. She always views the world in this way that makes it look beautiful. I click on her recent gallery, and I see a picture she took in Japan. It is a lady sitting at a table with a drink and a book in her hands with her legs crossed. The view is amazing overlooking the city. However, the model has sadness in her eyes. The caption read, ***What's a Good View Without a Good Page Turner to Read.*** I smile, and my eyes start to mist up. I miss her too! It has been too long. So, I pick up the phone to call the only person who I know will make me feel better.

"Well, well, it's about time you seen my damn Bat signal. I was about to march on down to that damn fancy ass building you work in and cut a fool in there just to get your attention," Synplicity answers.

"In order for you to march in here that would require you to be physically in town. And from the looks of it, you're a million miles away." I smile.

"And that's where you would be wrong. I'm only a few hours on a plane ride away. I'm back in NY now. That Batman signal was from two weeks ago. So, like I said, I was getting ready to come down there and act a fool."

"NY, that brings back memories," I say with a sadness in my voice.

"I know but it's not the same without you. Take some time off and come see your used to be favorite cousin. We can hang out and catch up. Or we can hit the clubs and pick up men and really have a good time."

"You are still crazy I see. Now you know I can't just drop everything and fly away just to hang out. And you must have forgotten I'm married, so I can't pick up no one."

"Well, I sure was hoping you had dumped that no good bastard by now. But I know, I know you love him. But come on, it'll be fun, and we don't have to club. We can eat at all our favorite places," Synplicity begs.

"Don't call him a bastard. Let me do that."

"Ohhh, that means he has done something. Spill it. Or do I really need to make a trip down there? Just say the word."

"No City." Everyone calls her City for short. She hated being called Syn when we were growing up. She said it made her feel funny and like Jesus wasn't going to let her in heaven. So, I called her City one day and she was City from then on.

"That's not spilling it. Come on, tell me what Kane's ass has done now. Or better yet, hop on the next thing smoking and come tell me over real tea or vodka. Whichever you prefer. Please, my little Paige Turner."

Just as I am about to say no again, my assistant walks in with one of those big edible arrangements. I looked at the card because I knew it was from Kane. This is his go-to method to get me to forgive him. Usually, he would send me flowers and make us plans for dinner. I open the card, and the words feel like a knife stabbing me in the heart. *Thanks for this weekend Kay, keep that box tasting fresh just the way I like it.* I should go to his office and fight him. But the thing is, I don't want to fight for him. Truth is, I am not even mad or shocked. This isn't the first time, so I am just numb to it. I don't know if that is a good or bad thing. Good or bad, I am about to escape it for a few days.

"Paige, you still there?"

"Yeah, I'm still here. I'll come," I say, barely above a whisper.

City starts screaming into the phone and I know she is jumping up and down. I can't wait to see her. I hung up with her and ask Danielle to clear my schedule for the rest of the day and the next four days. I tell her it is a family emergency. I know Kane is probably out of the house. I know I can make it home and pack without him knowing anything. I booked my flight on the elevator ride to the parking lot. I can't even remember the last time I took a trip for pleasure. Everything was Kane or business. I know the fight I will face when I get back. See the thing about Kane is he can dish it, but he can't take it. He likes control. If he can't control it, he wants nothing to do with it. What he doesn't realize is I'm about to snatch back my control. I'm not into games like him and I respect my vows, but I need a moment to feel like myself again. I want to feel something in my life like I felt in my dreams. I just want to feel alive again. And my dreams make me feel alive and free. Hell, they make me feel amazing. I hope this trip can wake up those feelings in me and it might make Kane wake up too. Just maybe he will realize how much I mean to him, and we can still save this marriage. But right now, I am about to start enjoying my life again.

Chapter Four

Pleasure and Pain
Synplicity "City" Walker

No, it isn't simple when it comes to you. It's complex just accepting you. The goals I made, the things I wanted, never included you. You, the one I never dreamed of and now I can't dream without.

"What's got you in here all smiles and screaming like a mad woman, beautiful?" Hakeem asks walking into the room. "It's only the fact that my awesome cousin has finally become aware of the asshole she married. She's coming to visit. And I don't mean like in a week or two. Like she'll be here today. I can't wait to see her," I answer, smiling hard as hell.

"That's great bae. What made her want to come this time? You've been asking to see her for a while."

"Well, like I said, I think she realizes she married an asshole."
"Listen, when she gets here don't do that, okay."

"Do what?"

"Don't give me those damn innocent eyes. You know how you do. You will harp on shit for years. That's how the divide came in between you and her."

"But you have to admit her coming on a moment's notice is strange. Well, maybe not strange. Because Paige was always moving and doing her own thing.

It was like the wind would blow and she would blow with it. Until. . ." I can't bring myself to complete the sentence without the thoughts going through my mind. The flashes of my cousin in my head make me close my eyes and hold my head in my hands.

I hear walking and I feel the soft dip next to me. Hakeem grabs my hands and encloses his hands around them. "I know what you're thinking about, but City, don't bring yourself back there. Let the past be the past. And let this be something good for you and her." He takes his hand and lifts my face until our eyes meet. He starts smiling. "You know you are still as beautiful as the first night I saw you." Looking into Hakeem's eyes, I remembered the first time I saw him. He was simply beautiful. If that word can be used to describe a man. He was my color, which usually was a turn off, but his skin was so smooth I just wanted to touch it to see if it was real. His eyes were light brown but not ordinary; they were a fiery cinnamon color, and I just couldn't pull myself away from looking then and even now.

"Just be there for her and listen to her. Ok?"

"Ok, I'll try."

"City!!!" He gives me a stern look.

"Ok, ok, I won't. I'll just relax and enjoy the time." Looking at Hakeem and feeling him near creates a sense of relaxation. No matter the situation or time or place, this feeling always makes me feel good. I stand up and make my way between his legs. Taking my hand, I started rubbing his head. Looking deep into his eyes, the lust is overwhelming. I need to feel him. Hakeem is far from what I want in my life. But he is everything I need.

The fact that we are completely opposite, I'm the hot-headed one and he is the calm and calculating one. He thinks things out and I just react. When we first met, I was reacting to how I wanted him. What keeps us together is how he made me realize I needed him. This feeling, this intense feeling with him is undeniable.

He became my shelter from every storm I had endured. That was unexpected after meeting him when I first came to NY to visit. He was my hero from the beginning and he's still my hero. It doesn't matter the state or country I travel to; I will always come back to him.

His hands go around my waist lifting my shirt. The way his hands move up and down my back and then to my breast has my legs weak. His fingers trace the red lace bra I am wearing and then slide back to my back, unsnapping it. My breast stands at attention as he starts caressing them softly and then sucking my nipples, twirling them around in his mouth. When he begins to bite them, it takes all my breath away. His hands move to the boy short panties I am wearing, removing them so quickly I barely notice. He stands up and I admire his chest. Yeah, I'm tall, but he's taller—6'4" with the body of a basketball player. He played basketball in high school only, but you can't tell that he stopped. His body is so well sculpted, it is like he just walked off the cover of NBA2K. His skin is like a Hershey's bar, just begging me to lick and take a bite of it. Sniffing him, I let his smell draw me in some more. I closed my eyes ready to take whatever he is about to give to me. He turns me so quickly I almost lose my balance, but with his arms wrapped so tight around me, I know I won't fall. I let him walk me over to the wall in the center of the room.

"Put your hands up!" He speaks the words so aggressively; I know if I still had my underwear on they would be soaked. "You're moving too damn slow." He doesn't give me a chance to move. He takes the lead and puts my hands up high, slamming my body against the wall. He presses his body so close I think we are going to become one. He doesn't speak again but I feel every word. This friendship, this relationship, this thing we share is so complex I can't explain it in any words. It is only a feeling. And I can't fight the feelings as he puts one hand around my wrists gripping them together, and the other travels down my body. My eyes are still closed but I know his eyes are on me, waiting for a reaction. I try to stay completely still, afraid to breathe too hard. I know what will happen if I don't. But the heat I am feeling has my heart feeling like it is about to beat right out of my chest. Just the thought of him inside of me makes me twitch just a little.

"I didn't say move. Did I? I see you like to do whatever you want. It's like you enjoy me punishing you. Turn around."

I turn and there, right in front of me, he stands completely naked. When did he take his clothes off? Never mind that, this man is everything. Every damn thing. From the way he stands so confident and so damn cocky as he strokes that monster between his legs. Again, I lick my lips in anticipation. I let my eyes travel every part of his frame. From the top of his head all the way down to his toes, fucking perfection. I smirk because I know my body is about to get worked.

"Oh, so did I give you permission to smile?"

"I didn't smile."

"I didn't give you permission to talk either. Now I have to show you who's boss before I give you this gift," he says, letting his package go and walking back over to me. That walk is even perfection. His hand is on my wrists again holding my hands in place over my head while the other travels my body. He caresses my face so softly it feels like I am dreaming. But this is all real. He slides his hand down to my breast and pinches my nipples, causing a moan to erupt from deep within me. I try to contain it, but I can't. And it is his turn to smirk. His fingers travel down my stomach, past my navel, and rest on my lady lips.

"Open your legs, and you better be wet for me."

I open my legs and bite my lip. I am more than wet; I am soaked. He toys with my opening and then finds my clit and rubs it for a moment before sliding his fingers in me. He is working his fingers in and out, while his thumb is still rubbing my clit. I bite my lip harder and close my eyes, trying to hold the orgasm that is building. I feel my body burning and wanting to move with his rhythm, but I can't. I want the gift he has for me, so I behave like a good girl.

"You are so fucking wet, Bae. Damn, I miss this when you're not here. Don't cum yet. Do you hear me? Keep your hands up and don't cum until I say so."

Whatever the question was I didn't hear it, and I am unable to answer it. And then I feel him release my wrists and open my legs a little more. Suddenly, it is not only his fingers, but it is also soft kisses I am feeling. He is kissing, licking and sucking the soul out of me. He wraps his hands around my legs, gripping my ass, and in one quick movement lifts me, hoisting my legs on his shoulders so he can stand and enjoy this meal a little better.

"Cum for me," he speaks in between all the slurping and sucking he is doing. That voice, and everything he is doing makes me lose control and I let loose an ocean. He drinks like he is thirsty and keeps going to pull another orgasm from me. It is a good thing he and the wall are holding me up because my legs are weak.

"Good girl, now I'll reward you." He lets me down easily and helps me when my legs wobble a little. "Since your legs are not working see if your knees are working, and you better make it good."

I love it when he demands what he wants. I am accustomed to being the boss with my business all the time. But this is different; I enjoy his control. I love the boss in him. Although, he thinks it is only sex he can command from me. If he only knew I would give him whatever he commands. I get down on my knees, all too eager to please him. Even his dick is all chocolate perfection. I am going to enjoy it more than him. Spitting on his dick to get it real nasty like he likes it, I stick my tongue out and let it move from the base of his dick to the tip.

I repeat the same motion underneath except I start at the tip and travel up to the base. I repeat the same motion underneath except I start at the tip and go to the base. I take his balls in my mouth, making sure not to use my hands, and hum on them for a minute and then return to the head and kiss the tip and put all of him in my mouth. I suck like my life depends on it. As I take more of him into my mouth, I feel him hit the back of my throat, my eyes start to water, and it feels like I will choke. I know I have him because I hear him moan and he puts his hand on the wall to balance himself. He is so large it is impossible to take all of him in, so I use my hands to work him a little more.

"Give me those hands. I told you to make it good. You can't handle me? I thought this was your dick. This not your dick?"

His eyes stare at me asking for confirmation. But I don't reply; I only comply. Yes, this is my dick, and I am never one to back down from a challenge, so I am going to prove it. I keep going even with the tears streaming down my face, taking in more and more of him. I want to give up, but when I look up at his face his eyes are closed, and he is in pure bliss, it makes me want to keep going. I feel him tighten the grip on my hands and push himself further into my mouth and moan while releasing his warm fluids. I swallow every drop.

"Shit, Bae, good fucking job."

He picks me up and carries me to the sofa where he bends me over and slams his dick into me, causing his name to slip from my lips. He slaps my ass and pulls my arms behind my back.

"Take this dick. Don't call my name now. You forget my name when you're all over the world so don't call it now. Just take it."

He slams in and out of me. I feel nothing but pleasure and pain. He lets my arms go and spreads my ass cheeks open more so he can get all of him inside of me. I can barely take it. All these years of having him inside me and still it always feels like I am a virgin again trying to compose myself. He hits my spot just right and I feel it in my chest. He pulls my hair that is in a ponytail and strokes like he is on a mission. "This shit so wet. Is it mine?"

"Yes," I scream. His strokes get slower and slower.

"It better be." And he releases again.

I am no good. I can't stand at all, so he carries me to the shower. He gently washes every part of me. I love this side of him too. The side that is gentle when I need it. I can feel how much he cares for me with every touch. When I turn to wash him, he lifts my chin and looks me in my eyes, placing a soft kiss on my lips.

"City, I love you."

I only respond with a smile. "I know." And just like that, I see the defeat in his eyes. He turns away, letting the water fall on his face.

This is the side of him that he doesn't show the world. And granted, he rarely says anything to me, but I know him well enough to read him. And I know he wants something solid from me, but I am content with the way we are. I am not one for titles and I enjoy my freedom. Yes, there are others, but Hakeem is my heart. I just know he isn't ready to accept all my sides, so I never show them all to him. I leave out the shower and I don't think he even notices. He is under the shower head allowing the water to run down his body, and I can tell he is deep in thought.

When he finally steps out, I have dried off and have my robe wrapped around me. I greet him with an open towel, ready to dry him off.

"Hakeem, you never have to question if I love you because I do. You know I have never been the sitting at home, waiting for you with dinner and your slippers type of girl. I enjoy the work I do and unfortunately, it requires a lot of travel. But distance doesn't change how I feel about you."

"I don't want you to be my dog, getting me slippers and shit. I want a real relationship with you. And I can't help it. I just like it when you're here and we can do this all the time."

Bending down drying off his legs, I look up and catch him smirking. "Aww, hell no. You mean what we did 10 minutes ago. Not this catering to the King mess."

"You know what I mean. But I like the extra too," he states, chuckling.

I stood and toss the towel at him, walking to the bedroom to get dressed. He walks behind me and kisses my neck. "Let's have dinner tonight."

"I would love to, but my favorite cousin is coming in town. It's about to be a party."

"Take it easy on her. Let her breathe first."

"Nope, I have her for a few days, maybe a week, so I want her to enjoy herself. I want to see some of the person she used to be come out, minus the bad memories. And maybe I can get her to stay with me just a little longer."

"What about the business trip this weekend to Paris?"

"I'm going to cancel it. I know it's a four-week project but if I get to spend one full week with her, losing out on this project is worth it. Besides, the owners really want my services, so they may wait."

"Well damn, now I feel played. You couldn't just stay for me. Just her?" Hakeem fake pouts.

"If you don't get out of here with that mess. You'll get to have me for three weeks. If that makes you feel better."

"Three weeks and you'll never want to leave me."

Tapping me on my ass, I turn, and he is fully dressed, looking good, and I feel my kitten purring again. *Calm down kitty.* "What are your plans today?"

"I just need to handle some business. You know, make this money. Money doesn't make itself. I'll call you. Have fun but not too much fun. And let me know when it's safe to come see her."

"Don't work too hard. And King, be safe." The concerned look I give him makes him stop in his tracks. I am not fooled by the legal businesses he holds. I know when he says make some money it involves something illegal and possibly dangerous. "Oh, and Hakeem, don't tell him that she's coming. I don't know if she can handle seeing him."

"City, I'm always safe. Don't you worry that pretty little head of yours. And I know. I won't say a word."

Kissing me on my cheek, he turns and walks out the door. Just like that, I feel the energy leave the room and want to open the door and tell him to come back. Instead of doing that, I prepare myself for this visit. I have a feeling it's about to be big trouble for me and her in this city for the next few days.

Chapter Five

Second Chances
Ace "Pharaoh" Mann

I never wanted some of you, I wanted all of you. I wanted to carry you in my arms and not just my mind. I wanted to touch your body and your soul. But those words I never did say and then you up and went away.

Meeting with this interior designer feels like a waste of my time. This is the fifth or sixth one I interviewed. Her reviews say she is the best, but so far, I can't tell. She is talking way too slowly and all the walking and bending in front of me is basically, doing the most. I want her to decorate my new restaurant not spread her damn legs. And everything in this presentation is saying nothing about her designs and everything about how she wants me. Her skirt is not only skintight, but also short as hell. Her shirt is so tight the buttons look like they are hanging on for dear life. At any moment, her boobs are going to pop out; she should've just let them hang. I hate when a woman offers herself like this. It shows as a form of desperation and makes her too easy. If she will offer it to me and she knows nothing about me, how many others will she give it to that easily? I feel my phone go off.

"Let's wrap this up," I state to her. Receiving the text from my brother has made me ready to get this little meeting over a lot quicker than this chic is moving.

"Ok, I haven't shown you the color scheme for the seats or tables. Do you want to continue another day?" she asks.

"No, I don't like the colors you're using to design the outside. They are too loud, so I can only imagine what you are trying to do in the inside. She likes pastel colors. It's softer and more appealing."

"She? I didn't see anything in your profile about a wife. Is she your head chef?"

Damn, did I say she? Come on dude, you slipping. "What does my profile have to do with colors?"

"Well, I like to know my clients before I work with them. That way I know how to approach the design. And your club has this similar color scheme. So, I assumed you wanted to stay with the same pallet. Is *she* your girlfriend? I knew a handsome man like yourself wasn't single."

Avoiding her question altogether, single, married or not, I don't want her. "If I wanted the same design as my club I would have gone with the same designer. I wanted something different, and it looks like you don't have what I want. Nothing I want. Thanks for coming out today." The shocked expression on her face says it all. But I'm a man about my business and right now she is wasting my time. I am ready to open this restaurant location, but I can't find the right designer. Either their designs are duplicating every place in New York, or they aren't speaking to me. My other location was easy to design and decorate myself because it was all me. It was symbolic of my moods.

Aces is three floors and a rooftop that is all of me. The first floor is a place to grab you some wings and beer. Of course, other food is served there as well, but my favorite is the wings. It is set up like a sports bar. A place where you can watch the game, grab some food, and hang for a minute. The second floor is my dance hall, a reggae club. You can leave from the first level and walk to the second floor and move to some reggae music or enjoy watching the ladies move to it. Now, the third floor is full of security, complete with velvet rope and a dress code. It is a top-of-the-line night club complete with elevated VIP sections.

The rooftop area is my favorite. There are huge, oversized sofas, with linen curtains draped around them. They surround the dance floor, and I positioned fans around that give the illusion of a breeze blowing so it reminds you of being on an island. I only open that area in the summer months. No one wants to freeze to death in the winter. Yeah, Aces is my baby.

I want my new place to have a distinctive look. When I purchased the building all I could think of was her. The way she looked, her smile and her smell. I remembered her telling me about this little eatery in France that she loved to spend hours at just people watching and sipping coffee and drawing. Her description of the booths was etched in my mind. She said it gave the place a homey feel even though she was a million miles away from home. I can still see the smile on her face as she spoke about it. That's the feeling I want. I want it to feel like her even if she wasn't there. I can replay that memory over and over in my mind. The only thing that is giving me peace is just thinking about the completion of it. I know nothing can replace her, but it is my dream and just maybe it will ease my pain of losing her.

As the designer is packing her things I hear the door open. And I see my brother walking my way. Hakeem is two years older than me, but I have him on the height at least by an inch. I'm 6'5. We both are chocolate. Standing next to him, anyone can tell we are brothers. He is the calm and cool one that loves attention. I am quiet and stand in the shadows. I just don't like all the attention. We both move the same in other ways. But I was ready to handle business all the time while he likes to play most of the time. The designer fly's pass without giving him a second look.

"I see you've been your sweet, charming self," he says, dapping me off and giving me a brotherly hug.

"You know how it goes. She wants what she can't have. And I don't have time for all that. I'm trying to get this money. All these chicks see is my money and their eyes start getting big and they start spending in their minds and thinking I only think with one head, so it'll be easy to get me."

"Shit, she was fine as hell. I was thinking with one head just now. Let me get her number; she got a fat ass. I need some decorating done," Hakeem says smiling.

"Now you know you already got your hands full. You don't need nothing or anybody else taking up your time."

"Hey, say less. But I see you been here working hard. I see it coming along." He gives my place a once over.

"Yeah, I was hoping to have it open in a few months. I just need the right designer to lay it out bring my vision to life for me." I can see this place competed in my mind. "You look relaxed."

"Well, you know I like to instruct people on what to do so I never need to look as dirty as you look right now."

"Nothing wrong with a little demanding work. Besides, I like working with my hands."

"Me too, just in a different way. That's what bosses do."

"I see. I see. Because I get my hands dirty, I'm not a boss?"

"I ain't say all that. I'm just saying your ass is cheap. You can hire people to take care of all this for you. Hire an assistant and let her pick out some designs."

"Fuck that, this my place. I'm the only one touching her."

"Her?"

"I didn't say her."

"Yeah, you said her. I heard you say her. So, you in here so much this is your new woman?"

"Man, shut your ass up." I chuckle, because if only he knew. I change the subject. "You got the info we need to move forward?"

"Yeah, I got everything on Mr. Fred Banks. He will be in Cali next month. I say we get it taken care of at that time because his security detail will be noticeably light. All the money he has and he's too cheap to pay for good security. Kind of sounds like you."

Shaking my head up and down. "Don't compare me to that pervert. It sounds like his loss and our gain. Get a copy of his itinerary and I'll get the designs of where he's staying and figure out the best spot to do it."

"Cool, we been on this one for a few months. I'm glad we finally got a break."

"I was getting ready to just take the chance and do him at his house." Holding my hands up, I already know what he is about to say. But I am a step ahead of him. I've seen the security detail at Mr. Banks' home in New Jersey a few nights a week. I don't have anything better to do anyway. I was getting to know his schedule well and I am sure I can pull it off with no problem. The crimes this man has committed, make me sick. He doesn't deserve to live. Now, Hakeem is in full lecture mode about planning. Stopping him in the middle of his sentence, I say, "I already know. I wasn't going to do anything without letting you know."

"I know you, Pharaoh. You like to do things on your own. But this time it's clean; we get in and get out. I want him dead too, but I want this money more. Get out your feelings."

"Man, go 'head with all that. If I wanted him gone sooner, it would have been done, and you know it. I only messed up once and it cost me a lot more than money. Miss me with that bs. I am not your child."

"Then stop acting like one."

Hakeem always took his big brother role a little too serious. I know he cared for me. But sometimes I just need him to be my brother. Hell, we have a daddy. He is locked up, but he is still our dad. And he took care of business very well. So, I don't need the lectures or him always pointing out my fuck ups. I know he cares. But I just need him to fall back and let me do me.

"I know I mess up sometimes. But you don't always need to bring it up. I'm reminded every day." My eyes scan the burn scars on my right arm that go from my shoulder to my hands.

"Sorry bro, I didn't mean it that way. I just need this job to be clean and performed exactly like the contract requests. Our reputations are on the line with this one. I want it to work seamless."

"His sick ass deserves to be shot and hung by his balls."

"I know, but to make this 2 million we make it look like a heart attack. Either way, the bastard dies."

"I get it. Don't worry, I'm keeping my cool."

"Ok, hey, let's go to Aces and get something to eat. I'm starving."

"Yeah, I could eat." I look around one more time, taking in all my hard work. This is going to be a great spot.

Sitting in Aces, I order the wings, and Hakeem wants the same but wants a beer. He keeps looking at me with concern, so I know he has some stuff on his mind and isn't sure how to tell me. Again, he is handling me as my dad and not my brother. "Bro, what's on your chest? Just say it."

"At the restaurant you said 'her.' Are you still thinking about her? I mean, I never really saw you as a café owner. But with all this gentrification going on I figured what the hell. It'll make dollars, so I know that makes sense. But I mean, are you trying to build this place to take the place of her?"

"First, nothing takes the place of her. And yes, I still think about her. She told me once about this café in Paris she loved visiting, and I just wanted a place like that here. It gave her peace so maybe it'll give me some too. I know it's dumb and you think I should move on. But I just need that peace."

"I'm your brother. I think everything your dumb ass does is dumb. But I understand it. I'm going to tell you something, but I need you to have a cool head about it. Plus, City told me not to say anything and she'll kill me if she knew I did. And you know she'll try it."

"You damn right she would. That girl is crazy. But go ahead, tell me."

"Paige is coming to New York. Just for a visit. Some shit going down with her and her husband, so she needed some space."

I can't speak, my mind is moving at such a quick pace, and I can't form any words. I trace the last thing in my mind I remember about her. Her last post was three days ago but I still scrolled through like it was my first time on her page. Her face was so beautiful and if I could go through the screen to get to her, I would. Her style is different now and I'll be damn if she hasn't grown into this fully developed woman that got thicker in all the right places. She was already fine, but the extra weight made her video vixen fine. The last picture she posted from three days ago simply said, *how can you feel so alone standing right next to a person.* She was unhappy, and I knew it. I wanted to reach out and comfort her. Maybe I should've DM'd her or commented. But the account I had was a ghost account so she wouldn't know I was watching her. I enjoyed watching her, but not in a stalker way, in a protective way. I wanted to know she was safe and happy even if it wasn't me making her happy. When I scrolled through her last few selfies, although she was smiling, her eyes weren't. The sparkle was gone. I swear if that stupid ass husband of hers did anything to hurt her, he will die a slow death. And that is a promise.

"Pharaoh, I need you to promise not to do anything. Let her be. I just wanted you to know. You know we don't keep secrets from each other, and I didn't want you to think I was hiding this from you. But City doesn't think she's ready to see you. So, give her some more time and space. No stalking her or following her."

"What did he do?"

"Who?" He has this look of confusion on his face.

"Her punk ass husband," I say with fire in my eyes. I don't like him for her. I don't care how happy she looks. I know he is a coward ass nigga. And I can't wait to hurt him the same way he hurt her. If in fact he did hurt, her. I never touched him because of her.

"Look bro, chill with all that. I don't know any details. All I know is City said she jumped at the chance of coming out here. City is excited too because they haven't talked or seen each other in years."

He is talking but I can't hear him; all I can think about is the sadness in her eyes and I want to make her smile again. I know I messed up in the past, but I've changed, and she needs to know.

"Aww shit, I never should have told you. Pharaoh, please don't go over there starting anything. And don't go killing her husband either. We don't know the situation. I need you to give me your word. She's been through enough and this trip means a lot to City. I don't need her on my back. I just got both of you back on good terms. So, give me your word."

I look at him for a minute, considering his words. He knows if I give him my word I will have to keep it. We believe a man's word is his bond and we stay true to that statement. Promising to stay away from Paige will be hard. I want her back in my life. I need her back in my life. But I also know me rushing her won't work either. After all, it's been almost seven years. I need to approach this the correct way.

"I give you my word, I won't do anything crazy." I won't do anything crazy, but I will get Paige back in my life. I just need to figure out how.

Chapter Six

Returning To You
Paige Turner-Daniels

Nothing changed but time. I'm still yours and you remain mine. I'll close my eyes and see yesterday. You're right here, next to me. When I reach my hand to touch you, I can't feel you. It's nothing but time that removed you.

The plane ride to New York was peaceful. It was peaceful because I felt free. I didn't worry about Kane. And that alone was freedom. I can't believe how much of my life just revolves around him. I think of how I am spending most of my days and how doing that doesn't involve anything I want to do or enjoy. I would wake up before him to make sure the coffee was ready. I knew he liked his clothes laid out and waiting for him when he got out the shower. I rushed home from work to make sure I had a hot dinner for him almost every night. Our weekends were spent going over by his friends or an event where we mingled so he could advance his career. And I would smile with all those fake wives. I don't have the same background as most of them, so I can't relate to them and no matter how hard I try to fit in, I don't. Yes, I'm well educated but I'm from the hood, and I don't hide it. I would stand there with a fake smile on my face dressed to impress, feeling lost and alone. I can't remember the last time we went to the movies or to dinner, just us. I love concerts and he refuses to go. Everything revolves around him and his needs. But the dumb part is, I allow it. So, I can't blame him for not pleasing me. I let the change come and did nothing to change it back. I didn't complain or voice my opinion. I didn't require him to put me first and it felt like it was too late. After all, you can't teach an old dog new tricks.

Getting my bags and walking through the airport, I spot City. Well, I spot the balloons and a big ass teddy bear and a sign that has my name on it. She is smiling so hard, and I admit that makes me feel so good. City's skin is a mocha chocolate, and she is flawless from head to toe. Her brown eyes are almond shaped and even her nose is perfect. She has perfect, full, pouty lips. Standing at 5'8, her body is slim, but she has curves. Her ass is perfect and so are her breast. I see she still doesn't like to wear a bra. I chuckle to myself. She could've easily been mistaken as a model, but she prefers to be behind the camera. She translates all her kindness and caring into the lens. In every frame, she captures this warm vision that speaks the story she wants to relay to everyone. It hits me how kind and loving she has always been to me. I drop all my stuff and run to her with my arms open wide. I hug her so hard. We are sitting in the middle of the airport crying and hugging each other. I missed the fuck out of my cousin.

"I missed you so much cousin." Finally letting her go, I started wiping my tears and getting myself together.

"I know. I missed you too, Paige," she says, trying to pick up all the stuff she has in her hands.

"I see you are still extra as hell. Why do you have all this stuff?"

"Oh, you don't want it? 'Cause, I wanted this bear anyway. It will look good on my bed."

"Umm, no ma'am!!! You can't give me a gift and take it back. Give me my shit." I take the bear out of her hand and press it against my body.

"I knew you would love it. Your ass hasn't changed one bit, you still like cheesy stuff."

I laugh, and it feels good to laugh. "You know I do. And don't call her cheesy. She's cute."

"Come on, let's get out of here before we have security shaking us down."

Riding through the streets of New York feels like a long-awaited homecoming. Except this isn't my home, but it feels like home. The sounds, the smell, the noise, everything about it makes me remember my first visit here.

"It's funny, everything looks the same, but different," I say more to myself than City.

"That's because our virgin Big Apple eyes were popped long ago. We've already taken our bite out of the apple. We chewed it up and loved it."

"Yeah, we did huh?"

We had just finished our second year of college at Tulane University, and I was excited about spending the whole summer in New York with my cousin City. We both had great opportunities that landed in our laps. I was attending an arts program, and she was attending a photography summit. We were so excited. It was really our first time traveling anywhere outside of our hometown New Orleans. My arts program was providing housing for us and City had a few photography internship interviews lined up after the summit to keep her busy while I attended my classes. My aunt Dana, City's mom, was so nervous about us traveling alone and being gone the whole summer. But we assured her we would be just fine. We were 22; you know, grown. My aunt Dana stepped in and raised me like her own daughter. My mom wasn't capable of raising me since she was serving life in prison. City and I were cousins, but we acted more like sisters. We were only months apart and extremely close. Seeing New York for the first time, I felt like my eyes would pop out. Everything was so big and bright and so busy. It was just like you imagined in the movies except I was able to reach out and touch everything.

"Let me hear you say, who's the bestest cousin of all." City walked into the apartment smiling and waving her hands.

"Well, I would say bestest, but that's not really a word," I replied, and she rolled her eyes.

"You know what, even you can't take this smile off my face. We are going to one of the hottest clubs tonight."

"No City, I don't have time for a club. I need to get my project finished and I have a meet-up with my group to work on our group project. I don't have time for one of your adventures."

"Look Paige, we did not come all the way to New York for you to keep your head buried in the books like you do at home. It's one night and I promise we'll leave early enough to get home, so you can make your meet-up. But we need this one night of fun. What harm can it do?"

I knew City well enough to know we were not leaving any party early. But I still agreed to go. We rolled together or not at all. "City, I better be able to get my project done or else your ass will be painting with me."

"Girl, I can't even color in the lines, so you know I'll have you back in time."

In the club, I sat at the bar. I wasn't much of a drinker; I preferred to watch. And the view from the bar was great. City was on the dance floor in her zone. My cousin could make friends in a minute. It always took me forever. I had trust issues. But City was this free spirit that attracted people to her like a magnet. She looked perfect dancing on the floor in a red spaghetti strap dress that was barely touched her thighs. She was tall and slender; her hair was down in curls, and she had her head back smiling so hard it looked like her jaws would crack. I held my small notepad in my hand and sketched the view I had of her. She didn't know it, but she was the perfect image for my project. I saw this guy walk up and start dancing with her and her smile disappeared. She turned to see him and there was that smile again. I knew she was pleased. So yep, it was gonna be a long night.

"Hey, Paige come sit upstairs with me in VIP."

"VIP, girl what?!!"

"Yes, the guy I was just dancing with invited me. Well us. We're a package deal."

"You can go, the view from here is good enough for me." I didn't want her to feel she needed to take care of me. I really was enjoying my view.

"Nope, can't do that. We do it together. Come on my little Paige Turner. Put the notebook up for one night and come on and have fun. I want you to dance with me. We get this moment only once. Let's enjoy it."

"Ok, ok. Let's go."

Walking up to the VIP section, it felt like someone was watching me. It was the same feeling I had at the bar. But when I looked around I didn't see anyone. Or no one with their eyes on me. It was a club, so a glance here and there was expected. The VIP section was very nice, but it was way too crowded. I guess everyone was getting an invite. All the girls kept eyeing me and City. They were staring at City, and I like they were *ready to fight, and I knew why, we were the best-looking ones up here. The guy City was with took us over to a sofa section and offered us both some glasses to drink. After the second drink, I swear he grew about eight arms because his hands were everywhere on City. She was trying to curve him, and it wasn't working. A bounce song came on and being from New Orleans that was right up our alley. I pulled her up to dance with me, away from Octopus arms. We were having a great time until he and his friend decided to come and dance on us. I was being groped by a guy who had his eyes closed and was displaying teeth that were yellow and chipped. At first, I thought it was golds. But nope, his teeth were that damn yellow. He smelled like ass and feet. I turned and whispered to City, "bathroom now."*

As we tried to make our way to the bathroom, he grabbed me by my waist and attempted to kiss me. I turned my head super quick. He said 'damn, don't be like that. Let me get a kiss'. His breath smelled worse than his body. It smelled like something had died in his mouth. I said, "I have to go to the lady's room. I'll be back." I grabbed City's hand and damn near dragged her to the restroom.

"Look City, I can't do it with him. He smells so bad. Who comes to the club dirty?"

"Girl, you? I can't do it with hands. He has just about touched everything on me. You know I like having a good time. But this is not fun. I just wanted to sit in VIP just so we can say we sat in VIP in NY."

"What kind of VIP was that? A VIP for rejects? They must give anybody a VIP out here."

"You're right, let's go."

We left the club but octopus arms and the clown with the body odor were right on us outside. I guess they were watching us. They stopped us and asked where we were going, and we tried to turn them down nicely. But they were not taking no for an answer. In fact, they felt like we owed them because we drunk their drinks and were hanging out in their VIP area. They were pulling at us and trying to drag us to a parking lot.

We heard a voice from nowhere say, "I think the ladies said no. Let them go." The guys were telling them a few other things, but my heart was beating so fast, and I was trying to get to my mace and my knife, so I barely heard what they were saying. Octopus arms dropped City's arm so fast you would have thought he had seen a ghost. He turned around and said, "We didn't know they were with you. It's all good." And then they disappeared right back into the club.

"Are you ladies okay?" the shortest one of them asked. He was staring directly at City.

"You dropped this shorty," the other one said and handed me my notebook.

"Well, it appears New York does have some gentlemen," City said.

"I wouldn't go as far as saying gentlemen. I'm Hakeem and this is my brother Ace. I know you were dipping on them clowns, but are you turning in? It's still early. My brother and I were going to grab something to eat. Why don't you join us?"

"We can't; we really need to get home," I answered, and City eyed me.

"But Paige I'm hungry and I know you are too. By the way, I'm Synplicity but call me City, and this is my cousin Paige. We can go but we can't stay out too long. I promised her I wouldn't make it a long night," City stated.

"We can grab something and go back to your place, that way we get to eat, get to know you and have you home at a decent time," Hakeem said.

"See Paige, sounds good right?" she said smiling at me. I looked at her and Hakeem both smiling, and then I looked at Ace who was glancing around at anything but me. I couldn't see his eyes but at least he smelled good. I felt like we were both just going along for the ride with them.

"Yeah, City. Sounds good," I said and faked a smile.

"Paige, we're here. Are you ok? Seemed like you were zoned out," City asks, unloading all our bags.

"Yeah, just thinking about the first time we came out here. We were so young and naïve. But listen, let's not talk about that. This place is beautiful. Your pictures really didn't do it justice. I'm starving; what do you have in here to eat?"

"Nothing right now, but I went to the store and got everything we need to make gumbo. Remember how we used to spend hours in the kitchen with Mom complaining about peeling, prepping and cooking?"

I laugh just thinking about it. "Yes, I hated peeling shrimp. They would always cut my damn hands. By the time we finished the gumbo I could barely hold the spoon to eat because my fingers would be cut and bruised from chopping and stirring."

"Don't worry, I got the easy peel shrimp, and I have prepped most of the things we need. But you still need to stir."

"Let me change into something comfortable and we can get started. Oh, I can almost taste it right now." I smile and start moving toward the room City said was be mine. This feels good. And it is much needed.

"Paige, we did the damn thing with this gumbo. I swear this tastes so good. Not as good as my mom's but damn it's good. We put our feet in this shit."

"It is good. I haven't had good gumbo in so long. At least not good homemade gumbo. So, tell me what's been going on with you other than travelling the world and taking all those wonderful pictures."

"Well, that's it."

"I see. No life, just travel and pictures."

"That's it. I travel, I take pictures, I make great money."

"I feel like there's a but in there."

"But something feels like it's missing."

"Don't I know it. I work, make money, but that's it. Remember when we could barely get a dollar together to get us a cold drink?"

"Yes, so you would go up to the corner store with 90 cents talking about, Mr. Charles my aunt gets paid on the third, can I get this drink now and I will come back and pay you 10 cents at that time? He would agree, and you would start counting them pennies slowly. Meanwhile, I was stealing us chips and a drink for myself," she says, making us both laugh.

"Wow, we did do that. It was a good thing he was old and damn near blind or else we would've gotten caught every time because you moved slow as hell."

"Oh no, you counted those pennies too damn fast. Trying to blame it on me."

"Man, as hard as those days were, I swear growing up got harder. I thought having money, having success and being married would be the answer to everything in life. It wasn't. I completely understand how you feel. I feel like, well, I'm not happy. City, you were right about him."

"Wait a minute, say it again? I need to record this. You saying I was right. And doing it of your own free will. This moment may never come again."

"You are crazy, but it's true. From the moment I said I do to him, he changed. He became this cold person that started to treat me like I was an option. But that wasn't the worst part. I know he's cheating, and I allowed it."

"Aww, Paige, you are more than an option. You are beautiful, smart, gifted and you are so much better than him. I knew from the beginning he was an asshole. But I let you do you because I knew the gap he was filling in your life. I need you to find who you are again. I didn't want to bring it up and I didn't want to say anything, but you haven't been yourself since the accident. I think you just need some time. You can stay here as long as it takes. Just don't be talking about how freaky me and Hakeem get."

I laugh, but I know she is telling the truth. I haven't been me. I haven't acted like me at all. "I can't believe you and him are not married yet."

"Well, it's not for lack of effort on his part. I'm just not ready to settle down. Don't get me wrong I still feel him, I love him. I also love who I am. I can't see myself being this stay-at-home mom. I like traveling and seeing the world. And I know Hakeem would want me here while he runs his businesses. So, we hook up when I'm home and sometimes he'll fly out to stay with me. Right now, that's good enough for me."

"How is he?"

"Girl, Hakeem is still crazy. You know he still likes bossing me around because that's his thing. He wants me to have a baby but like I said, I'm just not ready to do that. You have to see him. Girl, age just made him sexier."

"That's good but City, how is he?" She hears the seriousness in my voice and turns to face me. She starts shaking her head.

"No, no Paige. Guess what we are not doing? We are not going there. I think you should focus on you right now. I don't want you to. . . well, I want you to focus on you."

"That's why I got on a plane and flew here. I know I need to work on me. I know I need time to figure things out. But I also know my mind won't let me do that, knowing he's here in the same place as me. I swear when I got off the plane I smelled him and felt him. So just for peace of mind. How is he City?" I am serious. As soon as I touched down in New York I felt him because this city contains so many memories of him and I. In fact, he made me love it. I almost blush thinking about him. I look up and City is pacing and looking out all the windows.

"I told Hakeem not to tell him you were coming. But I knew he couldn't do that. Did you see him? I'll make sure he stays away from you. I don't want you to relapse. You know he does that thing. That creepy stalker thing. But he doesn't scare me. Okay, maybe a little."

"City, please calm down. I'm not relapsing. I'm not crazy or depressed. I didn't see him. I don't want his address to see him. I just need to know how he is. I want to know if he's ok. He was a huge part of my life, and I'm sure he's moved on with his life, so he probably isn't thinking about me. Just tell me how he's doing."

"He's doing fine now."

"Now?"

"Don't freak out or nothing, but after you left he went a lot crazier. He was already crazy, but you seemed to like it. Which I thought was weird because it seemed like you understood him. Which he doesn't seem like the type to open up at all."

"He was open. Just not with everyone."

"Hmmm, he opened up to you super-fast."

"Continue please. Tell me what happened."

"He came by looking for you a few times. I told him to give you time. He wouldn't accept that answer. I would see him standing on the corner, or he would be following me places. One night he knocked on the door; he was drunk and high. He wouldn't leave. He kept repeating how much he needed you and wanted to see you to make sure you were ok. Anyway, I called Hakeem over to get him. They had a big fight. He pulled out a gun on Hakeem and I thought for a second he would shoot him. It scared me, the look in his eyes when he kept saying how much he needed you. He just broke down and said how much he missed you. I wanted to tell you. But that would have kept you from healing. When you said you were done with him I knew you were done. At least for that moment."

"But he's better now?" He drunk socially but never to get drunk. I remember him being tipsy once. He just wasn't a drinker. He smoked to clear his mind. But that was it.

"Oh yeah, we've had dinners together with him. He apologized. We've even tried to set him up with a few women. Well, Hakeem, not me. I didn't think it was a good idea. We tried to double date. But he would find a way to ask if you were good then smile when I said yes and then ignore the girl for the rest of the night."

"I'm glad he's better. We weren't good for each other anyway."

"Is that so?"

"Yeah, that's so. Why are you looking at me like that?"

"Because your mouth is saying one thing, but your eyes are saying something else. This is a judgement free zone. But don't open a door you can't walk through. Close the other one first."

"I'm not walking through no doors. I'm married. And me being out here doesn't mean I'm leaving Kane. I just want him to get it together. Or maybe getting me together will make me finally close that door."

"Close the damn door and burn the damn entrance to it so you never go back to his ass. You know Paige, I always had a funny feeling about him. He just seemed sneaky, with his fake Boris Kodjoe looking ass."

I am laughing so hard. "Wait, if we're going to talk about him again I need another bowl of this comfort food."

"Not me, talking about Kane makes my stomach hurt. And thinking about him makes me want to throw up."

"Girl, you are so crazy," I say, moving toward the kitchen.

"You know, I know Ace was a little off. But I thought he was good for you. You were happier with him. Something about you two together worked. I honestly thought you and him would get back together after you took some time. When you came around again and you were with Kane, I just thought he was something to get your mind over Ace."

"Sometimes things don't go as planned." Kane came along when I was broken, and he didn't fix me; he put a Band-Aid on my scars. Do I miss Pharaoh? Yes, I think of him more than I care to admit, but it's a door I can't open again. There is too much pain there and I can't go backwards. And he isn't crazy, creepy or weird; he is misunderstood. He is kind, sweet and thoughtful. He is perfect, except when he isn't perfect. He lacks control. And I need someone who is controlled or can control themselves. Which is what I thought Kane would be. But he can't control shit, not even his dick. Now, I'm sitting wondering how I got to this junction in my life and wondering how to get out of it. Or just get through it. I drop my spoon and when I go to pick it up, I look at my thigh. Hell, I've made it through worse. I can get past this.

Chapter Seven

Unbreak My Heart

Ace "Pharaoh" Mann

My heart still remembers your sound. The sound of you breaking it. The sound of it shattering into pieces. I remember I was standing still but moving too fast to realize it was happening.

I know I told Hakeem I would stay away, but I can't help it. If she is coming I wanted to see her. I checked the airport schedules to figure out when she would arrive. I blend in well at the airport. I stay in the shadows. I see City waiting with all that damn silly stuff in her hands. I know Paige will eat it up; that is the type of person she is or used to be. She loves the small things people do for her. She used to say thank you so much it would make me dizzy. At the same time, it felt good because I knew she appreciated me.

I see her walking toward City. When she smiles, I almost drop the cup I am holding. It is the same as when I first met her at the club. I was mesmerized. Paige and City are laughing and crying together. When they hug and spin each other around in a circle I get a good look at her face. She is still incredibly beautiful. And still fine. She has on some dress slacks and her thighs are thick as hell and that ass is exactly right. The blouse she wore displays her breast perfectly. I feel my dick jump when she licks her lips. She must have traded those glasses for contacts because she isn't wearing them, and she isn't squinting. When she moves her hair behind her ear and out her face to pick up her bags, it reminds me of the night I first saw her.

Hakeem and I were at a club chilling for the night. We were upstairs in VIP. Our section had a great view of the dance floor, the bar and the other VIP sections. I stood in the shadows watching everything. That was me. I wasn't a drinker. I preferred to stay with my guard up at all times.

I had trust issues. I found when people drank too much they lost control. I liked keeping control of everything. My brother and I were always careful when we were out. Someone always wanted to try us. I stayed ready.

I was trying to watch everything but right now the bar had my attention. I noticed her sitting there with her legs crossed. She was watching the dance floor with a notepad in hand. Who brings a notepad to a club? That caught my attention. I wanted to know if she was a reporter or a cop or the FBI watching us. I wasn't paranoid just cautious. I told my brother I was headed to the bar for a minute. He barely heard me. His attention was on the dance floor. I would bet my last dollar it was the tall girl with the red dress that had his attention. He liked them tall. She was fine and beautiful too. She just wasn't my type. But the one at the bar. She was my type. She was thick as hell. She wasn't overly dressed, and her face didn't have a pound of make-up on it. She had on light blue jeans that fit her body like a glove and a yellow tie around half top. It looked like one of those mental hospital strait jackets. But on her it worked. Her stomach was flat and when she turns to the bar I saw that her naval was pierced. It was sexy as hell.

I stood next to her, but her attention was directly on the dance floor and then back to the notepad. She smelled like heaven. I ordered my drink and turned around and glanced at the notepad. She was drawing. The picture looked exactly like the dance floor except it was in pencil with no color. An artist. I didn't see that. She was so focused she didn't see me looking. She moved her hair behind her ear to get a good view of everything, and she was looking even better up close. She had on these big coke bottle glasses, but she took them off to clean them. Her eyes were small and slanted. But they fit her face perfectly. Her lips were full, and she had them glossed up, so they were shining. She would look at the dance floor smiling, showing the dimples in her cheeks. It was contagious because I wanted to smile too.

I saw the girl with the red dress coming toward her asking her to join her in VIP. She resisted but got up and went with her. When they were talking it was with a southern accent. So, I knew she wasn't from around here. When she stood up she was about 5'6 or 5'7. She had on heels that made her ass sit up just right and those thighs were thicker than I first thought.

But she wasn't fat, she was fit. Her legs, although thick, were toned. I was staring at her until a waitress blocked my view. I didn't see which section she went into, so I decided to go back into our section.

Hakeem said, "I saw you watching shorty at the bar."

I smiled and replied, "Maybe."

He smirks and shakes his head. "You like those nerdy ones. I ain't mad; she fine. They headed to that fool James's VIP section. I was just about to go holler at red dress. How her face look up close? They look young."

James was well known for flashing his money. He was a small-time dealer. Nothing major. But we heard stories about how he liked to drug women and rape them. "Yeah, they look young and green. They not from here so they don't know what's up. They have a southern accent."

"I think they about to turn black real quick. That fool James will welcome them to NY the wrong way."

"Not if I can help it."

"Oh, she got your nose open like that huh?"

"Come on bro, she just cute. Besides, no girl needs to be raped. That's some foul shit." True, my nose was open. I was interested in her. Still, no woman deserved to be raped.

About 20 minutes later I saw both of them heading to the restroom. Once they were out I saw them make their way to exit the club. I also noticed James right behind them. I tapped my brother. "Let's go."

We saw the girls standing on the corner and James and some guy he was with was right there too. We walked up behind him and heard them say, you owe us.

Hakeem spoke, "I think the ladies said no. Let them go. I know you don't think they owe you for those weak ass drinks you were giving out. Or owe you for sitting in that complimentary section your friend comped you tonight. Let her arm go or we can handle this a different way."

I didn't say anything. I let my eyes do the talking. And just like the cowards they were, they backed down. I looked at shorty who seemed like she was searching for something. The funny thing was, I saw no fear in her eyes. She just seemed annoyed by everything going on.

"Are you ladies okay?" Hakeem asked, staring right at red dress.

"You dropped this shorty," I said handing the notebook to her.

"Well, it appears New York does have some gentlemen," red dress said.

"I wouldn't go as far as saying gentlemen. I'm Hakeem and this is my brother Ace. I know you were dipping on them clowns, but are you turning in already? It's still early. My brother and I were going to grab something to eat. Why don't you join us?"

"We can't; we really need to get home," shorty answered, and red dress eyed her.

"But Paige I'm hungry and I know you are too. By the way, I'm Synplicity but call me City, and this is my cousin Paige. We can go but we can't stay out too long. I promised her I wouldn't make it a long night," City stated.

"We can grab something and go back to your place, that way we get to eat, get to know you and have you home you at a decent time," Hakeem said.

"See Paige, sounds good right?" she said smiling at me.

"Yeah, City. Sounds good," she said and faked a smile.

"Besides, you ladies are too beautiful to be roaming around New York this time of night. You're safe with us." I smiled but Paige just stared at me. I couldn't read her expression.

We stopped at a pizza place not far from the club and took the train back to their apartment. City and Hakeem were really hitting it off. But Paige wanted no part of me. She was quiet and kept looking out the window the whole train ride. Usually, girls would start talking to me before I could say anything, but here she was silent as hell. I felt like she wasn't feeling me. Once we got to their apartment, City explained why they were in New York. And I respected their hustle. They seemed to have their heads on right. I peeped shorty, or Paige, and she had salad instead of pizza.

"You watching your weight Shorty?" I asked.

"Oh, are you calling me fat?" She looked at me with what I was guessing was her mean face. But it was cute and sexy all at the same time to me.

I put my hands up in a surrender motion. "Not at all. I think you're sexy as hell." I watched her bite her lip to stop herself from smiling. I peeped Hakeem pulling City to the side, whispering in her ear. She moved and whispered something to Paige. Then they walked down the hall. "I guess that means they are really feeling each other."

"I guess, but don't get no ideas. I ain't feeling you like that." She sat on the sofa flipping through her notebook.

"I saw you at the bar drawing in the club. Can I see the picture?"

"So, you were watching me in the club?"

"Not watching, just noticing. And yeah, I'm nosey, so let me see." I reached for the notebook.

"Wait, let me flip to the club picture." She tried to grab it back, but it was too late. I saw the picture she started of me sitting on the train.

"This is really good Shorty. You have a great eye for detail. Except I'm a lot more handsome." I was joking; the picture looked exactly like me.

"Not really, in fact, I made the picture look better than you." She smiled.

"I see you got jokes too. I didn't even see you looking at me. I guess I'm slipping."

"I saw you through the glass on the train. Plus, I got a really good look at you in the pizza place. And I'm not on a diet I just think my body is a temple and I don't like putting all that grease in it."

I looked her up and down and kept thinking her body was a temple. "You right Shorty, it is a beautiful temple."

"Hold on Ace, I just met you. Keep your eyes on the notepad. And not this temple."

"I'm sorry, I wasn't trying to come at you like that, I just think you're beautiful. So let me see what else is in here." I flipped through the notebook and looked at all the pictures she had drawn. She really was talented. "How can you get such detailed pictures in this small notebook? Why not use something bigger?"

"This small one is easy to carry around. When I carry something big people tend to look over my shoulder or watch me, kind of like you did."

She smiled and looked a little more relaxed. We talked for another couple of hours and when Hakeem didn't come out of City's room, she offered me a blanket and the sofa for the night. It wasn't exactly what I had in mind, but I was feeling Shorty, and I didn't want to come off as a creep. I flipped on the TV until I fell asleep. The next morning, I heard someone in the kitchen and I opened my eyes to see shorty passing by the sofa in a nightgown that was barely touching her cheeks. I had a good view of just how fine and fit and crazy her body was. I checked my phone, and it was only 6 am. Damn she wakes up early. I went to the bathroom to handle my hygiene. She knocked on the door and said there's a pack of new toothbrushes under the sink. I hope I see you again Ace. And just like that, the front door closed. I hurried to finish what I was doing. I wanted to catch up with her. I saw her heading for the train platform.

"Hey Shorty, wait up. Where you going this early?"

"You do know my name is Paige? And why are you following me?"

"I'm concerned about your safety."

"I think I can handle myself."

"Come on Paige, I'm just trying to make sure you're safe."

"Let me find out you're a stalker. I wanted to get a view of the sun rising. I was thinking right over the bridge. It's for my class project."

"Well, I know the perfect place for you to see it."

"I don't know, I think the bridge would be good."

"I'm from here; take my word for it." She smiled, and I put my hand out for her to take it as we stepped on the train. The spot I had in mind would really be nice. The train was crowded

which made us stand close together. I swear she smelled like heaven. It was like a vanilla and coconuts with cinnamon smell. It was driving me wild. When we arrived at the destination, Paige started looking around excitedly.

"You're right, this is perfect."

I got her a chair. When she sat down her face got all serious and then she started drawing. I sat there and let her do her thing for a minute. About an hour or so later I knew she was hungry because I was, so I walked down to the café on the block and got her some fresh cut fruits and some green tea. She told me last night how she watched everything she put in her body. I listened to everything she told me. Shorty was smart and talented, but she also had this sweetness to her.

"Ace, this was a great spot. And thank you so much for the food. I see you were listening last night."

"Call me Pharaoh, it's my middle name and Ace is my street name. And yes, I was listening. You're a very interesting person. I respect that."

"Pharaoh, that's different."

"My parents were deep into black history. It's a play on words a little. Ace is first, Pharaoh means ruler and Mann means strong. So, it's one that rules strong. Well that's how my dad wanted it."

"I like that. It's different. It connects you to your roots in a way you may never understand. Our names give us purpose."

"They do. I don't run around telling everyone."

"You don't need to tell anyone. It shows in your actions. The way you stood up to those guys last night. It's in your eyes. You

have that type of aura." She smiled. "It's in the way you bullied me to let you tag along with me this morning."

"Well, I'm about to bully you into coming to my apartment so I can change. Got me out here feeling like I'm doing the walk of shame still in my last night clothes." She laughed so hard she almost choked on her fruit. I liked that she was just herself and free and easy to talk to, not stuck up or worried about her outfit. Today she had on some jean overalls that were loose and a half top shirt that matched the Nikes she was rocking. Her hair was pulled into a ponytail and her face was bare. She was beautiful in the sunlight. And the more she smiled the more those dimples drew me into her.

"That's fine. I need to meet my group for our class project in about two hours at the school and then after, can you take me to some more places around the city?"

"Sure Shorty. It would be my pleasure."

We spent that weekend together hanging out. I would take her to different places and let her draw anything she wanted. Our conversation flowed easily. It was Sunday night, and I was walking her to her apartment door, and I didn't want to let her go. This weekend was perfect. I didn't feel stressed about business. I felt like I was myself and she still liked it. To some people I could come off a little strange. I wasn't really a talker, I enjoyed the quiet, and I liked watching people because they always showed who they really were when they thought you weren't looking. I was enrolled in school and set to finish next spring getting my master's degree in architecture and design. Not a lot of people knew about me being in school. They only knew me from the street. I loved buildings and designing them. I had a few women here and there but nothing serious. Mostly I worked and studied. I took the summer off because my brother and I had a job to complete.

I liked Paige. I respected her passion for drawing; it matched my passion for designing. And I liked the fact she was taking it slow. Well, a little bit. Every move she made was sexy to me and I wanted to touch her every time we were together. I knew she was feeling the same way. She would brush up against me or when we talked she looked me directly in my eyes. When I spoke, she gave me her undivided attention. She turned to me to say goodnight and I got really close to her body. I put my hands above her head and trapped her between me and the door. There was nothing between us, not even space. Because she was shorter than me, her eyes were right at my chest. I lifted her chin and looked her dead in her eyes.

"I really am enjoying your company Shorty, but it's something I been dying to do since I saw you at the bar Friday night." She didn't back down or shy away like I expected her to do. Instead, she stood there and bit her lip, looking like she was considering her next words very carefully.

"Pharaoh, what have you been dying to do?"

At that point I had to fight with myself to control my dick. It was the way she said my name. I lifted her chin, and I pecked her lips. They were soft just like I imagined. I ran my tongue over her bottom lip and then I sucked on it. I started kissing her like it was the last time I would see her. I swear just the kiss had me so into her. I pulled back to see her face and she looked at me with lust in her eyes and did that lip biting thing that I found so sexy.

"I was dying to kiss those sexy lips of yours. Have a good day at school tomorrow. Call me, or else I may need to come back over and stalk you."

"Maybe I want you to stalk me. Thanks for a great weekend."

I turned and walked away fighting the urge to turn back and kiss her again. I knew if I did that I never would have let her go.

I fell hard for Paige. When she walked out my life it felt like my world stopped. She was everything I wanted in a friend, a lover and a queen. I want to apologize to her correctly for the accident. I was young and impulsive. I was a real hot head. I can still be that but losing her made me do a lot of growing up.

I take a picture of her with my phone. She still has those dimples and the smile she wore talking to City is one I haven't seen in any of her pictures on Instagram. She is happy. And that makes me happy. Now all I need to do is keep her happy. I want her happiness to include me. I want to see those smiles and dimples all the time.

Chapter Eight

Back in Time

Paige Turner Daniels
7 years ago New York

Time passed slow when I was with you. But the time away was even slower. We weren't meant to be, but we were. And then we weren't. Was it time still haunting me with memories of you? Or my heart still wanting you?

I heard the door open, and I knew it was City. I didn't know if she was alone or with Hakeem. They seemed to be one person since they met Friday night. Either she wasn't home, or they were in the room together. I saw her once alone this entire weekend. But I couldn't complain because Pharaoh kept me very busy. I blushed. Why was I blushing? I know why because he was so damn fine and sweet. Every place I wanted to go he took me. And he actually listened to me when I talked. It's probably just to get in my pants but he hadn't even tried until he kissed me. Just thinking about that kiss, I touched my lips. When he trapped me between the door and his body, I didn't know what to do. When he pecked at my lips and then bit my bottom lip, I almost moaned. When he tossed his tongue in my mouth my panties were soaked. It was a good thing I had the door to catch me, or my ass would have fallen backwards.

"It's just me Paige. Oh, what has you smiling? Is Ace here?" City said smirking and sitting down next to me grabbing some popcorn.

"No, he's not here. And where's Hakeem? You two were attached at the hip this whole weekend," I asked her.

"He's home and I'm here. But stop trying to change the subject. What has you in here smiling? I saw nasty thoughts spinning all in your mind."

"Nasty? You're the nasty one. City, you had that man calling your name on the first night. These walls are thin as hell."

"Well, you know I'm competitive and I couldn't let him win." I gave her a curious look.

"When we were at the table he whispered a dare to me. He said, 'I bet you'll scream my name.' And I said, I'll bet you'll call mine."

"Hoe, you said that like that changed the fact you fucked on the first night."

"Technically no. He ate and I sucked. That's not really sex."

"It's oral sex!" I looked at her and started cracking up.

"It still doesn't count as sex."

She started to pout then looked at me and we both started laughing together. City was City and since we were like sisters, I would never judge her. We were free to do as we pleased. City was just a little bit more open about sex. I was a little more reserved.

"So, tell me about him Paige."

"Pharaoh, is fine!!"

She put her hands up. *"Who is Pharaoh? You met someone else?"*

"No, keep up. His name is Ace Pharaoh Mann. He likes to be called Pharaoh."

"Hmm, I wonder if Hakeem's last name is Mann too?"

I just shook my head. "You don't even know his last name."

"Like I care. As fine as he was it didn't matter. But he did tell me to call him King and I thought it was a joke."

"They were fine! I had fun hanging out with him. He's different. But you know they are all different at the beginning."

"Well, give him a chance. Besides, I like Hakeem; he's fun and he's given me the best head ever. I may need to do a few yoga positions to take that monster he working with, but I never turn down a challenge."

"You are so nasty. I'm going to bed. I don't want any more of that popcorn. I know where your hands and mouth been all weekend." I laughed, walking out the room.

I was on campus at school eating my lunch outside. I was waiting on Pharaoh. We had plans to meet up today. And as much as I wanted to pretend I wasn't excited to see him, I was. I spent the last few nights flipping through my notebook looking at the pictures I had drawn of him. Thinking about that kiss. My head was down and suddenly a shadow was blocking out the sun. I smiled and looked up, thinking it was him. But it was some guy from my class who couldn't take no for an answer. I was annoyed. I told him several times I wasn't interested.

"You look nice today Paige. Your hair is different. But I like it," Randy said.

"Thanks. I was waiting on someone. Is there something you need?"

"I need you in my life. How about I give you my number and we can have dinner tonight?"

"I appreciate the offer but I'm seeing someone right now."

"How can that be when last week you said you were trying to focus? Listen, I really like you and I know if you gave me a chance you would like me too."

"Randy, I think you're probably a nice guy but like I said, I'm seeing someone right now." I started to gather my things when I felt Randy snatch my arm. I pulled back from him and turned to curse him, but I saw a figure moving quick as hell toward us. It was Pharaoh and he wore the same look on his face that he had the night I first saw him at the club.

Pharaoh grabbed Randy by his collar and had him lifted slightly off the ground. "Don't you ever in your life put your hands on her. She told you the deal. She's with me. And does it look like I like to share?" Randy couldn't say a word. He only shook his head from side to side. "Good, I think we have an understanding. Make this your last time looking at her and touching her, or when I come back I won't be so nice." It was at that moment I noticed the gun pushed against Randy's side. No one could see it, although a few people were staring. I knew Randy could feel it.

"Pharaoh, I'm good. I'm sure Randy understands. Don't you Randy?" I asked, and he nodded his head again. I was touching Pharaoh's hand and trying to get him to let him go. The grip he had on Randy's shirt was tight as hell. But he finally let it go. And Randy started fixing his clothes and moving away from us as fast as he could.

"You good Paige, did he hurt you?" He took my arm and started checking it for marks.

"I'm fine. You know I can handle myself. You don't have to keep saving me." He looked down and saw my can of mace and the knife I had dropped trying to get him to put Randy down. He started laughing.

"I see you got it alright. Put that thing away before you spray yourself or worse, me. Or give yourself a paper cut with that baby knife."

"Whatever, I know what I'm doing." I sat back down and started putting my spray and knife back in my bag. He then straddled the bench and when I turned around, we were face to face. The smell of his cologne was amazing and all I wanted to do was sniff every part of him. He wrapped his arms around my waist to pull me closer to him. The warmth and safety I felt with this man was unreal. We had just met but I felt like we'd been in each other's lives forever. *"Thank you, Pharaoh."* He leaned down and kissed my lips. And I melted all over again. Hell, he could save me any time. He faced me again and smiled. His teeth were so damn white, he could've done one of those whitening commercials. His goatee was cut to perfection, and his hair was cut low but had deep waves that were extra wavy today.

"So, Paige, tell me about this person you're seeing. I need to let him know his position is about to get taken."

"I'm not really seeing anyone right now. I just knew I didn't want to see him. He's not my type."

"What's your type?"

Shit, I knew he was going to ask me that. Did he just lick his lips? He's so damn fine. Get it together Paige, focus. "Well, it's not really a type. I like who I like. I like what feels good. I can't say it's a specific look or anything like that. It's how a person's energy goes with my energy." *I smiled, trying not to show how nervous he was making me.*

"You have a beautiful smile. What does energy have to do with how you feel?"

I wore some shorts today with a tank top. He was gently rubbing my leg, and I could feel the temperature going up, or maybe it was just me. "Energy is how a person reflects what they are asking the universe to bring back to them. You know how a person will walk in the room, and everything changes for good or bad? That is a person's energy. If you are positive everyone can feel it and they will want to be around you. If you give off bad energy no one wants to deal with you."

"So, is this some Voodoo stuff from New Orleans?"

I hit him and he faked like he was hurt. "No, it's not."

"Please don't put no spells on me. I like having hair and having all my limbs."

He was laughing so hard. I folded my arms and gave him my mean stare. But it was hard keeping it because his smile was making me weak.

"Don't be mad. I'm just kidding with you. How does my energy feel to you?"

He looked me right in the eyes when he asked me, and I swear my coochie jumped. I turned and started packing my bag, trying to avoid his eye contact. "Your energy is good." I felt his arms pull me closer.

"That's not what I asked. How does my energy feel to you?"

"Well." I put my head down. His eye contact was too intense for me.

Lifting my chin, he looked me right in the eyes again.

"Shorty, always be honest with me. I know you don't know me that well, but I'll be honest with you. My dad taught us a man's word is all he has. I don't speak much but when I do, I speak honestly. I want you to be able to express yourself. I'm feeling your energy, as you put it. Really, I'm feeling you. Speak on how you feel."

"I enjoy your energy. It's powerful. Even when you're quiet just your presence feels good. You feel good to me. It's so new and we barely know each other." He put his finger on my lips.

"Say less. Let's just let it feel good."

"Yeah, let's let it feel good." I was smiling way too hard.

"Let me walk you back to class. Can I feed you tonight?"

I wanted to say yes, feed me anything you want. "Yes, food sounds good." He walked me to class, and I noticed a few of the girls in my class watching him. Stare away girls, I'm keeping this one. I turned to say goodbye and he was right there pulling me by my waist closer to him. He planted a soft forehead kiss.

"This energy feels good. Don't sit next to your little friend in here. He might come up missing."

The coldness in Pharaoh's eyes let me know he was serious and then he smiled again and walked away. His coldness didn't scare me. I'd seen that look before. I'd never dated a bad boy before because I wasn't sure that was my type. The way he made me feel had me reconsidering seeing him. He seemed harmless to me. He didn't have that street dealer kind of feel to him, so I felt a little at ease. I'd seen too many girls get mixed up with a dealer and were either dead or in jail. I didn't want that kind of harm coming my way. My mom being in jail was enough for me. I liked my safe little boring life. Pharaoh didn't seem like the safe or boring type. I'd give it a little more time and then if it's not what I want, I wouldn't deal with it.

Chapter Nine

I am guided by a code that was written in my DNA. It's not up for debate. To rule, is to understand. I am not subject to you. You are subject to me. I am the ruler in the land filled with mad men.

I was in the barbershop getting a fresh cut, waiting on Hakeem who was late as usual. I swear he was never on time. I was almost done and out the chair when he walked into the shop smiling. "Well, King, nice of you to grace us with your presence today," I spoke to him.

Walking over to dap me off, he said, "You know I like to bless the little people every now and then."

This fool here was always clowning. But that was my brother, and I was proud of it. Hakeem, or King as we called him in the streets, was an enforcer for a few of the uptown major suppliers. Well, we both were. We started out as corner boys but neither one of us was good at taking orders. All that 'run it here,' 'pack it good,' 'my money better be right' wasn't our style. My father taught us at an early age a man who was a true leader answered to no one. King and I were leaders. He led in the front, and I preferred to lead quietly in the back. King was loud and outspoken. He loved attention and enjoyed having the spotlight. That just wasn't for me. I watched him as he walked through the shop dapping everyone off and hitting them with

jokes, making them laugh. He could run for mayor and win but we both had too many skeletons in our closets, and we couldn't make them disappear.

"Man, sit down, walking around here like you're some type of politician."

"A King has to speak with all his subjects."

"You're a straight fool! What you getting into today?"

"Nothing, I might pass and see City. But I need to make something shake on the west end so I'm not sure."

"You need me with you?"

"No, I got this one. Small time work."

"Ace, you're done man." Our barber Danny tapped me on the shoulder.

I took a seat to wait for Hakeem since I had a few things to run by him before we parted ways. I checked my watch to make sure I would make it on time to pick up Paige. It was raining today, and I didn't want her trying to take the train.

"You got some place to be Ace?" Hakeem asked.

"Just picking Shorty up."

"City said you two are together a lot. I see she still has your nose open."

"It's not like that. She's just cool to hang with and I like her energy." I chuckled when I said that last part. Just thinking about her saying that crazy mess to me had me smiling.

"Hold up Ace, you over there smiling? You see this man?" he said to Danny, making him look at me and laugh too. "Yeah, she definitely has your nose open. It's a good look for you. You don't smile that often baby boy. That other crazy bitch you was messing with didn't have your ass smiling like that."

"Man don't even bring her up. I told you we weren't together. She just thought we were in a relationship. Something she made up in her mind. What's going on with you and City?"

"She's wild. I like that. She doesn't question me on shit. She's just chill. And when I ask can I roll through she either says yes or no."

"What you do when she says no?"

"I roll through to the next one. You know how I do."

"All lies; you take your ass over there anyway."

"No man, I have options."

"Shorty told me how you drop by saying you just checking to see if City good. Trying to peep all in the door to see if somebody else there." The look on his face said it all. I was cracking up and so was Danny.

"Say it ain't so King. I thought you had options?" Danny asked laughing.

"Man, I don't have to explain nothing. I was just making sure she was ok. And that was only one time."

He wasn't slick at all. I could tell he liked her. He was always making an excuse to pop up by her. Or asking if we wanted to double date. I swear I didn't think he knew what a date was because he didn't date. He really did have options, and he usually used them all. Suddenly Danny stopped laughing and tapped King on the shoulder and gave me a head nod. We looked up to see Marcus and four members of the West End crew walking through the door. I stood up and so did King.

"Word on the street is I was being summoned by the King. So here I am, King," the head of the West End crew, Marcus, spoke.

"I'm confused. Did you come to talk or entertain me with your little court jesters," King said looking at the crew. One of them started moving past Marcus and I stepped in front of King.

"So, the King is that valuable, he has security? Look at this shit." He laughed and turned toward his boys.

The guy who stepped up turned to laugh too. That was his mistake. When he turned back I punched him right in the face and he stumbled. "He doesn't need security. I'm trying to save your ass. If he gets at you, you know it's lights out. And Danny here just got the shop painted this ugly ass blue color so I would hate to see it messed up with your blood." I felt King tap my arm as he was moving past me.

"King, get your brother man. I didn't come for all that," Marcus said, pulling his man back.

"Ace is fine. I don't need to tell him nothing. Let's get this straight right now. I wasn't looking for you; I told you I would come and see you if you didn't make your payments on schedule. According to my records, no payment has been made. That's a problem. No payment, no product. Nobody in your crew will eat. Did you tell them that when you brought them on this little mission?" His team was staring at him now with questioning eyes. "Why don't I let you address that later with them. You just wasting my time if you not ready to solve our problem. Are you ready to solve it now?" King said reaching for his piece.

"He's not," I answered for him.

"Nigga what?" He tried to step toward me, but when he felt King's gun on his temple, he stopped. Without speaking a word,

Jinx and our crew stood and locked the door and had their pieces pointed and ready to fire. I got ready to go to work too. I didn't like him anyway. And to step to us like he had no respect for who we were and what we did was unacceptable. Plus, I knew he didn't have the money because his ass was using all the product. I knew a cokehead when I saw one.

"I came here to talk to you about it, I just needed a little more time. But Ace is crazy; he didn't even let me get that out before he reacted. I really was coming in peace."

"How much time?"

"Give me a few days King. And I'll have it for you."

"Ok, you got it. But look, Marcus, don't make me come looking for you. Make this your last time showing up here trying to clown me. And apologize to Ace; he's sensitive and you calling him crazy and shit," King said with the gun still pointed at his head.

"Sorry Ace, we cool man," Marcus said through gritted teeth.

"See, that wasn't so hard. The King is pleased. You can leave now."

I just shook my head; my brother was crazy. People had the misconception because I didn't speak as much and reacted instantly, I was the crazy one. But King was on another level of crazy. My reactions were just that, reactions. My temper would get the best of me. However, King was calm and calculating which made for a deadly combination. Taking his seat again, he turned to me, and I saw the anger on his face.

"Times up, we take care of everything in a few days. I'll let Alexander know we'll get it done faster than expected."

"Keep me updated and I'll be ready. His dumb ass getting high off his own shit. When will they learn? I'm about to roll out. Has the King dismissed me?"

"You are dismissed."

"Hey Ace, before you go, you really think the blue ugly?" Danny asked.

Hakeem and I were co-owners of the shop. This was one of the businesses we invested in to keep our money flowing and appearing legal. I laughed while walking toward the door. "I wouldn't have picked it."

Chapter Ten

Changing Me
Ace "Pharaoh" Mann

To be honest, this is new for me. I didn't think it possible. And still can't believe. It's insane. I'm not this person, not this man. I swore I would never do these things.

I decided to drive to pick up Paige. It was raining pretty bad, and it was only going to get worse in a few hours. I sat in the car waiting on her. I knew her routine well and she rarely deviated from it. Sitting there gave me some time to think. I kept telling Hakeem once I went back to school I didn't want to handle any more jobs. Being an enforcer was easy but school took my full focus. Besides, unlike him, I didn't want to do this my whole life. King was smart; he had a degree in computer technology. But he wasn't using it the right way. Instead, he preferred to continue getting his hands dirty. I think he enjoyed the attention and the power and the money. Hell, I enjoyed the money. The work we were putting in this summer would allow me to purchase the building I wanted to redesign. I wanted to open a club. I wanted to sit down in my own club and know the building was crafted by me.

I spotted Paige; she didn't have an umbrella. Instead, she had a jacket holding it over her head trying to cover herself. I got ready to get out but seeing Randy running behind, I decided to watch to see how it would play out. She didn't know I was

coming today or that I would be in my car. This would be the second time I found them together and I wanted to know if something was going on with them. I didn't want to feel like I was being played. I really was feeling her, and I wanted to make sure she was really feeling me. He stood in front of her stopping her in her tracks, blocking the view I had of her face. I really wanted to see her reaction. She walked around him, and I saw the annoyed look on her face. I didn't know if it was the rain or him.

He ran in front of her path again, attempting to grab her arm. This fool really had a hand problem. Paige lowered the jacket she was using as a cover and suddenly Randy was falling in slow motion to his knees. I think she kicked him in the balls. He was holding his privates and rocking back and forth on the ground. She leaned over and said something to him and kicked his leg and started walking again. I could swear I saw her smirk. So, she has a bad side too. And I see she really can take care of herself. I like that in a woman. Getting out the car, I wanted to catch her before she crossed the street.

"Paige, Paige!" I screamed her name. When she turned around she had fire in her eyes, and she looked like she was ready to fight. When she saw it was me her face relaxed.

"Hey, I didn't know you were meeting me today. Come on, I don't want to miss the train."

"We don't need to take the train today. I drove. Come on, I'm parked over here." I started taking her bag and directing her toward the car. I opened the door and made sure she was in.

"You good Shorty?"

"Yes, thank you."

"You sure? You don't seem like yourself."

"It was a really long day. I'm not myself today. Honestly, I don't like storms"

"Sit back, I got you."

The drive to my apartment wasn't long but it was quiet. Which was unlike her. She didn't talk at all. Usually, she was drawing or jotting down ideas. Sometimes when we were together she would mark off places she wanted me to take her. But today she wasn't doing any of that. She was sitting with one of her knees bent up to her chest. Her head was resting on it, and she was looking out the window. I don't know why she didn't like storms. I had one mission now, her. I would do anything to get her back to herself. Even if it means just being here when she's ready to tell me the story of why she doesn't like storms.

"Where are we?" she asked.

"This is my place. My own space. I wanted to spend some time with you if that's okay."

"I don't know if I'm the best company today. But I don't want to be alone either. This is really a nice place. It didn't look like much outside, but this modern look inside is different. I love the bookshelves."

"Thank you, I designed and built them." The apartment I took her to when I first met her was a place that Hakeem and I shared. Even though we both have separate places, we shared a common place, so no one knew where we lived.

"Wow, this is great work. I see you work well with your hands."

She had no idea. I watched her walk around touching the shelves so lightly, almost like she thought they would fall. She stood reading the titles of the books. She wore a dress today and it had gotten wet from the rain and was clinging to her thighs. I walked over and wrapped my arms around her.

"You're wet. You want a towel or something?"

"You mind if I shower? I just want to freshen up."

"My bedroom is to the left. I have towels in the bathroom already. Take your time." While I watched her walk down the hall I walked to the kitchen to find a menu to order some food. I wanted to have something for us to eat. I put on some music and waited for the food.

"It smells good in here."

"I ordered you some veggies from the Chinese place. I don't have any wine or anything else to drink, but I got you some tea. Come sit down so you can eat." I turned around and she was wearing one of my t-shirts. She was shorter than me, so my shirt looked like a dress on her. She didn't have on a bra, and I could swear... nah couldn't be, her nipples were simply hard as hell. Her hair was pulled up in a ponytail. Her thighs were on full display as she sat at the table and tucked the shirt between her legs. She started digging in. I had to catch myself; I knew I was staring. She was so beautiful to me, and it was so effortless.

"So, what has you out of whack today?"

"Nothing I can't handle."

"That's not what I asked you. Paige, if something is wrong you can talk to me about it. I would hope over these past few weeks I earned a little of your trust." She takes a deep breathe.

"Are you a drug dealer?"

"No, I'm not. Why would you think that?"

"I know you're in the streets in some form, but I don't date street niggas. And today Randy came at me talking about how all the girls fall for the thugs of NY. And how I was just another hoe to you. And when you were done with me, you'd pass me to your other drug dealing buddies to turn me out. He said I could come back to him, and he would still accept me."

I laughed knowing Randy was about to come up missing. "Interesting. I'm not a street nigga or a nigga. What did you say?"

"That's not what I mean. But anyway, I told him if I got turned out I would continue sucking the dick of any and everyone but his ass. He tried to touch me, and I couldn't pull out my knife fast enough. So, I kicked him in the nuts."

"I saw."

"You saw? So, you knew."

"I didn't know what he said to you. But I saw how you handled his ass. And he deserved it. No, I'm not a dealer, or a street nigga, but I am in the streets. Just not the way you may think. I'm not trying to turn you out. And I would never call you a hoe. I would hope you see a different side of me. I don't plan on being in the streets my whole life but right now it's a means to an end. And I won't leave my brother behind. Family is important to me."

"Good, because I'm not one you know."

"I know."

"I don't want details on what you do. Just know I never want it to touch me. I do see you differently, which is why I've allowed you in my life. You are smart, and talented and caring."

"If I'm all those things then don't let someone else give you your opinion of me. I won't let it touch you. I promise."

"Don't make promises you can't keep. I've enjoyed every minute we spent together. I really like you."

"Oh yeah? Then come closer to me. I don't want you to be afraid of me. I hate that he got in your head about me. When I'm with you, I'm Pharaoh; in the streets, I'm Ace. They are not the same." She straddled me and laid her head on my chest. I held her for a minute.

"I'm not afraid of you, I'm afraid of how I feel about you."

She looked me right in the eyes when she said it. Her arms circled my neck, and she started with a kiss to my forehead, then my cheeks and my lips. When she kissed me, I felt so much passion in that one kiss. I ran my hands up and down her thighs. I returned her kiss, biting and sucking on her lips. I tilted her head to the side and started kissing her neck. She was so damn soft, and she smelled like that vanilla scent she always wore. I didn't have vanilla soap, so maybe she brought it over. My hands moved from her thighs to her ass. She didn't have any underwear on, and I couldn't help but squeeze her cheeks together. Her ass was so soft. I wanted to feel and see if it was as soft as her thighs, but the shirt was in my way.

"Can I have you?"

"Just tonight."

"Nah shorty, it doesn't work that way. You treating me like I'm a one-night stand or some shit. Can I have all of you?"

"Yes, Pharaoh, do whatever you want with all of me."

"Are you sure? That could be deadly."

"I trust you."

When she said that, my dick got harder, and I was ready to take her at that moment. But I wanted to take my time. I pulled the t-shirt off she was wearing. I sat back and looked at the view for a minute. She was completely naked, and her body was amazing. Her breasts weren't huge; I would say she was a good size C. But right there staring me in my face was conformation of something I peeped earlier; her nipples were pierced. I thought I saw that when she walked in the room. I never saw it before today. Hmmm, so she likes a little pain. They were standing at attention begging for me to touch them. So that's what I did. I grabbed them gently and placed soft kisses on each one. I placed my tongue on her nipple and licked around it and then kissed it. When I felt her squirm a little, I pulled on her nipple ring with my teeth. When she moaned it was the sexist sound I had ever heard. I lifted her from my lap and sat her on the table. Her body was amazing. Her stomach was so flat, and I admired her belly ring; it was just a stub today, not the normal hoop. I kissed it and looked at her. She sat with her palms pressed against the table. I admired the way she had all the confidence in the world about her body. Most women would try to cover themselves or be bashful, but not her. All I saw was lust in her eyes. That let me know she wanted me just as much as I wanted her. "Open them legs, let me see it."

She smiled and slowly spread her legs. And right there in full view was perfection. She had three butterflies tattooed on her stomach right above her vagina. They were small but so detailed. They looked so real. She leaned back on her elbows and licked her lips, smiling at me. I was almost jealous just thinking of the man who got to see this view while doing her tat. Her hair was shaved on the sides and neatly trimmed into a landing strip. I wasn't like most guys my age who preferred a bald vagina. I liked hair on mine. It was something sexy about it. I felt like I was fucking a woman and not a little girl. I chuckled. She wanted to direct me, but little did she know, I didn't need any direction. I knew which direction I was going. I ran my hands on her nipples again, making her tremble. I started kissing those butterflies and then I lifted her right foot and admired how soft her feet were. They were so tiny and almost disappeared in my hands. I kissed them and moved to her ankles. I rubbed and kissed every inch of each one of her legs. She was ticklish so she was laughing and giggling. I was enjoying this way too much. Her smile, her laughter and her soft moans were contagious. When I got to her inner thigh I placed her legs over my shoulders, and I got ready to touch her lips. She was wet, I saw it. Moving my hands to spread her open more, I wanted to see just how wet she was. I wanted to know if she was truly ready. And she was; her pussy was glistening with juices. I moved closer to her center and kissed her lips. She smelled so good. I started sliding my tongue up and down her slit. Her wetness had me turned on so much I wanted to skip this foreplay. I changed my mind when I started sucking on her clit. She tasted even better. I was licking and sucking until I heard her breathing getting heavier and heavier. She was calling my name, and I knew she was coming.

"Fuck Pharaoh, I'm coming."

That only made me want to go harder. "You said you want me stop?" I lifted my head, fucking with her. "Because I need you to say more than that to me. Tell me what you want me to do." She pushed my head back down and stumbled over her words when she spoke again.

"Keep sucking right there. Yes, Pharaoh, oh shit, right there. Please, I'm about to . . ."

She came right in mouth. I tried to make sure nothing went to waste. I stood up to remove my pants and slipped the condom on I had in my pocket. I stood over her staring at her face. She was sweating, and her cheeks were red. She was now leaning up again on her palms and smiling. I went for those breasts again. I think the piercings she had were turning me on even more. It was the innocent looking ones that surprised you. I swear I never would have guessed it. But that's what I liked about her; she was a mystery, and I was still having fun solving it. I was ready to enter her, so I slid her to the edge of the table. I had my dick trying to get inside of her. She was so damn tight. I didn't think she was a virgin, but she was tight as hell.

"You want me, Paige?" She didn't answer. "Let me know if you can handle it; if not, I'll take care of it. I don't want to hurt

you." She sat up and placed her hands on my dick, stroking it and placing it back at her entrance.

"You're so damn big. But I like that. I like the pain. Stop treating me like I'm a fucking flower and fuck me."

I rammed right into her when she said that. I had never been so turned on in my life before. She was taking all of me and moaning and screaming my name. She was so tight I was about to nut. But I wanted her to cum first. Watching her arch her back a little more. She was grinding on me with her eyes closed. I grabbed her by neck, lightly choking her, and said, "Don't talk shit if you can't back it up. Look at me."

She opened her eyes looking directly at me. "Cum on this dick." Her eyes rolled back in her head. With my hand still on her throat I stroked until I felt her body shake and she released a damn ocean. I could feel her juices dripping down my legs. I wanted to see her cum again, but the pleasure in her face and the grip she had on me was making it hard for me to continue. I picked her up and took her to my bedroom.

"Get on your knees. I been wanting to see that ass from behind."

"You sure you could handle all this ass?"

She bit her lip and smiled. I took that as a challenge. She got down on her knees. Her ass made a perfect heart shape. I rubbed my hands all over it. I felt like a pervert for thinking about the things I wanted to do to her. I spread her cheeks and started kissing her pussy again. I wanted her to ride my face, so I turned over and laid on the bed then lowered her until it was nothing between us, not even space. I slapped her cheeks, and she started riding my face and I almost lost my life when she tightened my face in between those thick ass thighs. But death would be worth it. When she loosened up, I stood up and entered her from the back. I pressed her more into the bed and I gently pulled those nip rings. I started rubbing her clit and she was talking in tongues because I couldn't understand nothing she was saying to me. I swear she felt amazing. When I felt her tighten and squeeze me again, I could no longer hold it. I came and stayed behind her for a few minutes rubbing and admiring her ass. "Paige, you good?"

"Better than good. I feel amazing. You are good with your hands, lips and mouth too. I need another shower now that you got me all dirty and out of my character."

"I got you all dirty? Please, you took advantage of me. Coming out here in here with my t-shirt and no panties on. You knew what your ass was doing."

"What? I'm the innocent one. I was just letting my clothes dry. And I really couldn't find anything else to fit me."

"You're not innocent at all. I see you with them nipple rings." She blushed. "Nah, don't act shy now. I didn't notice before and I didn't feel them."

"I keep them covered because I don't like the attention. My piercings and my tattoos are my personal choice."

"I like them, that shit is sexy as hell. Come on get in this shower. Let me clean you up so I can get you dirty again."

"No, let me clean you up so I can get you dirty again." She stood up from the bed. And I couldn't help but to smack her ass. She smiled and stood in front of me making me hard all over

again. She motioned with her finger for me to follow and turned toward the bathroom. I smiled to myself. This was not good. She had me all excited and happy; this wasn't me. But I liked it. I felt myself doing something I thought I was against. I tossed those feelings right out my head. Nah, I'm just having fun with her. I got up and walked toward the shower. This was so much more than fun, and I knew it. She had no clue how close she was getting to my heart.

Chapter Eleven

Moved By You
Paige Turner

I saw the sky in purple and blue when I opened myself to you. My vision wasn't clear, but my heart was guiding the way. It gave false directions. I didn't know if I wanted to leave or stay.

It was the day after, or the morning after the day after. I don't know; I was confused and high off sex. Every part of my body was sore. I'd been in positions that stretched my body to the max. Pharaoh, and I had been locked up in his apartment exploring each other for days. He ordered food when we were hungry and would feed me, or I would feed him. We would talk or dance or just lay with each other in silence. I hadn't been so moved by a man before ever in my life. He knew exactly what I needed without me saying a word. One moment he was caring and gentle, washing my hair in the shower and helping me dry off. And the next moment he was throwing me against a wall fucking me like his life depended on it. It was the perfect combination of what I needed.

He was still asleep. I got closer to him to caress his face. His goatee was trimmed to perfection, and it complemented the shape of his face. His skin, blemish free, was smooth and so chocolate I just wanted to take another bite of him. He had a few tattoos; the Ace of spades stood out the most. I came to the

realization that I would have to care for Ace too. I didn't care what he said, they were one person.

His whole body was like a work of art. He was 6'5, toned but not slim. He was built perfectly. I knew he had to work out because he was lifting me like I weighed nothing, and I'm a thick girl. It was like he sculpted every inch of himself to match his personality. His parents gave him the right name. He was like an Egyptian Pharaoh living and breathing in our time. When he walked he demanded attention, and if he decided to speak to you it was with such conviction you didn't know what to say back.

When we were first getting to know each other, his silence almost freaked me out. And the way he would pop up out of nowhere had me a little on defense. The more I got to know him the more I understood him. When he was quiet he was thinking. A lot like me, his creative side was always working. I think that made us closer. Whatever street business he did made him stay on guard all the time. I watched him check our surroundings all the time. He said he always arrived early to check out things. For some reason that didn't scare me. It only made me feel more secure with him. As crazy as that sounded I liked knowing he was somewhere around me. I could take care of myself just fine but him being close just made me feel better.

I really needed to get back to my apartment. I had to finish my paintings. I had to let City know I was okay. Hell, I needed to get a change of clothing. But I didn't want to leave him. I wanted to stay right here. This close to him. I started running my fingers down his chest.

"Is that what we doing now? Taking advantage of me while I sleep?" His eyes were still closed. But he was smiling.

"Nobody trying to take advantage of you. I don't have to ask; I know you'll give it feely."

"You're damn right I would."

He opened his eyes and stared at me. It was like he was looking into my soul.

"What's wrong?"

"Nothing, I have work I need to do. I need to let City know I'm good, and I need a change of clothes. I hate to go but you know—" He interrupted me before I could finish.

"Then don't. I told Hakeem to let City know you were in good hands. I can take you to grab your painting supplies and your clothes."

"No, I've consumed enough of your time. But this was fun." I didn't know what else to say. I mean, the sex was amazing. Mind blowing in fact, but I didn't want to look stupid by making it out to be more than what it was. I started to move to get out the bed. He pulled me back down and this time, his hands were caressing my face. The way he looked at me, I couldn't read his reaction. His face was a cross between resentment and frustration.

"Paige, do you think this was only fun?"

"Well, I didn't want to make it out to be something it's not. And you know?"

"No, I don't know. I don't think you've dealt with a man like me before. I don't open up to everyone because I have trust issues. I brought you to the place where I actually lay my head, *not a hotel or your place. I could have hit it and been done. But I wanted to explore and experience all of you. We did more than have some random, fun sex. I'll be honest with you. That wasn't just fun. That was me expressing my feelings. I'm trying to build a relationship with you."*

Wow, I was pretty sure my mouth was wide open. "Why do you want me?" I was confident in who I was; that's not a question. I wanted to know if he wanted me for me or all the pleasure I just gave him. I wanted no confusion about it.

"Why wouldn't I want you? You're amazing. You are smart and beautiful. You're open and honest and sweet when you're not trying to cut me with that small ass knife."

He chuckled and smiled. Damn, that smile. Focus Paige, focus.

"You have this ability to make me feel at ease and relaxed even when I'm having a hard day. I feel comfortable just being me with you. You're like no one I've met before. Whenever I take you to a new place, the look on your face says exactly how you feel and that brings pleasure to me. I love watching you work. Your pieces are created with care, and they are just as beautiful as you. Just like I want one of your pieces on my wall to admire and enjoy, I also want you here to admire and enjoy you."

Yep, that was pretty much all he needed to say to me. He had me. "Thank you for your honesty. But, you do know I don't live here in NY?"

"An easy fix. Do you want me?"

The intensity in his eyes was killing me. I had more than butterflies in my stomach. I wanted everything about him. I wanted whatever came with him. His energy matched mine and his passion did too. I knew this was moving fast but I just wanted to go with this feeling.

"Yes, I want you. I want everything about you."

"Ok, so you can stay here for the rest of the summer. And after that we'll figure it out. Let's shower and get dressed. You can get your stuff." He kissed me and started getting out the bed. I pulled him back and kissed him some more. My hands were all over him, touching and feeling every part of him. I was so turned on by his words. I admired a man who could express himself so freely. He just didn't know I was already working on a way to stay in New York. If my artwork was selected at the end of the summer showcase, I would win a scholarship to the art school of my choice. And my choice was here in New York and now with him. I was sliding under the covers searching for what I needed. Found it. I kissed his dick first before spitting on it and then I tried to swallow him whole. Yeah, I wanted all of him. We could get my stuff after this session.

****

"WELL, well, well, if it isn't my little cousin Paige coming through the door doing her little walk of shame. Still in Friday's, make that Thursday's, clothes and everything. Such a slut!" City greeted me as I walked in the apartment. Pharaoh needed to take care of some business, and I needed to get my stuff together.

"Takes one to know one." I laughed and walked into the kitchen to get me some juice and started walking toward my room.

"So, it's like that now? You're about to keep all the juicy details to yourself, huh? Hot, nasty ass."

"Ask nicely."

"Nope, I don't need to know."

"Ok." I kept walking. I knew she wanted to know. I was counting down in my head. Any minute.

"Come on my little Page Turner, let me read all about the weekend. Your little nasty, extended weekend," she begged and smiled, patting the sofa so I would sit next to her.

I walked slowly back toward her and took my time sitting down. I crossed my legs and blew on my nails like I was drying them. *"Since you asked so nicely."*

"If your extra ass don't get to talking."

I started laughing and shaking my head. *"City, that man was too good to put into words. I saw, walked and took a seat in heaven. I was sipping tea with the angels. "*

"Damn, it was like that?"

"It was better than that. He was attentive and aggressive all at the same time. He washed my damn hair so intense and gentle it was like he was making love to it."

"So that explains that bird's nest on top your head. Your hair was fucking too."

"Well, I didn't have my shampoo. All I had was my purse with my lotion."

"Wait, hold up, did you say washed your hair like he was making love? Paige, are you falling for him?"

"*Falling, no.*" *She gave me a look.* "*Ok, maybe.*"

"*No, no, no Paige, we are not doing this. You're the focused one. Remember you said men will knock you off focus and that we have goals. So, what now?*"

"*I don't know. I enjoy being around him. He doesn't knock me off my focus. In fact, I've done some of my best work with him. I just really love his energy. He's the first man to come along and make me feel this way. City, I just want to follow it. Is that wrong?*"

"*No, baby girl. You've always followed your feelings. Your feelings led us to Tulane University. Your feelings led you to apply for this program. They haven't been wrong so far. Follow this one, too. You haven't smiled this hard in a long time. You are glowing. I want you to do you. Does he know we plan to stay?*"

"*No, I'm waiting to see if I will win the showcase. Then, I'll tell him.*"

"*Well, we already know you winning, so that's not a problem. But there is a problem.*"

"*What?*"

"*And I say this with love, go wash all that damn sex off your ass. Sitting on this couch with that nest on top your head and your draws in your purse smelling like men's shower gel.*"

"*You work on my nerves. I'm going.*" *I did have my panties in my purse. How the hell did she know?*

"*I still love you.*"

"*Kick rocks.*"

City and I had been working on a way to stay in New York since the first night we got here. We thought we would get homesick, but we just fell in love with everything. The food wasn't the same but that wasn't a big deal for now. Besides, this was exactly where we needed to be right now. City was making great connections, and she was offered an internship to work with a photographer who took photos with Vogue magazine. She would still be able to do school, and this would count as a credit toward her degree. If I won the showcase I would be able to display my artwork in gallery out here. New York gave me life. It made me feel free to do me and not be judged. I didn't always fit in with the in crowd back home. I was different, I dressed differently, I was quiet, and I liked to move to my own beat. This was the perfect place for me. I wanted to shower and start on my last piece to my collection. It came to me being with Pharaoh this weekend. I had three weeks to get everything done. I wanted it to be perfect. I wanted to win more than ever now.

Chapter Twelve

It All Falls Down
Ace "Pharaoh" Mann

And when it falls, it falls like leaves in Autumn.
Slowly blowing in the wind until it finally hits the ground.
From green to orange to brown, like London bridges, they all
fall down.

Today was Hakeem's birthday celebration. He had a big celebration set up for the club tonight. I was excited but not about the party. I was excited because Paige was returning today. After winning the showcase, like I knew she would, we got to spend the next two semesters together. At the end of the spring semester, she was offered an opportunity to travel to Paris for a few months to study with an International Art Exchange program. It was only two months and a couple of weeks, but it felt like a year. I even flew out to Paris one weekend to see her before I started my internship with one of the top architectural firms in Manhattan. I missed her. She didn't want me picking her up from the airport because she said we never would've made it to the party. That was true, so I agreed to just meet up with her there. I still needed to get my hair cut and pick up Hakeem's gift and the gift I had for her. I designed a butterfly necklace just for her and I planned on giving it to her tonight.

I was ready for her to move in with me. She kept using City as an excuse but now that City had a new roommate, she had

nothing holding her back. Falling in love with Paige was so easy to do. She was everything I wanted and more. Not having her here these past few months made me feel like I was losing my mind. She would call me on the phone, and we talked for hours while she painted, and I designed. She would tell me about this little café she went to almost every day. Before she left, she asked if I was okay with her going. I explained to her I would never hold her back from her dreams. I would support her with everything she wanted to do. If that meant me just getting to hear her voice I was ok with it because I could hear the happiness in her voice when she described all the new places she visited. Her happiness was something I never wanted to take away from her. She told me about her childhood. She cried many nights in my arms about her mom being in jail. Her dad was a big-time drug dealer, and he killed a guy one night who was trying to break into their home. Paige's mom took the charge, so her dad could stay free to run the business and get her out with his lawyer. At least that was the plan. Her dad disappeared a few months later and hadn't been heard from since. That left her mom in jail. She said her mom would never turn on her dad even if that meant being away from her only child. She felt rejected and unloved. She explained why she never wanted the street life to touch her again. She already felt like it took so much away from her.

I understood, and I made sure to limit my time on the street and tried my best to transition into something completely legal. Not just for her but for myself. Hakeem loved being feared in the street life. It only made me more paranoid than I already was if that was possible. I only enjoyed the money. The more people we killed the more I couldn't sleep at night. Sure, the money was good, but I couldn't rest at night. The only time I slept soundly was when Paige was next to me. She calmed me, and I calmed her. She didn't sleep good at night either. We would both be wide awake talking about anything that came to mind. Sometimes she would paint, and I would design something and then her ass would try to paint my shit some girly pastel color. More than a few nights she painted me, or we played with body paint. I swear the things she had me doing had me feeling soft, but I loved it. Especially when I got to paint her body. She was so sensual, just touching her was a turn on. Most nights we ended up making love until we were exhausted and fell asleep. Those were my favorite nights. Her body was amazing, and her sex drive matched mine. I couldn't wait to have her all to myself again.

I arrived at the club extra early. I wanted to make sure security was tight. I wanted to scope out our section and make sure it was located where I could see everything and everyone. If it wasn't, I would change our section. Little things like that mattered to me. I always wanted to feel safe. This club thing was more of Hakeem's thing than mine. I preferred smaller places with less crowds. It was his birthday, so I went along with it. It was after 11 and I was drinking my third bottle of water. I wasn't into alcohol. It made me lose focus and I like keeping focus. I wanted to relax and maybe have a beer but not until I knew she was here. She hadn't called, and I was starting to worry. I looked over at Hakeem and he was getting his fifth or sixth lap dance from some girl he probably didn't even know. He better enjoy it now. City will come and shut that shit down. She demanded respect even if they weren't in an official relationship. And the funny part was, "the King" gave it to her. He didn't do that with any other woman. They knew their place and stayed in it. If they got out of hand he cut them off.

I turned to face the door again. I felt like I had been watching it all night. And there she was, finally. She walked in looking good as hell. She wore a skirt, and it fit her like a glove with a split on each side; it sat below her belly button. I couldn't wait to kiss it. She wore a half top that was barely covering her breasts, and I could see her piercings through her shirt. Her breast looked a little bigger because they were sitting up just right. If she lifted her hands everyone would have seen what I saw. She couldn't be wearing shit like that; I'd have to kill someone tonight. She looked like she had gotten tattoos around her waist that went up to her side and on her back. I wanted a closer look. Her hair was in these big, fluffy curls that almost looked like an afro. It was so big; it covered half her face and came to stop at her shoulders. She looked amazing. Her and City were walking together giggling with each other. One of the members of our crew stood up and rubbed his hands together and said, "Damn, I got to get her tonight!" I walked up to him and looked him right in his eyes and said, "and if you do you'll die." He put his hands up in surrender and said, "Chill Ace, that's you?" I started walking away but turned back to say, "all day." I tapped Hakeem on his leg on my way out the section.

Walking toward her, we made eye contact. She was so fucking beautiful. I wanted to grab her and walk right out the club and go to the house. I wanted to be inside her. Not only that, but I also saw all the stares she was getting. As I got closer, I saw a guy grab her arm and try to pull her toward him. I picked up my pace and pushed him when I got to her. I moved her and City behind me.

"Man, you got a problem with your hands?" he said.

"No, but you do, clearly. Touching something that's not yours," I said, moving closer to him.

"I don't see no rings on her finger. She free to me."

"No ring needed; my mark is imprinted on her soul. Look real good and you'll see a Pharaoh, not a bitch ass nigga." I got ready to hit him, but I felt her soft hand on my arm. Hakeem and our crew were at my side.

"I know we don't have a problem?" Hakeem said.

"We can make it one," this fool had the nerve to say.

"Bet," I said, moving her hand off my arm and closing in on him. But before I could get to him a familiar face was between us.

"Ace, man, I'm sorry. We don't want no problems. This my cousin; he's from out of town. Daniel, man chill out," Mac came over and said and started pulling his cousin back.

"Mac, I'll chill out, but he needs to apologize to my shorty." I turned to his cousin, folded my arms and smirked.

"Dan come over and apologize," Mac said. Dan wasn't going for it. He was shaking his head and pointing his finger at me as if that shit intimidated me. I was only backing down because Mac,

Hakeem and I all grew up in the same neighborhood. Mac leaned over and whispered something in his ear and Dan ran his hand over his face. He walked a little closer and said, "My bad, no disrespect at all."

"Listen; to show no hard feelings I'll send over a bottle for the ladies. Happy birthday King." Mac dapped me and Hakeem off and pulled his cousin back toward their section.

I turned my attention back to Paige. "Shorty, why do you have that on?" She had that look like she wanted to kill me. She turned and stormed off toward the bathroom. City rolled her eyes and walked behind her.

"Ace, you always got to fuck up a good time?" Hakeem pushed me and walked toward the bathroom.

I knew I shouldn't have said it, but I was thinking it. Her clothes were always borderline something. Too sexy, too colorful, too manly or like tonight, too sexy. She was barely wearing anything at all. I didn't want everyone looking at her like that; she was mine. She was only for me to think about and touch. She really wanted me to kill everyone in here. I walked toward the bathroom and knocked. No one opened it, but I could hear them talking.

"Shorty let me in."

"Fuck you Ace." The way she said Ace hurt my feelings. I'm Pharaoh to her.

"Paige, please, I'm sorry. I shouldn't have said that to you. You look beautiful."

The door opened and I smiled, but it was Hakeem looking me at me with a smirk. City pushed past him and looked me up and down. "Don't think you scare me. She can wear whateva she wants, asshole. Go in there and kiss her ass with your rude self. Come on Hakeem, I need a drink."

He followed right behind her. "Coming baby. Get in there and fix this shit. It's my birthday, I'm trying to enjoy it." He waited until City was a few feet away and whispered, "I know how she got you; those breasts and nipple rings are nice." He tapped me on my arm lightly and walked away smiling and shaking his head.

I walked in then closed and locked the door behind me. She had her back turned to me. I walked behind her and the first thing I smelled was vanilla. I missed that damn smell. I wanted to run my fingers through her hair like I did so many times when we showered, and she let me wash it. But she would fuck me up if I messed up her hair.

"Your hair looks amazing. I just want to run my fingers through it."

"Nah, Ace, don't touch it. I'm glad something about me has your approval."

She turned and faced me. She was pissed, and she was holding back tears. "I'm sorry, I didn't mean it that way. I think you look sexy as hell. I just, I don't know. I got in my feelings about other men looking and touching on you." I went to touch her face, and she smacked my hand away.

"Ace, I express myself in all forms. Through my words, my art, my hair and my clothes. It's all linked to how I feel. This is me. No one will tell me how to look, how to act or how to dress. If I can't be myself, and be free to do it, I can't be with you."

She stepped back and motioned her hands over her body. "I need you to be secure in knowing, if I have given this to you, it's only for you. All of this is yours only. It doesn't matter who was looking at me. It matters who I was looking at, and that was you, Ace."

I got closer to her and leaned my head down until our foreheads were touching. "Stop calling me Ace. Call me Pharaoh. You smell so good. I missed you so damn much." I took her hands and then I turned her around. I got down on my knees and kissed her ass.

"What are you doing, Ace?"

"City told me to make sure I kissed your ass. So that's what I'm doing, kissing ass. Say Pharaoh, not Ace."

"Make me say it."

"Bet." I turned her around and lifted her skirt. I admired the thong she was wearing. I noticed it wasn't tattoos I saw but something else, like ink the Indian people wore, Henna. It was beautiful. I couldn't wait to get home and explore it in detail. Right now, I knew we didn't have time. I lifted her and positioned her on the counter. I kissed her thighs and then I kissed her center. I took my teeth and pulled her thong to the side. I started to eat like I was starving. In no time she was calling me Pharaoh. When I was done, I wiped her off and she looked at me with so much passion in her eyes, and I knew I was in love. "I'm sorry Paige, I love you." She wrapped her arms around me and kissed me.

"Pharaoh, I love you too. And I missed you more. I have something to tell you when we get back home. But for now, let's enjoy the night."

The way she said home, made me know this was real. And I felt like she was ready to move on to the next step.

"Yeah, let's enjoy the rest of the night."

It was three something in the morning and we were getting ready to leave the club. I never really had fun at the club but being with Paige allowed me to have a good time. Her and City would dance and then she would dance on me. A couple of times I had to warn her to stop, or I was taking her in the bathroom again. I drank a few beers and even did some shots with Hakeem. Right now, we were in search of food and then headed home. We were headed to our cars, and I couldn't keep my hands off her. I didn't know if it was the drinks or just being that close to her. I was laughing like a little schoolgirl. Hakeem stopped in his tracks and turned around and looked at me.

"Man, you back there laughing and smiling like a damn schoolgirl. Who the hell are you right now?"

"Mind your damn business and turn around. Can't you see I'm trying to explore this beautiful temple." We all started laughing.

"Man, get your ass in the car with me. I'll have someone take your car home," Hakeem said. I wasn't about to put up a fight. I was a little twisted and I just wanted to keep my hands on Paige.

"You act like you any better than me. You can't even walk straight. We gone ride with Jinx and you ride with Desmond. Let me get some food in me and I'll be good." I dapped him and got in

the car with Jinx. I was trying to put Paige on my lap in the front seat, but she wasn't having it so we both got in the back. Driving to our destination, I was kissing her neck when I heard a BOOM!!! I looked up and someone had hit Desmond's car. They were directly in front of us. We stopped, and Jinx and I jumped out, running toward them to make sure they were good. I heard another BOOM!!! I turned around and the car we were just in was spinning and crashed into the side of the wall of the bridge we were riding on. I heard gunshots break out and I felt a bullet hit my arm and then my leg. I fell to the ground trying to get out the line of fire. I heard footsteps and running and a voice that sounded familiar say, I want that nigga Ace to back up all that shit he was talking in the barbershop. It was that nigga Marcus and his crew. The footsteps were getting closer. I pulled out my gun waiting on them to get closer, until I heard Paige scream. I heard them say get her. And I came out blasting. I didn't care who I hit but they weren't getting my baby. I heard shots coming from every direction and then I heard a blast, and I saw the car with Paige still in it on fire.

In my mind I wasn't processing everything that was going on. I started running toward the car and I felt a hand on my shoulder trying to stop me. It was Hakeem trying to stop me. He was saying something, but I wasn't trying to listen. I ran toward the burning car and tried pulling the door, but it wouldn't open. I started kicking the glass in and saw her passed out and part of her body was on fire. I couldn't get to her because the flames were in the way. I took my shirt off and wrapped it around my head, covering everything but my eyes. I could feel the heat and fire on my skin, but I needed to keep going because I had to save her. When I got her out the car she was barely breathing and all I could see was her flesh exposed. I didn't know what to do. City was behind me screaming and Hakeem was trying to put out the flames that was still on my shirt. My vision started getting blurry and I kept hearing a ringing in my ears. I passed out and when I woke up, I was being rushed to the hospital. I was trying to get up, but I couldn't. I needed to see if Paige was good. I passed out again. The next time I woke up I was in a hospital bed. I focused my eyes and scanned the room. Hakeem was sitting in a chair next to the bed watching tv. I tried to talk but for some reason, my throat was killing me.

"Ace, don't try and talk man. Let me call the nurse." Hakeem jumped up, running out the room.

The nurse came in and checked my vitals and gave me some juice. She explained I had a tube down my throat, so it would take some time for the pain to go away but I should be able to talk in a few hours as long as I kept drinking juice and eating some ice. When she left I looked at Hakeem.

"I'm glad you're feeling better. You scared me bro. You been out for a while. You got hit three times and your arm got burned pretty bad. You were in surgery for so long and they say you coded. I'm sorry Ace. I should have taken care of Marcus. I let it go because he came up with the money. I didn't see him coming back at us like that at all."

I motioned for some paper, and I saw my left arm was wrapped in a bandage. It hurt my body to twist and move. When he saw what I was reaching for he handed it to me. I wrote one word, Paige.

"She had surgery too. She was shot in the arm, and she had a few broken bones from the car accident and being pinned in the car. Her left leg was burned extremely badly. I don't know how you got her out the car. But you saved her life."

I wrote down my fault.

"Nah, Ace, we never saw that coming and her and City just got caught in the middle."

I wrote some more. Where is she? He looked at the paper and turned his head. "She's doing better but um, well, she hasn't woken up yet."

How long?

"It's been a month. They saying she'll make a full recovery, but her body just needs time to heal."

I pushed the back of my head down hard into the pillow. It was all I could do. All I wanted to do was cry. She made me promise my street life would never touch her, and it did. And now her life depended on it. I felt like shit. What if she never woke up?

Chapter Thirteen

We Need to Talk

Paige Turner-Daniels

Present Day

A different place, a different time but still the same you're on my mind. I can't escape you as hard as I've tried. And I've tried a million and one times. But each time you still appear in my mind.

I woke up from the same dream I'd been having for the past few weeks. I can't understand how I was having the same dream repeatedly. Or how the dream feels so damn real. I walk to the kitchen to grab a water, and I overhear City on the phone arguing with someone. I assume it is Hakeem. She turns, sees me and I swear she looks lost and scared. She abruptly ends her phone call.

"You good Paige?"

She asks, looking like she is wiping away tears. "I think I should be asking you the same question. I didn't mean to disturb you. Do you want to talk about it?"

"You didn't. The conversation was over anyway. It's a guy I'm seeing. He's upset that we can't meet this weekend in Paris because I cancelled the trip. He wants to come to New York, and I don't know how to really tell him no. He thinks we're in a relationship. He knows nothing about Hakeem. I can't have him come here and mess everything up, you know."

"Nah, I don't know. Explain it to me. Because I thought you and Hakeem were in a relationship."

"We are and we're not."

"Yep, I'm lost again."

"When I'm here I'm all his. But when I travel, well I'm with whomever makes me feel good. But Kaleb and I have been seeing each other for over a year and he's ready to get serious now. He's sick of the cat and mouse game with me. I keep him at arm's length because I feel like I'm starting to fall for him. I really like him."

"I'm not a relationship expert but usually when you like someone that means you want to explore your options with them and possibly take it further."

"True and all, and I can't understand what's holding me back. He's good to me. And I know he loves me. He makes me feel like I'm the only woman in the world."

"The question is, do you love him?"

"I don't know. But anyone can learn to love a person right? I mean look at you and Kane."

What? No, she didn't. I gave her the side eye. "Totally different, City. Kane and I happened, and I loved him. I didn't need to grow to love him. The only thing that's grown between us is my hate for him. I'll ask you this, do you love Hakeem?"

"Yes. But I know he won't accept all of me. And besides, he wants a relationship on his terms."

"You mean he won't let you keep running around the globe like you're free? Do you mean he won't let you keep sleeping with men and women as you please? You mean he wants to be the man in the relationship? You mean he wants your spoiled ass to produce a miniature spoiled you?" The look on her face is priceless. I am calling her on her bullshit. She isn't ready to settle down with anyone because she is selfish, spoiled and free loving as she puts it.

"Yep, that part and that part and especially that part. I'm not spoiled. I like having things my way and there's nothing wrong with that at all. He wants me here. Wants a family and all. I still have parts of the world I want to see and things I want to do. And his stubborn ass won't leave this damn city except to visit me for a weekend. I love it here but sometimes I feel trapped. I like traveling, I just wish he would come with me, instead of trying to play the King of New York."

"Have you told him? I mean, expressed how you really feel?"

"Once, a very long time ago. He didn't really hear me, so I don't know about trying to say it again. Kaleb is willing to travel with me. In fact, we travel many places together and I like it. I like how it makes me feel secure and like I'm not by myself in the world. If only Hakeem understood that part of it. I do want a baby, but I want to show him some of the places I've been and eat in a different city and walk hand in hand together and just be us outside of New York."

"Oh, so you do want a relationship. Because that pretty much sounds like a relationship. Just tell him City before you make any decisions. Give him a chance. See where his head is at. We've gotten a little older and he might be ready."

"Maybe I will. Speaking of chance. Do you think you can give him a chance again?"

"Who Kane?"

"Hell no, not that ass. Cut your losses and keep it moving. Ace. I passed by your room, and I heard you fighting in your sleep. I thought you were having a bad dream, but you were having an old freaky ass dream, with your nasty ass. You called his name. Well, not really called it. You moaned it."

"Did I? Stop playing. Why would I call Ace's name?"

"Again, you moaned it. You moaned Pharaoh's name. And girl that dream seemed very intense."

"It was. I've been having the same dream for the past few weeks. I just figured I was horny because I haven't slept with Kane in over six months. But the dream seems so realistic. And it's always the same person. I couldn't really make out his face until I got here. But I knew it was him from the way he moved and from… well, the sex. Nobody made my body feel like he did."

"Six months? Hell, yes your ass is horny. Probably beyond horny. I don't know how you're doing it. Damn."

"Me either, I just can't bring myself to keep giving myself to him knowing he's spreading all of himself to everybody else. Marriage was supposed to be good and happy. I just feel so stupid and so alone."

"Aww, Paige. That's not how it's supposed to be at all. I'mma say this because you need to hear this; you never should have opened that door, and you didn't really close the other door. Go and see Ace. Talk with him. Get the closure you need. Forgive him so you can move on. You are stuck, and you need to get pass this portion of your life."

"The way I left, the way I just walked away. I don't know if I can just walk back in and say, hey Pharaoh, what's up."

"Well don't say that shit. You sound lame."

We laugh together. "I guess I'm a little rusty."

"Hell, yes your ass rusty and your coochie dusty. My poor little Page Turner. You're love deprived, dick deprived, and sleep deprived with them bags under your eyes. You lucky you got me here to help you."

"Aww no, don't do me like that. And City, I'm not up for one of your crazy ass plans." She has that look in her eyes.

"I got you cousin!!!! Let's get some sleep. We going out tonight and we about to get you right."

"City, don't be trying to hook me up. I'm still married."

"Fuck that marriage, fuck Kane and fuck that innocent act. Get your shit together. You're grown, and you need to act like it."

She twirls her ass out of the room and slams her door. I know I'm grown. I know I need to get my shit together. But she's not about to call me on my bullshit like I just did her. Damn, she's right though. Six months is a long ass time. She's right; get your shit together Paige and yeah, fuck this marriage. He says fuck me all the damn time.

****

"You look sexy Paige. I like it. Turn around, let me see what that ass looks like."

City turns me around and gasps when she sees my ass. I am wearing some high-waisted pants, that showed every curve of my body. She swore I looked great in the store. I'm not so sure now. I feel like it is too much. And the top is a V-neck cut. It is cut so damn low I just know I'm getting ready to do one of those *Love and Hip-Hop* interviews. The ones where everyone got new breasts and wanted to show them off. "I think it's too much. My ass is huge. And my breasts about to make their appearance at any damn time. I think I should just change."

"Please girl, don't tell me that nigga took your confidence too?"

"No, I'm just saying I've gained a lot of weight."

"You are what, an 18 or 20? Do you understand you look perfect right now? Women pay all the time for an ass like yours. And you still have no damn waist at all."

"Look at my stomach. It's poking out."

"Girl put them heels on and let's go. I can't believe you. Judging that perfect ass body, that beautiful face and that just right ass. You look amazing. But I knew you would. We related. And I look amazing too!"

She does look amazing. She is wearing some flared pants that make her thighs look thick even though she is slender. The halter top she is wearing only covers her front. Her back is out. Her heels make her even taller. She really could've been a model. We do look good, and it feels like old times. Laughing and talking in the back of the Uber. I missed her so much. I'll never let this happen to us again. We need to stay close. I need her and maybe she needs me too.

Getting out the Uber, I look at the line. I don't know if these heels will stand up to standing in line all night. In true City form, she marches right up to the security guy. She gives her name, and they march us in so fast I don't have time to see the name of the club. The stairs are dimly lit, but they keep a flashlight guiding our way. We come to another line that has more security and a velvet rope. I keep thinking this place must be very fancy. They move the rope, and we walk right into more stairs and a roped off, elevated section. The view is amazing, you can see the whole place, the dance floor, the bar in the middle and all the other elevated sections.

"This is nice City. How many levels does it have?"

"I think three or four. If you want, we can go up to the patio later. But for now, this is good. They'll bring us a bottle over real soon. I'm a regular. Plus, I know the owner and he made sure to have everything just right for me tonight."

"Look at you, knowing club owners and getting us the VIP treatment. This is by far than our first VIP experience." We both start laughing. I see bottles heading our way and I can't wait to let go for the night. I haven't hung out, freely, in years. I always had to make sure not to drink too much, not to dance too much, not to eat too much. It was exhausting living up to Kane's crazy ass idea of perfection. But not tonight, I am going to be me and enjoy all of it.

Two bottles and several dances later, City and I are both feeling good. I love this club. The music is perfect. The drinks are mixed just right. And the owner kept us snacking on everything. It was like a buffet, and it is only us two. I am looking over the dance floor and dancing to the music when it feels like someone is watching me. I search the whole floor, and I catch a few guys smiling at me. But nothing else. I feel a tap on my shoulder and turn around and come face to face with Hakeem.

"Look at you Paige. You look good baby girl. Give me a hug," he greets me with the warmest smile.

I hug him and glance behind him to see if Pharaoh is there. For some reason I am excited about finally seeing him. But he isn't. "Hakeem, I'm far from a damn baby girl. You look good too."

"I see City has you feeling good."

I'm tipsy as hell. "Nah, it's the owner. They've been sending drinks all night. Look at all this damn food. It's just us and we have our own person buffet."

"He tends to take care of City and I very well. How have you been? I wanted to come around sooner, but your personal bodyguard was keeping you very secure."

"I'm good. Better now."

"That's good. I don't really know how to say it but I'm so sorry for everything that happened. I take full responsibility for what happen."

"It's been years and it's water under the bridge now."

"I know but I just wanted you to know it. City told me you're ready to talk to him. I'm glad. He blamed himself a lot. I've already told him to keep his distance and if you need me back there with you, I'll come."

"Wait, what? What are you talking about?" I am confused as hell.

"City didn't tell you? This is his place. Ace's club."

I look at City and she stands behind Hakeem. I look around the club and I start to notice the ace of spades everywhere. On the walls, the napkins, the tables. I can't believe I am partying and loving HIS club.

"Ok Paige, don't get mad at me. This is your chance. You've had a few drinks to loosen you up. Go and talk with him. Get your closure," she says, stepping from behind Hakeem and hugging me. "Do you want me to come with you?"

"No, I'm good. You're right, it's a good time right now to get it done."

"Ok, this is Tara. She'll take you to his office," Hakeem says. "Y'all both dirty for this, but I got it. Lead the way Tara."

I hear Hakeem ask if I am drunk. I am good, just tipsy. Nah, a little drunk, but if I wasn't I would not have had the courage. I follow behind Tara. We walk down the stairs and through the dance floor. I look up and see City and Hakeem watching me. I want to make a run for the door. But I realize I want to see him. We walk pass the bar and through the kitchen and down a hall. With each footstep, I sober up. I think I might pass out. I am trying to think of something to say.

"You must be special. No one is allowed back here except King," she says, popping on some gum.

"I think I need to stop at the restroom for a minute. Let me make sure I look ok," I whisper.

"Nervous huh? You look fine. Ace, can be very mean. He's very short with women he doesn't like. You don't really seem like his type but who knows. There's one right there. I'll wait right here."

Is she jealous and coming for me? "He does have a certain type. And he's not mean, he's cautious with whom he spends his time. I guess you didn't make the cut?"

"Hold up—" she starts to say but is cut off.

"I see you haven't lost that smart ass mouth of yours. Thanks Tara, I can take it from here," Pharaoh walks behind me and speaks.

Shit, shit, shit!!! My palms are sweating, and I stand there for a moment. Unable to turn around. Come on Paige, you can do this. Stop being afraid. Just turn around. I turn and there he is; well, there we are face to face. This man is still too damn fine. His body is still so perfect, so fucking perfect. He stands there and I take all of him in. He is still tall and handsome. His hair is still cut low with waves that go on for days. He is dressed casually with jeans and a button-down shirt. And he smells amazing. Nothing about him changed but time. He aged but he aged well. My legs feel like jelly. Get it together Paige, say something.

"Hi Ace." That is so lame. City's going to kill me.

"It's Pharaoh, and hi Shorty. I figured I would make this less awkward and meet you. Can I get a hug, or will your bodyguard City fight me?"

"That damn City. Sure, a hug won't hurt." We embrace and he squeezes me so tight. I am trying not to inhale his smell. But it is all I can do. I'm trying not to feel how good his arms feel or how my temperature is rising. Again, it is all I can do. He is holding on to me and I can't help but almost melt into his arms. I catch myself and I let him go. He grabs me by the face and looks me in my eyes.

"I thought I would never see those beautiful brown eyes again. I don't want to be forward but just let me look at you for minute." He hugs me again and then he gently runs his hands down my face and to my neck. He is tracing the outline of my body. Here I am a married woman, letting this man feel me up like this. But I can't move. It's like his touch has a spell on me. This wasn't a good idea. I don't know how to close this door because all I want to do is keep it wide open. I finally stepped back and smiled at him. He is still standing so close to me I can barely breathe. I can't step back anymore because I am between him and the wall. When I see his hands lift again I don't want to be rude, but I can't take his touch again. I am more than positive that my panties are already soaked.

"This is a very nice club. City and I were having a good time. The music, the food, the drinks, everything was perfect."

"I'm glad you are enjoying it. Come on, we can talk in my office."

"Look at you all official, your office." I'm trying to find humor in the situation but really, my nerves and emotions are getting the best of me.

"You got jokes. If you're uncomfortable we can go back in the club area. You seem nervous."

"Just a little bit. I was having a good time. I haven't had that in a long time. I didn't want to get into a serious discussion about anything."

"Listen, I completely understand. Come on, let's go back to the VIP area and just chill. How long will you be here? Maybe we could grab some tea or something another day."

You can't go out with him; you're out of your mind. And you're married. Girl, fuck that marriage, do you smell him? And just look at his fine ass opening doors and walking through this club like a boss. I should've just gone back to the office with him. But I knew I would end up spread eagle on his desk.

"I'm not sure how long I'll be here. But tea sounds good."

Back in VIP, City runs over to me and pulls me away from the men. They are talking and busy getting the waitress over to the section.

"Are you good?" City whispers.

"No, girl you didn't tell me how fine he still was. Shit, I need another drink." I am fanning myself, but I still feel like I am on fire.

"Did you guys talk?"

"No, I can't talk to him right now. My body is doing all the thinking."

"And I can guess what it's thinking. Ole nasty ass."

"I can't even deny it."

"Well, I ain't stopping or judging you. But again, don't keep walking through doors you can't close." I look up and Pharaoh and I catch eyes. The door is wide open, and I have already walked through it.

Chapter Fourteen

Desires and Consequences

Paige Turner-Daniels

My mind is running in circles thinking of you. I can't keep running from this feeling. I can't keep running from you. I'm spinning out of control.
And where I'll stop only my heart knows.

Being in New York for two weeks has changed me. I woke up each day excited. I wasn't sure if it was the city itself, being away from Kane or that Pharaoh and I had spoken every day since the club. We weren't really talking about much, just general stuff. We sat and had tea, but he didn't bring up the past and neither did I. My mind was playing with me because it felt like old times. Except, we weren't lovers, we weren't having sex, and we weren't young as hell anymore. I got a call from my office. I need to go back and handle a few projects, so I am getting myself prepared to go back to Atlanta. I'm not ready. I want to stay here. However, I have responsibilities, and I need to handle things instead of running from them. I'm not great at facing my problems. And I need to change that. I don't know what I will do about Kane. Can I really give up on my marriage? I still love him even after all the shit he put me through.

I'm headed over to Pharaoh's place to let him know I am leaving. I felt like it was something I couldn't say on the phone. Besides, I need to let him know why I left the hospital so abruptly. I am sick of running from everything. I want all my cards on the table. Like City said, I need to close some doors.

"Hey Paige, you look beautiful today," Pharaoh says as he opens the door.

"Thanks, did I interrupt your workout?" He is shirtless and I'm sure I'm drooling.

"No, come on in. What can I get you to drink? Water, coffee, tea?"

"Coffee please."

"Have a seat, let me put on a shirt and one coffee coming up."

While he is in the back putting on a shirt, I walk around checking out his home. His designs got better. His work is on whole other scale. I see the shelves he used to have in his apartment, and I had a flashback of him fucking me on the side of it. Alright Paige let's not go there. That's not why you're here.

"What are you over there smiling about, Shorty?"

"Nothing, I see you still designing a lot of stuff. It looks great in here."

"I still play around with a few things. Not as much as I used to. I design buildings now. Do you still paint and draw?"

"No, I lost a lot of motion in my hands when they were broken. I haven't touched a paint brush in years."

I see the sadness in his eyes. He is walking toward me, and his hands are on my face. "Paige, I'm so sorry. I never, never wanted to hurt you. I made a promise to you, and I feel like I let you down. Can you ever forgive me?

"Listen it happened, and I'll admit I blamed you for a long time. City and I were talking, and something became clear to me. I haven't closed the door on you because I haven't forgiven you. I hated you for a minute." He moves his hands, and I walk to the window because I need to say everything, and I can't do that looking in his eyes. "When I came out that coma, I saw all your flowers and cards and notes. The nurse told me how you tried to come and see me every day. I was so hurt especially when I lifted my hands, and they were both broken. The doctors told me I would heal but they didn't know how much damage was done. Then, I saw the burn on my leg, and I freaked out because they told me about all the surgeries I would need."

"Paige." He is coming toward me; I hear his footsteps. I turn to face him.

"No, let me finish. The thing that hurt the most was when they told me I lost the baby. I had to come to terms with a lot of things in that hospital that day. I had to realize I didn't want to become my mom and sacrifice myself for a man who loved the streets and money more than he loved me. I made the decision to leave. And I fell into a deep depression, along with all the hospital stays and rehab I went through. The hardest part was not being able to talk to or see you. City sent me pictures of your progress until I begged her to stop. I knew you were good. But I just wasn't. I want to apologize for running. I should have stayed and faced you." I look at him holding his head down and shaking it. And he walks closer to me.

"A baby? Why didn't you tell me?"

"I didn't know how. It was so much at one time. I blamed you. I blamed me. I blamed everything. It took me a long time to accept it.

"You still should have told me! It was my baby too! I knew you were hurt and in pain, but I didn't do it on purpose. I wanted to be there and help you through everything, but you shut me out. We lost a baby? You didn't have the right to keep that from me."

"Yes, I did!" I got emotional. "I dealt with it; you didn't have to deal with it. Listen, I want you to know I forgive you. And I'm really sorry for laying all of this on you. I just wanted to clear the air once and for all." I grab my purse and start toward the door when I feel him wrapping his arms around me.

"No, you don't get run again. You stay and face me this time. Do you really think I didn't do everything in my power to protect you? I never meant for anything to happen to you. I did everything I could to save you that night. You weren't the only one who went through pain and suffering. I lost you. I felt like shit for so long. I tried my hardest to find you and when you finally resurfaced you up and married someone. It was like I never existed in your life. Here I was hurting, and you were off getting happily married. Now, you come in here and drop this information on me and you want to run back to your little happy life. Do you understand what you're doing?"

"I didn't mean to hurt you. I just thought you should know. I want you to move on with your life too. I wanted nothing to hold you back like it's been holding me back. And who told you my life was happy?"

"I saw you. I saw you on your wedding day. You were smiling and laughing, and it felt like I was dying because that should have been us."

"You were there?"

"Yes, I wanted to make sure he was what you wanted. And I saw for myself he was. I witnessed the only woman I've ever loved, love someone else. So don't walk in here talking about your closure and feeling better. I didn't get closure. I didn't get to grieve our baby, and I didn't get a happy ending. You're still as selfish as ever."

"Selfish! Selfish, is thinking your lifestyle wouldn't touch me and it did. Selfish is you still getting to live out your dream while I can't. Selfish, is thinking I could ever be happy without you."

He hugs me. He is holding me so tightly I thought I was going to stop breathing. I didn't even realize how hard I was crying. It is finally out. Everything I thought about him. Everything I felt. Everything that happened. I am relieved and overwhelmed at the same time. I don't know how long we stand like that, but I feel myself being lifted bridal style and carried to his bedroom.

He sits me down on his bed and starts kissing my hands. I thought they were wet from his kisses, but it was his tears. He moves my hair out of my face and starts kissing me. I should have protested, I know, but I don't. His mouth on my mouth feels like heaven and I've missed heaven. I stand to let him undress me and I undress him. He stands up and pulls me up too. He stood back and just looked at me.

I try to cover myself. I wasn't the smaller Paige from years ago. I had grown, and I was fat in some places and had stretch marks in other places. He gently moves my hands.

"You are still as beautiful as I remember. Don't try and hide anything from me. I want to see everything. Let me, please."

I can't answer because his touch on my body feels incredible and I am afraid if I say anything he will stop. I watch as his fingers trace every part of my body. When he gets to my nipples he smiles and looks at me. He goes lower to my stomach that I am trying to suck it in, but I can't. He gets on his knees and kisses it. When he gets to my thighs and sees the tattoo covering the scar on my leg, he pauses for a minute and traces every design contained in the tattoo.

"Paige, this is every place we used to travel when I first met you. It's beautiful. Is this me?"

"Yes, it's you." The burn scars on my thigh were so bad they were unable to be fixed. I covered the scar with something positive. All the things I loved and right in middle, buried but still visible, was a picture of Pharaoh dressed as an Egyptian Pharaoh. You really had to look close to see it. The tattoo artist I had to do it was very good and very detailed. It was beautiful. I turned something ugly into something beautiful. Kane hated it and he hated my nipple rings too. He told me I should thank him for coming along and showing me something other than hood shit. I made sure I always wore skirts long enough to cover it, so no one saw it. He made me feel ashamed of who I used to be as a person and here Pharaoh is making me feel so beautiful.

"It's beautiful and so are you."

"I gained some weight."

"And? It's all beautiful to me. Let me show you. Sit down. On the bed."

I sit down and he stands in front of me. I can tell he still works out because his body is cut everywhere. I reach out to run my fingers across his abs and when I look down his dick is rock-hard and asking for me to touch it. So that's what I did. I touch it and stroke it. It has been so long since I was this excited about a man. Hell, about sex. I want to continue touching him, but he moves my hand.

"As good as your hands feel, this is about you and not me."

He starts touching and kissing every part of my body. I swear he doesn't leave a spot untouched. I have my eyes closed enjoying every minute of it. When I feel him kissing my tattoo, I can't help but start moaning because his hand is touching my inner thigh.

"At last, a real reaction. You want me to kiss you here?"

His fingers are gliding against my lady lips, and my voice is caught.

"Don't be shy, say kiss me Pharaoh."

I feel him slowly opening me up. I can feel his breathe on me.

"You smell so good. Tell me to kiss it. Let me know you want me to do."

"Pharaoh, please."

"Please what?"

"Please kiss me." And just like that I feel extremely soft kisses and then his tongue circles my clit. I lose it when his finger slips in me. I am cumming and he wasn't even down there for two minutes. "Right there Pharaoh, right there." When I say his name, it's like he goes harder. I moan and scream his name like a mad woman when I reach my orgasm. I am beyond myself. It had been so long since I'd had one and before I can recover he is hovering over me. He is biting and licking my nipple and when he pulls on my nip ring, I lose it again. I can't believe I came just from that sensation. The look on his face is a curious one. I can't read it. I feel him spreading my legs and entering me so slowly, I almost come again.

"Paige, you're tight. Does he even touch you?"

I don't want to think about Kane right now. Not at this moment. Not when I feel like I am losing my mind. Not when I am in the midst of sin. I close my eyes because I just want the moment to last forever.

"Open your eyes, look at me, feel me. You were giving him my pussy?"

I don't know how he wants me to answer that.

"Don't get quiet now."

I feel him pushing in and out of me with more intensity. I am biting my lips, trying not to scream.

"You couldn't have been giving him anything, you feel so tight. You're so damn wet. Whose pussy is this, Paige?"

Fuck, my eyes are rolling back, and I feel another orgasm coming on again, when I feel him pull out causing my eyes to pop open and look at him.

"I asked you a question. Turnover, get on your knees." I do exactly what he says when I feel a slap on my ass and then I feel him tapping his dick on my butt.

"I shouldn't even give you this dick. You out here giving this pussy to that lame ass nigga. I'll ask you again, and if you don't answer you not getting this dick. Whose pussy?"

"It's yours Pharaoh." When I feel him enter me again, it's like the earth has moved. "It's always been yours."

"Damn right, stop giving my pussy to him, it's mine again. All mine. I'll kill him if he touches this again."

Pharaoh and I had sex in every position, in every room in his home. I watched the sun set and rise again. He's sleeping, and I am standing looking out his window. The guilt of everything I had done with him hits me so hard. I can't believe what I had done. This isn't me. I respect my vows. And then there is this part of me that feels alive again. I had to face myself. Either I want this, or I want my life back in Atlanta. This is complex. I don't know anything about Pharaoh and years change people because I was changed. Sure, the sex was good but what else do we have in common now? I can't draw with him anymore. What the hell will we talk about? And who walks away from their marriage after a fling? You really did it this time Paige.

"Why you over there overthinking everything? Come get back in this bed."

"I would like to do that, but I have to get ready. I have a flight booked to get back to Atlanta. I have some projects due, and I have to get back to my life. Pharaoh, this was. . ."

"It was too short. Can't you work remotely from here? Or I can hire you to work."

"Do you even know what I do?"

"You're an excellent accountant at one of the top firms in Atlanta. Just because I'm not in your life doesn't mean I didn't care enough to know about your life."

I smile. This man here is everything I need; it just isn't the right time. "Let me go and get showered and changed. Call me and we can get together tonight and have dinner. It's not fair you know everything about me and I know nothing about you."

"Sounds good, just don't hop on a plane and disappear on me again. I have something for you."

He gets up and I take in his body once again because he is naked. He walks toward me, dick just swinging, and everything in me is saying get back in the damn bed. He goes in his closet and comes out wearing a pair of basketball shorts. He has something in his hands. When he reaches it to me I know what it is, my old notebook.

"I wanted to send it to you, but I'll admit I held on to a lot of your things. I feel like you need to have it back now."

My hands are trembling just holding it. I haven't looked at any of my work from the past because it held too many memories. Flipping through the pages, I touch all the pictures I had drawn. They were my very first moments in New York. I smile when I get to the picture of City at the club and Pharaoh on the train. This is everything to me. I close it and press the book to my heart. "Thank you, this means a lot to me."

"I wasn't able to design anything after the accident. It took me some time. Those months were the hardest for me. I can't imagine how tough these years have been for you. Creativity was your backbone."

"It's been different. I put myself in my work. I work hard at managing accounts, so I don't have to think of drawing or painting. This really does mean a lot to me."

"Paige, don't go getting on a plane and jetting away on me again." He leans down and gives me a forehead kiss. "This time I will come and get you."

"I won't, I'll see you for dinner tonight." I clutch the notebook close to my chest again and then I walk out of his home feeling on top of the world. How can something so wrong feel so right? For the first time in years, I am going to go with my feeling. I am going to follow something that makes me feel good. City was right. I need closure, but first I am going to figure out how to do it my way.

Chapter Fifteen

If We Are Being Honest

Hakeem "King" Mann

I made a way to be honest with you. But I wasn't always honest with you. You want all of me and I said ok. But this feeling in my heart is not speaking the same way.

Sitting in my office, I was thinking about the other night at the club with City, Ace and Paige. It was just like old times.

The only difference this time was there wasn't an accident, and no one got hurt. City insisted they get an Uber home, and I was against it, but I completely understood. I want City here 24/7 but she is so damn stubborn I know she will never agree. Having her here these past few weeks has been refreshing. Well, it was until I got that last text.

"Hey King, I'm headed out. You need something before I go?" Jinx walks into my office and announces.

"Umm, no, I don't need anything."

"You good man, is there a problem?"

"I got a little something I need to deal with but nothing I can't handle."

"I hope it doesn't involve any gun play. Ace walking around here on cloud nine, I would hate for anything to happen with him and Shorty again. Let me know right now if we got any problems."

"Nothing like that but I may need for you to take someone out."

"Let me know who and I'll get it done."

"Cola."

"Man, here I thought you were serious. Just stop fooling with her. I told you that a long time ago. I guess with City in town you can't give her all the attention she requires?"

"She knows the rules. That's not the problem; she just sent me a pic of a positive pregnancy test." I can't believe I fucked up. I never went in Cola raw. I want to think this is some type of mistake, but I know a couple of months ago I went over to her place really fucked up, so it is possible.

"Damn King, what you gone do?"

"What you gone do about what?" Ace walks in and takes a seat.

"He done fucked up and got that crazy girl Cola knocked up."

"Damn, Jinx, let me tell my own business. I fucked up Ace and Cola might be having my baby."

Jinx looks at me. "I just told him already."

"You want Jinx to get rid of her?" Ace says with his face all serious.

"I told him I'll do it. I don't have any problem doing it. I never liked her anyway," Jinx says.

"I told this fool to let her go years ago. She's not right in the head if you ask me. People like that can't be trusted."

Me and Jinx look at Ace and start cracking up laughing. "Ace, your ass is not right in the head. What the hell are you talking about?"

"Yeah Ace, you the last one to talk about somebody. But I told him the same thing. I told him to leave her alone. Check this, I won't have to do any killing. City about to kill both of them."

"You got a point Jinx. She'll take care of this whole situation. King, you sure it's yours?"

I run my hand over my face. "I don't know. I don't remember going up in her raw but a couple of months ago I spent the night, I was real fucked up and anything could have happened. I don't even want to think about what City will do. She'll leave me." I get up from my desk and start pacing the floor. I am so in love with City. She is everything to me. I pictured us having little chocolate babies together. Not me having a baby with someone else. City is a lot of things, but she is very unforgiving. Once, a girl popped up on us having dinner and she didn't speak to me for six months. It wasn't like I was unfaithful. Our only rule was when we were together it was about us. That meant no one surfaced. No one. I won't be able to keep a baby hidden. This will crush her.

"Calm down Hakeem. Sit down man. Let's think about this. You can always get a blood test. If the baby is yours City would have to understand. Besides, both you and her are in this fake relationship. She bounces all over the globe and you bounce around New York. Once she comes back in town, you guys act like the perfect King and Queen. I just don't get it," Ace says shaking his head.

"It's not for anyone to get. That's just how we want it to be."

"Sounds like you guys are in an open relationship. The rules in open relationships mean anything can happen. Get a blood test before you open your mouth. I got to roll." Jinx gets up and daps me and Ace then walks out the room.

"How do you really feel?"

"I feel like I might be having a prince or princess, and I can't be excited about it because it's not with the person I really want."

"Nah, don't give me that bullshit. You have feelings for Cola. You just don't want to admit it. You've been on and off with her for years. When City's not here you two are all in love and when City comes back in town you run back to City. You always liked having options. Your options may have just run out."

What he said is true. I don't hate Cola. I just don't get the same feeling with her as I get with City. Cola gives me what I need when City is absent. But she was never a replacement for her. She was only a placeholder.

"Let me think it out. I'll figure something out. What's going on with you and Paige?"

"Just seeing her walk into my club the other night, I almost lost it. She's still so beautiful. Every damn part of her."

Ace has this glazed look in his eyes. My brother is so in love with her, and I don't want her to break his heart again. But I'm not going to say that to him. Paige is a sensitive subject for him. He loves her so much he was willing to give up our business relationship to keep her in his life. At least that's what he wanted to do after the accident. I worked without him for about a year. Until we finally found Marcus. What Ace did to him made me cringe and we're both professional killers. With Paige being back I know he is ready to get out again. He is successful in his field. I was thinking about getting out, but I love the money too much. "Don't fall too hard, Pharaoh, she still has a situation."

"Yeah she does, but that lame ass nigga can't be handling her right."

"You did have sex with her. When was it? Me and City had a bet that it would happen that night. I told her give you a day."

"It's none of your business. That's crazy. I can't believe you and her discussing us like that."

"Please, the look you two were giving each other all night gave it away. I'm just glad you're relaxed a little. Take it slow."

"I am. In fact, we are having dinner tonight. I'm on my way over right now."

"Perfect, let's double date like we used to back in the day. It'll help with my nerves being around City."

"You just trying to bring me along for security. You scared of City's ass."

"You're damn right I am. I'll sleep on it and decide what I want to do."

"I support you either way big bro."

Chapter Sixteen

Not So Damn Fast
Kane Daniels

You underestimate the hold I have on you. The ability I have to make you do what I want you to do. I have shown you love and respect. But just enough to keep you in check. You can't walk away. It's safer to stay.

It had been almost three weeks since I'd heard from Paige. I sent a private investigator to watch her and get me pictures of her every move. I didn't miss her or care if she was good. I needed one thing from her, her money. Paige had made excellent money off not only her investments but also her paintings she sold to a gallery before we married. She wasn't rich but very well off. She assumed my financial status matched hers. That wasn't the case. I only gave the appearance of having money. I was in debt, deep in debt. Doing an internship with a life insurance company had its benefits. It was boring but in their computer system I learned everything about who was due to inherit money and who wasn't. Meeting her that day wasn't by chance at Whole Foods. I had done great research on her and her father. She was due to inherit more money from the death of her father. His body was unearth in some swap area in Louisiana. Once he was identified and declared dead my company was in charge of contacting the next of kin. He had a very large insurance policy, and she was the beneficiary. That was something no one knew, not even her. I saw Paige listed one day in an article for an up-and-coming Atlanta professional as a woman to watch under 30. She was beautiful, so I researched her. And boy did I hit the jackpot. She was damaged and alone when I met her making her an extra easy mark.

I picked Paige not only for her money but because she had all the right investor connections. I made sure I got to know each and every one of them. I was planning on making a run for District Attorney next year. I knew with all the dirt I had on some of my clients, Paige's money and all the investor connections I had, my financing would be secured. I wasn't about to let her mess up my plan. I was hoping the investigator would come back with some dirt on her but so far her ass was being good. Only shopping, eating and hanging out with her bat shit crazy cousin. I couldn't stand City. She had forced Paige to get a prenup. Telling her it was better safer than sorry. I was sorry I signed it. If Paige could prove I cheated I would walk away with nothing from this marriage. If she ever cheated I was set to be extremely rich.

I wanted to schedule my announcement to run for DA next month. The exclusive club I wanted to have the announcement party was going to cost me a pretty penny. I needed Paige to co-sign on transfers I needed done to make my big event happen. If I didn't need her I would've let her ass stay in New York. It was peaceful without all her damn nagging. But I did, so here I am standing outside of her cousin's City's door ready to beg her to come back home. I was prepared to put my best acting skills into action. I heard them both having a conversation. I put my ear to the door and listened.

"You're looking cute my little Paige Turner. Tell me what's on the menu tonight. No wait, let me guess, Pharaoh," I heard her loud ass cousin say.

"Is your mind always in the gutter?" She asked.

"Most of the time it is," she answered. "Sorry to disappoint you but we agreed not to have sex again until I felt ready. Right now, we are just getting to know each other."

"Just childish. I thought after you came in here glowing the other day this cat and mouse game would be over."

"Let's not go there ok. I never should have crossed that line."

"Too late, you already did, and you can't turn back time. Just keep doing you until you lose that little voice of reason in the back of your head. Hell, I would."

"It's not that simple. And you keep forgetting I'm still married."

"Nah, you need to forget it. He cheated; you got a get out of jail free card. Let that shit go and move on. Don't feel guilty. He hurt you first."

"You know what Aunt Dana would say, two wrongs don't make it right."

"I know, I know. His dumb ass deserved it and your dried up coochie needed it. Besides, has he even called you? Sent a text asking why you're here and not home?"

"No, he sent a text to ask if I was on working on an account for one of our sister firms out here and I told him yes."

"Why didn't you tell him the truth?"

"I didn't want to fuss over the phone. I would rather handle it in person."

"And when do you plan to handle it?"

"I don't know. Stop pressuring me. I'll do it when I have to I guess. Now leave it alone."

I see my sneaky wife has been sneaking around. She's planning to leave me. I won't let that happen right now. I want to get all my money first. I knocked on the door and City opened it looking at me all disgusted. "City it's good to see you. Where's my wife?"

"Paige, get ready. There's something at the door you need to handle."

"City, stop playing." I heard Paige say. When she turned the corner she had the same look as City.

"Hey baby, you look amazing."

"She should she dropped some stress," City said staring at me. "As always it's good to see you too City. May I come in?"

"I don't know. Paige, can he?"

Paige just stood there looking at me. "Well Paige, I came a long way, are you going to let me in?"

"Kane, how did you get here?"

"By plane and then taxi. Come here baby." I walked over to her trying to hug her. "You really do look good. Did you change your hair or something?"

I couldn't tell what Paige had done to herself, but she really did look astonishing. I may not have been in love with her, but the sex was always good. And right now, she looked good enough for me to take back to the hotel and bang her back out.

"No, I haven't changed my hair. And again, what are you doing here?"

"Why don't you come back with me to the hotel room, and we can sit down and talk. I know everything between us hasn't been perfect, but I miss you and I want you to come back home." I was trying to lay it on thick. I took her hand, but she pulled it back.

"Everything between us is far from perfect. I doubt you missed me at all. What's the real reason you're here?"

"That is the real reason. The last time we spoke you were angry; I was upset and then you just up and left. I was giving you time to yourself, but now you've been gone too long. I really do miss you and I want you to come back home." I walked toward her, and she backed away. What the hell was going on with her? She's been around City too long.

"I wasn't angry, I was hurt when we spoke. I was angry when I got the fruit basket for your little bitch."

Damn, my secretary was getting fired once I got back to Atlanta. This was her second time sending the wrong shit to my women. I knew I shouldn't have slept with her. She wanted me to herself and that was never going to happen. "I don't know what you're talking about, I sent you roses and swung by your office for lunch. But you weren't available."

"Roses and fruit are two different things. I am sick of you trying to play me."

"Paige, I wouldn't play you. I'll admit I have taken you for granted and for that I'm sorry. We're married, and things happen. When they do, we need to work on it not run away from it."

"I don't feel like there's anything for us to work on. You don't respect me; you don't value me and I'm still wondering do you even love me. If I have to wonder, that's a big problem. I think you should leave."

"Yes, leave now!" City said.

"Paige, we're married. You can't just call it quits after one thing. Just give me a chance to explain."

"I think the ladies asked you to leave." I turned around and saw two guys standing behind City.

"Yep, so leave. She doesn't want your ass anymore. Keep it moving," City said.

"Look, calm your big, dumb, ghetto ass down City. This is between me and my wife."

"Did this fool just call me dumb and ghetto? Oh no, not today. You got the right one. I'mma show you who's ghetto." The guy who spoke earlier grabbed her as she lunged at me. "No Hakeem, let me go. He has it coming."

"Man, you are not going to be disrespectful to my woman. Now the ladies asked your ass to leave. I suggest you do so before I really have to welcome you to New York," Hakeem said, moving City behind him.

"Paige, please. I was there for you when you needed me. I got you through a lot. We shared vows together. We made a promise to each other." Again, I reached for her, and I saw what I said was getting through to her. If I could just get her out of here I would be home free. "What we have, doesn't have to do with anyone else. Let's just discuss this in private."

"Paige you don't have to discuss anything with him. You say the word and I'll make him leave. It's your decision." The other guy came and stepped closer to Paige.

"Who the fuck are you?" The way he was staring at her made me become possessive of her. All she was doing was standing there looking confused.

"I'm Ace and really, you don't want to know me," He answered.

"Paige, is this the clown that gave you those ugly scars? Are we really doing this right now? Do you really want to go back down that road again? I've never hurt you like he did." She was still standing there looking from me to this clown.

"Shorty, those scars have healed. The emotional scars he's inflicting on you won't heal if you keep letting him control and hurt you."

"Paige, dammit, say something." I yelled to her.

Chapter Seventeen

Decisions
Paige Turner Daniels

I was stuck between a rock and a hard place. I couldn't make my heart, and my head agree. I closed my eyes and screamed. I felt like the hard place and the rock were crushing me.

I was standing there listening to Kane and Pharaoh. I was looking back and forth between them both, my present and my past. This should be an easy choice. Pharaoh was right, Kane was hurting me and the pain I was feeling was internal. No one could see it but me. No one knew how I was really feeling. I didn't even express myself to Pharaoh; he said he could see the unhappiness in my eyes. I felt dead and empty inside. I felt like the life had been sucked out of me. At first, I thought it was because I missed doing my art but when City and I were talking and laughing, I felt like I missed another part of me. She was always more than a cousin; she was like my sister. She was a part of me that was irreplaceable. And what did I do? I let Kane separate us. I could say a million times I didn't, but I did. I chose to love my husband and let my sister go. I wasn't about to allow that to happen again. I loved and missed her way too much. I needed her, and she needed me. Our relationship was important.

I also missed love. I realized it when I felt Pharaoh's touch. His touch was so authentic. The way he made me feel was like nothing in this world I'd ever felt before. His kindness was amazing and the way we were able to communicate with each other, Kane and I just didn't have that. Our conversations flowed so easy without being forced. I felt so comfortable talking with him. He wasn't judging me or calling me hood. He wasn't telling me I was nagging him or requiring too much of his attention. As a woman, I needed and longed for that feeling. I felt warm inside and that was a big change from the cold and distant person I had become. It made me wonder did I change for me, or did I change for Kane?

On the other hand, Kane was also right. The scars on my body from my time with Pharaoh had healed, but was I healed? There was still so much pain and hurt. Dare I say I was a little jealous, too. I couldn't figure that part out. I didn't have a jealous bone in my body. Yet, here I was jealous because he was actually living out his dream. I couldn't watch him do that every day. We were going to be artists together. At least that was our plan in the past. He wanted to design buildings, and I wanted to paint them, or at least have my art designs hanging in them. He promised he would design an art gallery just for me. When I looked at him that's all I saw sometimes, past promises, past hurt, past dreams and past failures. None of those things would happen now. And what about my life? I almost died and several pieces of me did die that night. Not just my hands, but our baby. Could I really take that kind of chance again? Talking with him, he never said if he was still in the streets, and like a fool, I didn't ask. I saw his home and his car, hell that watch on his arm. He and Hakeem were big in the streets. I heard the rumors. I felt the stares and the whispers when we were dating. I remembered how cautiously he used to move. Even at the club the other night, I still felt like the street boss in him never died. I saw the way people moved and jumped when he spoke. How they scattered out of his way when he walked. He still even walked like a boss; his whole demeanor was screaming boss. I couldn't trust that he didn't still have enemies. I couldn't trust my safety with him anymore. I didn't know him anymore and he didn't know me. How could we get back together without knowing each other?

I guess the same could be said about Kane. When I met him, he was so different from Pharaoh. He came in my life and just made sense. By that I mean he was my grown-up relationship. He didn't know the artist; he knew the accountant only. He didn't mind that I buried myself in my work. He never complained that most nights I was at work late because his grind was just as hard as mine. We were a perfect couple, with the perfect home, perfect cars and perfect jobs. But perfection was just an illusion. We worked so hard at being perfect, we forgot to be us. The man that once held me when I had nightmares was now barely in the same bed as me. The man that overlooked my scars now made me feel ashamed of them. The man who vowed to love me was now giving his love to someone else. That hurt me. I wanted the man who would share his dreams with me. I wanted the man that would take me on dates, and I wanted the man who would love me again. I knew Kane seemed cold and insensitive, but I knew the funny side of him. The side that was kind and caring. The side that didn't have much growing up like me and was just as alone in this world as I was. The side that wasn't this cocky ass attorney, but a man who would change his clothes a million times to try and make himself look confident, just so he could feel confident. The side that made me fall in love with him. How could I walk away from that man? He had a hand at molding me into this strong, hard-working businesswoman. He was a big reason for my success. How could I just up and leave for one mistake? We took vows.

I was confused and angry and I felt like I was being forced to decide. All I wanted to do was run. I covered my face with my hands and turned my back to all of them in frustration. How could I choose? I couldn't choose; both of these relationships had hurt and scared me. Both of these men had brought me pleasure and pain. Could I even make the right decision? Hell, was there a right decision?

I felt a hand touch me on my shoulder and I jumped. "Paige, it's ok, it's me, City. You don't have to decide anything right now. I need both of you to step away from my cousin and let her breath."

Hearing her speak, I wanted and needed her protection. I wanted to hide behind her and remain safe. I couldn't live my life like that. I was always running from my problems. It was a bad habit I had developed, and it needed to stop. Knowing it was time to stop running, I turned around. "No, City, let me handle this, please. I've avoided so many situations in my life by running and I'm sick of running. I can't run anymore."

"Don't let them rush you. You have the right to take all the time you need to take. Just say the word and I'll put them all out."

"I know and I'm not letting them rush me. I know what I need to do City." I gently moved her out of the way. I wanted the resolution in my mind to be like a math equation, if I subtract the right one the remaining one would be the solution to everything. But this wasn't math, and I didn't know if the resolution I was deciding on would be the best. I took a deep breath and finally spoke. "Kane, can you wait for me outside please."

"Paige, I'll wait outside but not for long. Our marriage shouldn't be up for debate. We have a wonderful, perfect life in Atlanta. Since I've met you, I've done nothing but rebuild what he tore down. Don't let one mistake break us. We are stronger than that. We vowed for better or worse. Just give us another chance and I promise I will change. I love you." Kane walked up to me and kissed me on my forehead and ran his hands down my arms and stood there staring at me. He leaned down and whispered, "You can't leave me now, you promised, and I need you."

His words hit me so hard. I did promise. I did take vows. "Kane, I know, just please give me a minute and wait outside."

"You heard my cousin. Wait your ass outside," City said opening the door for him to exit.

When City closed the door, I took another deep breath, and my eyes met Pharaoh's eyes. Why did he still have to be so damn sexy? He was dressed down today in some dark-colored blue jeans and a button-down white shirt and some Timberlands. He looked so New York, and I admired that about him. As smart as he was, he blended in, in any environment. The way he was looking at me, I wanted to run into his arms and melt. He should have gotten old and ugly, that way I could say this was an easy choice. That wasn't the case. He was still handsome, still fine and I saw the growth in him. The thing was, he'd grown past our hurt. I was still living in it. I couldn't lose everything I worked so hard to get. I wasn't a young girl anymore. I was a woman, with a real life and real bills and a real career. I no longer held my vision of love in a naïve way. I knew love couldn't conquer all. I knew love wasn't the solution to everything. I knew just living off love wasn't possible. As much as I wanted to give everything up, I just couldn't. I knew I didn't know this Pharaoh. I was holding on to the man I meet and knew years ago. And he was still holding on to the girl he met years ago. I had changed. I was different. He was different. I couldn't turn my back on my husband for a dream. As much as I wanted the dream, I had said vows and for a moment I forgot we vowed until death do us part. I needed to give us another chance. I needed to fight for my marriage. Fight for the life I had worked so hard to build. After all, Kane needed me.

"Paige, these past few days with you have been perfect. Don't walk away from me now," Pharaoh said moving toward me. His eyes were pleading with me to stay.

"Pharaoh, for years I never wanted to look at you again. In fact, I avoided anything that had something to do with you. Deep down inside, I blamed you for the accident and me losing my ability to draw. I know now, and I guess I've always known you would never purposely hurt me. I'm so sorry I blamed you. You didn't deserve that from me." I grabbed his hands and ran my fingers across his scars.

"Paige, I'm so sorry about the accident and if I could take it all back I would. I would change everything about that night. If I could, I would take all your scars away."

"I know you would. But we can't undo that night. I can say seeing you, spending time with you has given me something I didn't get years ago. It has given me strength to let go of my hurt. I was wrong for sleeping with you—"

"Wrong? Nothing about what we did was wrong. Did it really feel wrong to you? The way I touched you, the way you touched me. The way your body responded. No shorty, nothing about that was wrong."

Hearing him call me shorty and remembering him touching me almost made me spread my legs for him again. "I'm married, and I don't care how angry I was with him, it didn't give me the right to spread my legs with someone else. I should have respected my vows the same way I want him to respect me."

"I knew your situation and I'm man enough to admit I didn't give a fuck about it. Fuck his punk ass. What happened between us wasn't a mistake. We were drawn to each other. That's how it's always been for us. I respect you because I know you're a good person. You're a good woman who deserves more than what he's giving you—"

I interrupted him, "You don't really know me. You know who I used to be. And I'm not her anymore. I've grown and so have you. We can't go back to the past and just rekindle something thinking it will be the same. It was crazy of me to think that way. I have a life that doesn't involve the creative me and you have a life that's all creative. In a way, I'm jealous of that. You're living your dream. I created a new dream and I'm living it. I'm so proud of the man you've grown into. But Pharaoh, understand that I have to continue to write this chapter in my life before I start a new one."

"He can't love you like I can. I can get some of the best surgeons to work on your hands. Or we can try some computer programs. I just don't want to lose you again Paige." He caressed my face so gently and I felt my heart breaking.

"Listen to yourself. You want me to be that Paige again, and I'm not. I lost a piece of me that a doctor can't bring back. I lost a part of us that I can never get back. You don't know this Paige. I've accepted this me and so has Kane. I will always love you Pharaoh. But I have to go back to my life."

"I've never stopped loving you. And I won't ever stop. I understand how you feel, and I won't make you choose me. Even though we know I'm the better man." He smiled, but I saw the hurt in his eyes. "Don't let him keep controlling you. The Paige I met was a fighter and free thinker. That had nothing to do with your art. I've learned that life doesn't have the greatest timing but given enough time you can change, even prepare for just the right time. I believe in what I feel, and I've learned to act on it not react on it. You're right, we don't know each other anymore."

"Exactly, I'm so glad you understand. Good luck with everything." I hugged him, and he smelled so damn good I didn't want to let go. But I did. I walked over to City, and she looked so mad with me. "City."

"Don't you City me. You know I hate him. I hate him for you. You looked so miserable when you got here. I don't want him stealing your joy and your soul again. He makes you so unhappy. If you want, I can tell King to make him disappear. He'll do it and I know Pharaoh will help. You won't have to worry about divorcing him," she said, serious as hell.

"No City, please don't do that. Remember we had this big talk about closure. About me not walking through another door before I close the other one. Well, let me work through this please."

"But I missed you."

"Aww, I missed you too. And I promise nothing will keep me away from you again. Not even Kane this time."

"Promise?"

"I promise. But you promise me you'll start taking some of your own advice. Talk to him," I whispered in her ear as I hugged her.

"Ok my little Paige Turner. Are you sure we can't kick his ass one good time?"

"Yeah, Paige, please let me kick his ass. I want to show him a real thug, all that damn court talking his ass was doing up in here," Hakeem said.

"Calm down Bonnie and Clyde." I laughed and walked toward the door. I looked back at the three people standing there looking at me, and my heart hurt. I was finally closing the door, and I didn't know how to feel about it. I was walking back into a life I built without them, and I didn't like the way that was making me feel. I wanted to take each one of them with me. City for her beauty and her ability to make me laugh and smile. Hakeem for his wisdom. He had this presence that spoke louder than any words could ever speak about him. I understood why he was King on the streets. And Pharaoh, he was once air to me and now he was a breath of fresh air. He showed me what I was missing with Kane. I was missing passion, and fun, and love. I knew I had to change us. I wanted those things in my life. If this marriage was going to work, I needed him to provide those things. I needed the Kane I first met and fell in love with again. I needed dates and quality time. I needed so much; I hope he was prepared to give it all to me. "I'll see you guys later." I walked out the door and hopefully into a bright future with my husband.

Chapter Eighteen

I Can't Let Go

Ace Pharaoh Mann

I miss you more today than yesterday. If that's possible. I miss you like my next breath and I'm finding it hard to breathe. I'm gasping for air, please come back and save me.

King and I were headed to board our jet. He and I were about to fly out to Cali. We were finally going to take care of our target. I was glad. I was ready to be done with it. I had better things to focus on. Since Paige left New York, I couldn't get her off my mind. I went through every emotion possible over the past couple of months. I was hurt, upset, angry, sad and lost. I couldn't understand how I let her walk out of my life again. I felt our connection and it was strong as hell; it wasn't just physical. After we would have sex we would lay together and just talk. We talked about everything except how she felt. She was good at avoiding telling me how she felt about me. Then I started to think maybe she was just using me to get back at her husband. But I was good at reading people and her eyes were telling me they loved me. I wasn't imagining that, and I was sure of it.

"Ace, you good man? You been quiet the whole ride. No smart-ass remarks. No comments about my shoes. You feeling ok?" King asked while trying to feel my forehead.

I was trying to dodge his hands. "Man, if you don't go ahead with all that bullshit. I'm good, just thinking about something.

"Something or someone? I can't believe she still has your head so gone."

"She's special."

"Take her husband out and be done with it."

"That won't do nothing but hurt her. For some reason she loves him, and I can't figure out why."

"You can't figure it out because she doesn't love him. Baby brother, you're still wet behind the ears when it comes to women. I need you to get out more or something."

"You get out enough for the both of us. What are you seeing that I'm not seeing? Because I saw her walk out with him. That could only be love."

"You think it's love because that's the only emotion you think she understands. Women are crazy, but they are also complex. She's married to the man, she feels obligated to him. At this moment, he's her comfort zone. She's herself with him. She knows what to expect and how to deal with it."

"I know they're complex. Especially Paige. But she knows me too. She can be herself around me."

"You mean her old self?"

"Her old self or her new self. She can be anything around me. It wouldn't change the way I feel for her. I tried to make that clear. I wanted her to understand, past or present, I love her."

"Did you really make it clear? Before you say yes, do you remember what she said to you that day? She said you love the artist in her, and she wasn't an artist anymore. All you came back with was you could fix it."

"Because I can fix it. I can get her to see the best doctors or help her learn those computer programs. I can get her doing art again."

"She was right, all you know is the girl from your past. Are you in love with a memory?"

"Come on King, I love her for her. I don't care if she can create art or not. I love everything about her. All I have is memories. I can't help I hold them so close to my heart. It's all I have left."

"Create new ones."

"I was trying to do that with her. That's why I wanted to meet at the club, so she wouldn't always have bad memories of us at a club. I planned on doing more, I just didn't plan on her leaving so soon."

"What, if nothing else, have you learned in our line of work?"

"When you fail to plan, you plan to fail." I was nodding my head because I understood what he was saying to me. I didn't plan it out good. I was just hoping she would see me, and everything would fall in line. I should have known better. That wasn't how she operated.

"Take a step and think this out in your head. If she's worth it to you, find out who she is now. Stop trying to force her to be who she used to be. I think the past is still hurting her, so you need to move in the present. You need to find a way to get to know this Paige. What does she do for fun now? What do you both still have in common?"

"Ok, ok, look at you coming with some knowledge. You may have a point."

"Once in a while I need to break you off with the King's point of view."

"Can the King view when the prince or princess is coming?"

I watched King start shifting in his seat. My brother didn't get nervous often but right now, I could tell he was. I knew this thing with Cola was driving him crazy. He wouldn't admit it, but I saw it.

"In the next five months or so. I heard the heartbeat Ace; it almost broke me down. I didn't want this child. But just thinking about it, I'm getting excited. I never thought of a little me running around, but now I can see it. Part of me feels bad about it because I know how much this will hurt City, but the other part of me doesn't give a fuck. I feel like it's my child and we already have a connection. I don't care that Cola's the mom. That won't make me be with her. I just care about my child."

"A little you, I get it. Paige told me she lost our baby the night of the accident. Just the thought that we shared a life together had me looking at her different. It made me look at life different. I could have a little me running around right now. But we don't."

"Damn man, that's rough. You really need to take it easy with her. She lost a lot that night. I know you love her, but maybe—"

"I can't let her go again. Just like I don't understand your relationships with City and Cola, you don't understand how deep this feeling in me flows for her." He held his hands up in surrender motion.

"You're right, relationships are complicated and anyone looking from the outside won't get what's going on because they only see, they don't feel it."

"When do you plan on telling City?"

"That's the magic question. When's the right time to say baby I fucked up but whether you like it or not, we about to all be a family. Can you really see City and Cola in the same room together?"

I laughed so hard because those two were complete opposites. Cola was the basic hood chick. She lived in a nice area, but her ghetto ass still acted like she was in the projects. She wore cheap knock off anything. Her hair reminded me of a chia pet; one day she would be bald as hell, and the next day she would have hair down to her ass. She was skinny and shapeless. She had big breasts and a tiny ass. Her ass was so small if you blinked you missed it. I didn't know what King saw in her. She didn't work, didn't have an education and she didn't have any goals. Wait, she did have one goal, trapping my brother. I knew King was paying for her apartment or she would still be living with her mom. When her and King met she gave him head right there in the club in front of everyone. He liked it. Whenever he was chilling with any other women in the club, she would fight the girl, and he enjoyed it. When he called she dropped everything to cater to him, he loved it.

City was still City. She was beautiful, smart and well educated. When City walked in a room I swear she would take your breath away with her confidence and her charm. Her and Paige had that in common. She owned a successful business where she was the boss. My brother loved her for everything Cola wasn't. She was a freak but in private, she would never fight over him and when he called she checked her schedule before answering. She made him work and kept him on his toes. She suggested he invest in a few business ventures worldwide and it made him a ton of money. She enhanced him. Cola took from him, and she was getting ready to take even more with this baby.

"Nah, I can't see them two in the same room together. Ghetto and bougie. City trying to ignore Cola and Cola jumping up and down trying to get City's attention. It would be a mess."

"Don't let City fool you. She got a lot of ghetto still in her ass too! She just hides it better."

He had a dazed look in his eyes when he said it. "Oh, I know. I've seen it for myself a few times. It's not hidden at all. It's just when I see the two of them, I see a queen and a peasant. I think City would look at her as beneath her."

"She is beneath her. I don't know what I was thinking. I can't turn back time now any more than you can with you and Paige. Whatever happens will happen. I'm not ready for it but I plan on getting ready."

"I got you either way. Let's get off this plane and get this job done. I got something I need to start planning."

Talking with King gave me a focus. It always did. He'd always been a good big brother. He's just misguided on women. He got that part of him from our dad. Our dad was a ladies' man. He had this coldness towards woman; all except one, our mom. He respected her and treated her like a queen, he just never committed to her or should I say, she never committed to him. I watched and listened to him cater to her and love her. He asked her to marry him more than once and she always said no. She said she knew my dad loved her, but he couldn't love only her. She never wanted to place him in that position. And she said she didn't want to be treated out of a real relationship always watching what he was doing. One time we were out at dinner together and a woman came up to my dad and tried to confront him in front of us and he shut her down and she vowed to make him pay. And she did. She called the police on him when he was out making a drop. He had more than a few keys in the trunk and a gun that was used in a murder. He was arrested and sentenced to 40 years to life. My mom was heartbroken, and she passed a few years later from cancer. King took over raising us. His first kill was the bitch that locked our dad up. It killed us that he was behind bars, and we had to watch our mom suffer and die alone. He's just like dad when you think about it. He loves City, but she knows he's not ready to commit. I just didn't want Cola to be his downfall.

I wanted to take a nap after we arrived. Tonight was going to be a long night. Instead, I pulled up Paige's Instagram page and saw she posted some pics of her and a friend. I was relieved there were none with her husband. I thought about the butterfly necklace I wanted to give her. I contacted my tech person, Ronnie. He was a wiz at getting all the intel I needed on any job King, and I did together. I just needed different intel right now. I didn't want to send the necklace to her home. I just wanted to send it to a safe place. I sent him a quick text and he called me.

"Ace, I'm confused, is this a job or personal?"

I could hear the confusion in his voice. "Both, why?"

"I get to searching her up. Up pops this beautiful woman. I've worked for you and King for years and there's never been a woman, unless she's the girlfriend of the person."

"Maybe we are doing something different this time." I wanted to laugh because Ronnie was this big computer geek that always worked without question. He was good at what he did. Once he looked up who we needed to kill, he would commend us on getting the job done because he felt they deserved it. Not only were we killing people who owed the Cartel, but a few of the sick bastards were child molesters. Ronnie could pull anything up on anybody. In this world of nothing but technology, everyone left a footprint somewhere. I could tell with this one he was having a change of heart.

"Listen, I don't usually object." He cleared his throat. "Umm, I'm not doing this one. She's seems like a good person. She gives to charity. She's smart. Even her social media is classy and clean. I didn't find any nudes on her or anything. Although I was hoping. I'm asking you to rethink this one."

I chuckled to myself. "No nudes, huh? That's just surface stuff. She's stone-cold deep down."

"Ace, I've never not done what you ask but today, I'm going to try and reason with you. I know you're about your money and you and King take this very seriously, but all jobs are not good jobs. I'm saying no to this one."

"If that's your final answer, I can let King know, and we can cut our losses with you."

"Now Ace, I don't mind the work I do for you. But most of the people deserve it. I'm asking you to look at her picture and you'll know she's innocent. I don't want no problems with you or King. I just don't want innocent blood on me."

I started to laugh. I couldn't hold it anymore. "Ronnie, I was just joking with you. This is a personal job. But I like how you were going all out for what you believe in. That takes guts. I didn't know you had it in you."

"Oh God, good. I like our arrangement; it keeps my pockets right and me safe. If she's not a usual client, what do you need on her?"

"Just basic stuff. I need to send her something and I didn't want to send it to her home."

He cleared his throat again. "So, it is personal? You like her? I see why, she's beautiful and smart."

"I just told you it's personal. And stop asking questions, it's not your business. Oh, if you find any nudes, delete them or else." I was friendly with him, but we weren't friends.

"Ok, ok, I get it. Give me a few hours and I'll have all you need."

"Thanks Ronnie. You're right, she is beautiful and smart." She was all those things. And I had made the mistake of boxing her into the role of just an artist. I missed the other sides of her. The funny side, the side that enjoyed books, the side that liked music, the side that enjoyed cooking and the side that I could sit and listen to for hours talking about anything and everything. I missed all those things about her, and I needed her.

Chapter Nineteen

Far From Perfect
Paige Turner Daniels

I'm far from perfect you see. I can't be your perfection 'cause it just ain't me. I'm perfectly imperfect and that's just perfect for me.

Sitting in my office, I was trying to get some work done. However, my focus was off. I opened my purse and grabbed the notebook I had been carrying around since I returned from New York over three months ago. I flipped through the pages of my old artwork and my hands started to shake. This was my reaction each and every time I pulled this notebook out. I didn't know if it was my nerves or the fact I wanted and needed to draw. I stood up and started pacing the floor. The view outside my window was perfect. I wanted to go outside and do what I used to do, create art, draw everything. My nerves wouldn't let me do it. I sat back down and continued working on my reports.

"Paige, I have a couple of packages for you. Also, Mr. Thomas has requested to speak with you in about 30 minutes. I made sure your schedule was clear. Do you need me to prepare anything for you?"

Danielle, my assistant, walked in my office and announced.

When I came back from New York, she and I started talking more and more on a non-business level. I enjoyed our talks; she was cool and real down to earth. "Start a set of new files for me. I bet he wants me to take on a new account. That man acts like I'm the only one that works around here. And if you can put these files away, that would be great." I pointed to the side of my desk. When she moved the files, she knocked the notebook down. Before I could reach it, she was already flipping through the pages.

"Girl, you know why. You're the best and your workaholic ass will continue to take on more and more clients. Doing the exact opposite of what you said you wouldn't do when you returned from your trip a few months ago. I figured that wouldn't last. Did you draw these?"

"Yes, I did. I know I said I wouldn't continue working so late and so much, but honestly, it keeps me busy."

"I can't believe it. I mean it just looks professional. The detail is amazing. It looks so real. I never got an artist vibe from you."

"They are from a very long, long time ago."

"Let me see the new work."

"I haven't done anything new in years. Like I said, those are from a long time ago. Different time, different place and a different person, Danni." I laughed and turned to look out the window again.

"Hmmm, I think I got a glimpse of her when you came back a few months ago. Now her, she seemed fun."

"What? I'm fun."

"You are, but the more time passes, the more you become that stuck-up, serious, work, work, work Paige."

"I am not stuck-up, and I am fun."

"Yes, you are. I don't mean it in a bad way. It's just you're all about your business. You are no nonsense in here. I don't blame you; that's why you're the best at what you do. Before you left, we never said more than a few words to each other. Everything was professional. Nothing like right now. But when you came back to work a few months ago after your break, you looked so refreshed. You were vibrant and upbeat. You were someone I'd never seen before. That person, I could see as an artist."

"Well, the artist is dead."

"Damn, I bet the artist would have approved all my vacation time."

"Nope, I need you here with me."

"I have an idea. Why don't we both take a vacation and then you would have time to create some more drawings."

"Not a chance. Besides, I don't do art anymore." I held my hand up before she could say another word. "Don't ask, it's a long story. I just don't do it anymore."

"Long story or not, that was real talent. Don't let talent like that go to waste. Besides, art is a passion, and you never lose passion. It's only hidden beneath the covers we toss over it. Uncover it and let it go free. I'll get your new files started."

She walked out and closed the door. I started to spin in my chair just thinking about what she said. *Uncover my passion. Uncover my passion.* I kept repeating it in my head. She said that like it was so easy. My passion for art was replaced with my love of accounting. My other passion was love. If I'm honest, my passion was him. And I missed him. My decision didn't involve passion, it involved doing the right thing. When you do the right thing, everything else should fall in place. At least that's what I thought. The past few months have been hell on me. I came back expecting a big change in Kane. The only thing that changed was how I viewed him. Sure, he was home more but he wasn't really home. He was on his phone or his laptop planning his announcement to run for DA. I was trying to be supportive of his plans, but there was something that just didn't seem right. I couldn't quite put my finger on it, but it was something. Let's just say it was far from the perfect dream he sold me before we left New York together.

I was about to head to my meeting when I received a text alert from my bank that a large withdrawal was taken. It was the way I had my settings. Anything over $15,000 and I would get an alert. I logged into my account while walking toward the meeting and to my surprise, I saw a withdrawal for $20,000 done today. I knew it was Kane because he had to sign for it and his signature was listed in the information section. He had his own account. Why would he need that much money out of our joint account? He and I needed to talk.

The meeting was basically what I already knew. We were getting a new client, and they would need me to oversee the account. This was a huge client who had numerous businesses and needed me to clean up all their finances. I had Danni start pulling everything, so I could go through it with a fine-tooth comb. The client was coming for a meeting in a few weeks, and I needed projections, cost analysis and budget planning. This was going to be a big project.

Back in my office, I picked up the two packages on my desk and one had no return sender. I opened it and it was a jewelry box. When I opened the box, it was a necklace with three butterflies with white diamonds surrounded by blue and black stones. It was amazing how the butterflies on the necklace resembled the butterflies in my tattoo. The only difference was my tattoo had more colors. I found a card and read the note. ***I'm still jealous of the person who got to spend hours drawing these on you. I miss you! Don't think about returning it. It's something I had made a long time ago. It belongs to you.***

He didn't need to sign his name. I knew it was his design. I could tell from the details. It was so beautiful. I couldn't wait to put it on. Wait, wait, wait, I couldn't wear this; it's from another man. But it was so beautiful, and I really wanted to wear it. I couldn't believe he remembered my tattoo and in such detail. That meant so much to me.

"Paige, I have some of the reports pulled but I'm about to head out to lunch and I will pull the rest when I return. Do you want anything?"

"No Danni, I'm good. I was planning on stopping by Kane's office today."

"Wait, why are you smiling so hard?"

"Nothing it's nothing. Just a gift from a friend."

"Let me see. Wow this is beautiful. It's so unique. A friend or a *friend*?"

"An old friend and get your mind out the gutter. It's not like that at all."

"If you say so."

"Yes, I say so. Get out of here and have a good lunch."

"Ok, and if you're trying to freak Kane on lunch, don't wear that gift from your *friend*."

****

I was sitting in the lobby of Kane's office waiting on him to return from lunch and I called City to entertain me while I waited. I missed her so much. I needed another trip with just me and her. I knew she still hadn't addressed her situation with King because she was still living. There was no way he was ever letting her go. He really did love her, and she really loved him. They were two Alphas and that made a bad combination because they both wanted to be the boss.

"Hey, my favorite cousin," I sang in City's ear.

"Hey boo! I miss you. Did Kane fuck up yet? Are you on a plane back?"

I swear this was how she answered the phone every time I called her. "You are so damn silly. Stop wishing for the failure of my marriage. I told you he's trying."

"I know, I know. And I ain't wishing, I'm just saying a leopard doesn't change his spots."

"Let's change the subject. How is the shoot going?"

"Paige, I think this will be some of my best work. I know Chicago has been seen from every angle, but this is one is so beautiful. I didn't use any professional models just real people. I wanted to catch the genuine feel of the streets."

"I can't wait to see it. You are still coming to visit soon, right?"

"Yes, I have to do some candid shoots of Atlanta for a Superbowl promo. A little business and a little pleasure."

"I can't wait. I have something I want to show you."

"Give me a hint."

"Ok, don't make a big deal out of it—"

"Me, make a big deal out of something? Come on, you know me."

"Exactly, that's why I said it. Pharaoh sent me a necklace."

"I knew that man couldn't stay away from you again. You put that voodoo on him again. He's probably watching you from a corner or something right now."

"I said sent, not personally handed it to me. You so damn stupid, got me in here cracking up." I was laughing so hard the receptionist started clearing her throat. I hated visiting Kane at work for this very reason; everyone was so prim and proper.

"It's only a matter of time."

"It's beautiful, it looks like my butterfly tattoo. I can't believe he remembered it. The detail is amazing."

"I told you, that's that boom, bam voodoo! That man loves you."

"He loves the old me. She and I are two different people. How are things with you and King?"

"Fine."

"What happened?"

"He's being bossy as usual. I heard some rumors in New York before I left, and I think he got with someone else. And not just sexually, like in a relationship. When I get back I am launching a full-on investigation."

"Don't get mad if that man has moved on. Remember, you're the one who didn't want a relationship."

"I know what I said, but still. I didn't expect him to move on so fast. I want him to miss me a little and beg me to come back like he always does."

"Stop playing games with him. I told you to tell him how you felt but no, you had to do it your way."

"I told you to leave Kane, but no, you had to do it your way."

When she said Kane's name, I looked up and saw Leslie strolling through the doors of the building like she owned it. I didn't understand what he saw in her. She was the total opposite of me. She had a great body, but her lace front looked like a bird's nest. She was plain at best, and basic. She was that girl in high school that all the boys were crazy about, and you didn't know why until you finally realized they were passing her around. I couldn't believe he risked our marriage for that. Looking at her, I started to feel self-conscious about my body. I knew I had gained some weight. Maybe that was the reason Kane stopped wanting me. But I'd never been a thin girl, so I couldn't comprehend the change now. Maybe I should try dieting or exercising. I was getting in my head again. Something I said I wouldn't do. When I looked back at the door again, there was Kane walking in fixing his tie. He was still cheating on me. He promised. The wife in me wanted it to believe it was a fluke, but the woman in me knew. I just knew.

"City, let me call you back."

"Is everything ok Paige? You sound strange."

I wasn't good. I felt like a fool all over again. I really believed he would change. "I'm fine, I'll talk with you later, love you." I hung up before she could ask me another question. It's clear he and I needed to talk about more than just the money.

Chapter Twenty

I had goals set and things in mind to do. I was about my business and my business wasn't about you.

"Leslie, that was amazing. You always know how to relax me," I said, getting ready to hop in the shower. I was on an extended lunch break because I needed my fix. Since returning from New York with Paige, I was spending more time at home. That cut off a lot of my extra activities. Since I didn't have evenings free anymore, I adjusted; this was just one of them.

"Kane, how long are we going to keep doing this lunch time thing?" Leslie asked.

"Not long. I thought it would spontaneous. You don't like it?" I wasn't about to play this game with her. This shit was on my terms and my terms only.

"Don't get me wrong, I enjoy it. I enjoy you, but I'm falling behind at work and I hate staying late. I don't get why we can't go back to our weekends. I loved when you were able to spend the night, and I could wake up with your dick in my mouth."

Just like that, my dick was standing at attention again. "I know, I miss it too. And we will get back to doing just that when it's time. And right now, is not the right time."

"When will it be the right time? When you become the DA? Or after you divorce little Miss Perfect? Because I've been waiting for a very long time for that to happen."

And bam, she messed it up just that quickly. "I know you have, that's why I feel how I feel for you. You know I need to play this out exactly right. I need her right now and believe me, she's far from perfect."

"I want you to need me too, Kane."

"Don't nag me Leslie. I get enough of that at home." I walked away from her to take my shower. I needed to figure who I needed to move up on my roaster to take her place. I could tell Leslie was getting her feelings in the mix, and that's never good. Next thing you know, she'd be making demands and requesting when she wanted to see me on her terms. That's not how this worked. I was in control, not her. She didn't understand how easy it was to replace her. So many women made it easy for me to promise little or nothing just for them to spread their legs. I barely did any work. I was a straight, black, successful man in Atlanta. Hell, I was like a unicorn to them, and they all wanted to touch it and play with it and ride it. I'd been with Leslie this long because her head game was top notch and no matter what, she never told me no or put any demands or labels on our arrangement. That worked. Now that I'm running for DA, I could see the look in her eyes. She wanted what most women wanted, a commitment. I wasn't willing to give her that right now or any time in the future.

****

I walked back into my office building and there in the lobby was Paige. I wondered why she was here and how long she had been waiting because she looked comfortable. I fixed my tie and walked over to her.

"Well, what did I do to deserve this visit today?"

"Hey Kane, I was close to the area, and I just thought I'd pass by and talk to you for just a moment."

Here she goes again with this bullshit. I pulled her in for a hug and then gave her a forehead kiss. I grabbed her hand and walked her toward the elevators. I was hoping she didn't notice that Leslie walked into the building about ten minutes before I did. I opened the door to my office and told her to have a seat. I sat in my chair behind my desk preparing myself for the bs that was about to come out of her mouth. "Tell me what's on your mind. I know you and you are never on my side of town. What's so important?"

"You're right, I dropped by to see what's up with you. You've been making some very large withdrawals from our account lately and I want to know why."

"Paige, we could have discussed this at home. It didn't deserve a visit. Not that I'm not happy to see you."

"To be perfectly honest, you don't look happy to see me. You look like a kid who got caught with his hand in the cookie jar. The only thing is, I don't know which cookie jar, Leslie's or our account."

"Don't come in here starting your mess today. I don't know why you still feel the need to accuse me of cheating."

"I feel the need because I've been waiting for you for over an hour. And ten minutes before you walk in smelling like you just got out the shower, she walks in the door."

"I don't know how things work at that little accounting firm but here, we are adults, and we don't have time frames for lunch. I'm so high up here my boss never questions me. But if you must know, I went to visit a client and I shot some basketball over at the LA Fitness, so I freshened up before coming back to work. So now there's a play by play of my day. Do I need to provide receipts for the lunch too?"

"I didn't ask for play by play. I asked a question. Considering all that we've been going through, you should be willing to give this information; instead, you get so damn defensive."

"I'm defensive not from the question but from your assumptions and accusations. I've been doing nothing but proving myself to you and you still come to my office doing pop-up visits, almost trying to smell my balls and telling me when I can and can't take money out of our joint account."

"I wasn't trying to do a pop-up visit as you call it. I've been assigned a new client, and it will require a lot of my time, so I thought before I become swamped with work I would come and visit my husband and he and I could have lunch and sit down and talk. I can't help that I notice the obvious."

"That's just it, Paige, you assume without asking. You could have sent me a text to let me know you were here. It's almost like you want to catch me doing something wrong." This was where my defense attorney skills came into play. If I could create a little shadow of doubt, I had her.

"You're right."

Got her! "Listen Paige, the only thing I'm trying to do is build a better life for you and me. I'm busy handling a full case load and I'm trying to run this campaign. I withdraw some money to cover some additional expenses for the campaign. I want to have a certain balance in my separate account, so no one goes digging into your account and our joint account. I was only looking out for us. If it's a problem, let me know and I'll cover everything with my personal funds."

"No, it's not a problem. I just. . . Well, I get a little controlling when it comes to finances. I know I shouldn't be that way."

"Right, because it's our money."

"I get it, I'm doing too much."

"You always do. Just relax and understand I'm doing this for our future." As she shook her head up and down in compliance, I knew she was feeling everything I was saying to her. She made this too easy. "Now, what else do you need from me today?" I moved closer to her, ready to see if I could get her to bend over physically as easy as I got her to bend over emotionally.

"How about you take me out to dinner tonight? I want to discuss us making an appointment for couple's counseling."

"I would love to, but tonight I need to get this deposition turned into the judge. This will be a big win under my belt, and I want to get it done before the big event in the next few weeks. How about I get a raincheck?"

"Of course, but for the next few weeks my schedule will be tight. I have a new client that will be keeping me very busy. I'm not sure when I'll have some free time."

"Do what you need to do. I completely understand; we will rise to the top together. We'll be Atlanta's most admired and most esteemed couple. We'll be the envy of everyone."

"That's your goals, not mine. I didn't even know running for DA was so important to you. I figured you loved being a defense attorney and dreamed of owning your own firm one day. I didn't see you crossing to the other side of the table."

"I just think owning my own firm can come later. Right now, I have my eyes on bigger things. Better options that will put me in a better position to become a governor. Just think, after one year of being DA, I will have the power to run for any office in the state. Paige, we could be living in the governor's mansion." I couldn't read her expression. I knew it wasn't excitement. This was what I kept talking about; this dumb bitch didn't get what type of power we could have. She was okay with being mediocre. Power was everything to me. I wanted my name known worldwide. I wasn't going to depend on the man for everything. I was never going to be poor again. I worked too damn hard to get everything I got. Truth is, I was sick of doing all these underhanded deals for these criminals. I wanted to work smarter not harder. I needed Paige, I needed her money, I needed her because a family man looked better for the office of DA. I needed her to get on board. I was ready for this game to end, and I needed her to end it. "I think a governor's wife would fit your fine ass just right. Just think about it. You can finally have some free time to do whatever you want to do. You could even start your own accounting firm. Just support me Paige. That's what I need from you, support like I supported you through all your things."

"I support you. And if you want it then I want it for you too! I won't hold you; I need to get back to the office anyway. I'll see you when you get home."

"Okay sweetheart, don't wait up. This could be a long night."

I walked her to the door and kissed her on her cheek. I watched her fine ass walk down the hallway. I was glad she was gone but damn, just thinking of her bent over my desk was making my dick hard again. I made a mental note to make sure to keep my withdrawals under $15,000. I'd be damned if she was about to start keeping tabs on my money. I couldn't understand why she was watching the money so hard. Unless the money was drying up. I think it was time for me to make something shake. I knew what I needed to do. I also knew it was about to shake Paige to the core. That wasn't my concern. My concern was keeping my pockets fat. I opened my laptop and sent the information I had on Paige's dad to my reporter friend. She would report on anything to advance her career. Once the news of his death and how he died came out, it would free up the insurance policy for her to collect on it. Then, we wouldn't have any more problems with me keeping my pockets fat and getting the rest of the money I needed.

Chapter Twenty-One

Broken Rules

Synplicity 'City' Walker

Not only did you the break the rules, you broke me.

I flew back into New York just for a few days to grab some things to take on my trip to Atlanta. I needed more than work clothes. I'd be damned if little miss Paige Turner didn't take me out to party while I'm there. Even if I had to force her to do it. I missed her so much and I couldn't wait to see her. I was passing by my favorite Chinese restaurant to grab a bite. I sat at one of the booths to wait for my order. They were packed so I knew it would be a few minutes. While waiting, I overheard King's name, so I moved to the edge of the booth to hear just a little better.

"Why we need to come way over on this side of town to get some damn food? We could've just picked up something on your side."

"I know, but this is King's favorite place, and I like getting him what he enjoys. I want to have it waiting for him when he gets there. You know my ass can't cook. So, this will do."

"I know you love pleasing him but really Cola, an Uber ride here and one back is doing too much."

"Look Shay, I know you don't get it, but I would do anything for him, and he'll do anything for me. This is a small sacrifice," Cola said blowing on her nails.

"He'll do anything for you? Girl please. He needs to do more. You know, like getting you a car. How are you and the baby going to get back and forth still taking Ubers?" Shay replied.

"Damn, you always stressing me about him doing more. He does so much for me already. Since I stopped stripping, he keeps my pockets fat, he pays for my apartment, and he lets me be me. Now that I'm about to bless him with his little prince or princess, there's nothing he won't do for me," Cola said smiling.

"Please, that's nothing. With all the money he makes, you should have more. I heard that bitch of his has a beautiful, fully paid off brownstone and the new Infiniti QX60. She didn't even need it because she was rolling around in that champagne color Range Rover. That's how you should be rolling. You'll need that for you and the baby. Just tell him to get you one of those. You're usually the best at getting things out these tricks, but you're slipping."

"She got another new car? That's so stupid. She's never even in town to drive anywhere. That's a waste of his money. I swear he spoils that bitch. I can't wait until she's out the picture. I'm still on my game, that's why I made sure to secure the bag with this baby. I want my crib paid off and I want a new car every year. Having his baby will guarantee it."

"Don't be dumb Cola. He ain't leaving her. You and the baby will still be playing your part on the side. Watch boo, he'll try and continue to keep you a secret. What you need to do is drop in on that bougie bitch and let her know what's going on. Nobody wants to know they man having a baby with another woman."

"I can't do that. King would kill me. He said he would tell her. And when he does, she'll leave. From what I heard, she can't produce babies which is why he's so excited about ours. She's the dumb one; she been should've popped out a baby. After all the years they've been together, she'll walk away with just the car and house. I'll walk away with the King of New York, and I will be his queen. Don't worry, I've planned this out too long for this not to work."

I heard them high fiving and laughing together. While I was sitting here trying not to have a panic attack. I couldn't believe King. A baby? A fucking baby? My heart was hurting, and it was taking everything in me to not get up and say something. I heard them get their food order and getting ready to leave. I needed to see her. I needed to see this woman because as confident as I was, I felt small and insignificant compared to her. She was doing something I had dreams of one day doing, carrying his child. I peeped through the plastic plants that surrounded the booth to see if I could get a good look. I didn't want them to see me. I saw two women headed toward the door. I didn't know which one she was until she turned around to wave goodbye to the hostess. She was light-skin and slender with two huge afro puffs in her head. She had overdone it on the make-up, but she was still cute. Her boobs were almost busting out her shirt. She had on one of those Fashion Nova outfits, a pattern shirt and matching pants. I was slim, but she was skinny. There was nothing about her that stood out to me except her belly. It was small, but I saw it. I couldn't breathe. How could he? I knew our relationship was complicated, but we always agreed to use protection. We agreed if there was someone else he was serious about, he would say it to me. He knew a baby was a deal breaker. He knew. He broke all the rules. He broke us.

I wasn't angry at her. I'm ghetto and hood, but I didn't fight over a man. She wasn't the one in a relationship with me, King was. Which was why I needed to address him directly. I found him sitting in the barbershop laughing like everything was ok. How could he do that to me? All the things he promised over the years, all the plans we made, I'm so glad I never dedicated myself to him. But thinking about it, I did in some form. I dated other men, but I never let them get close. King was my world. I just knew he wasn't ready. He kept saying he was, but this just confirmed it. I was a fool to ever believe he loved me. When you loved someone you just didn't hurt them.

I stormed in the barbershop like a mad woman. I knew I looked crazy. I was crying, and my make-up was a mess, and I was on fire with anger. "Hakeem, how could you?"

"City, baby what's wrong? Wait, I didn't know you were town. What happened?" He looked at me like he cared and was so concerned. I swear he was so good at faking it.

"Don't baby me, you low down, dirty ass nigga. And don't worry about why I'm in town. I didn't know I need to inform you I was here. I guess it's easier to play house with your baby mama when I'm away." I launched toward him, but someone caught me. The look on his face said it all, he was caught.

"City, calm down and let me explain. Let's go in the back and talk."

"So, it's true. You got that anorexic, cheap, watered down, wanna be version of me pregnant?" The whole way there I kept wishing it wasn't true. That maybe it was a different King because New York had so many of them. Deep down, I knew it was true because they knew too much about me.

"Please City, not here. Let's just go in the back." He tried to grab my hand, and I snatched it back from him.

"Why Hakeem? All the promises we made about our future together. All the things we were planning to do. Every time I went away on business, and you begged me to stay, telling me you needed me, and the whole time you were replacing me and starting a family."

"It's not like that at all. It just happened. It was an accident. I would never purposely start a family without you. You're my world."

"How long?"

"What?"

"Don't play stupid now. How long have you been seeing her?"

"It doesn't matter. Let's just sit down and talk. Please City."

"That long? You were in a relationship with her and me at the same time? I guess every time I left she stepped in, so you weren't without." I felt someone tap me on my shoulder and I turned to see Ace looking at me with pity in his eyes. I guess he knew he was about to become an uncle.

"Take it to the back City, not out here in front of everyone." He gently took my hand and walked me to the back room. King came right behind us and Ace gave him a look that I couldn't read before he walked out and closed the door.

"I didn't want you to find out this way. It was never my intention to hurt you. I love you City. This baby was a surprise. It wasn't planned. I—"

"Don't give me that crap. You were clearly in a relationship with this Cola heifer. Paying for her apartment, giving her money and going home to her. That's more than just fucking somebody. That's never what we agreed. It doesn't matter if you planned it or not. You're playing house so what did you expect?"

"I'm not playing house with her. I don't go home to her. I go to my own damn house. And don't come in here acting all innocent. You think I don't know about Kaleb. You been seeing him for some time now. Was that part of our agreement too? From the look on your face, I could tell you didn't know I knew. Don't come in here pointing fingers like you was just fucking him and walking away. You were overseas playing house. Traveling with him and cooking dinners for him and meeting his family."

He was right. Kaleb and I were getting closer. I did a photoshoot in Mali which was his hometown, and he flew in to show me around and introduced me to a few of his family members. It was nothing big. What King didn't know was I cut it off with Kaleb last month. He wanted a relationship, and I wanted one too, just not with him. Now I felt like a fool. I let go of a man who really wanted me for me for a man that had me out here looking like a fool. I went to him and told him about me and King. I made it clear King was who I wanted. I knew he kept tabs on me, but I didn't know he was watching me that hard. I guess I should've been watching him too, instead of trusting him. "Don't you dare turn this around on me. I stopped seeing him, check your facts. I was stupid for cutting him off. He did something you wouldn't do; he was willing to travel with me and see the world."

"You mean he was willing to follow behind you. That's not me City. After all these years, you still don't get it."

"I don't get what? That you want me here waiting on you to show me some attention. Grateful that the King decided to bless me with his presence. That's not me either."

"I just wanted you to be here."

"You want me to give up my career. It's who I am. I couldn't give up me. He understood that, why don't you?"

"I know who you are, and I accepted it for years. Don't come in here telling me about some other nigga accepting and understanding you. That's like me saying she understands me more than you do."

"Obviously it's something because you're allowing her to keep this baby."

"It was a mistake City, I'm sorry."

My whole body felt like it was weak each time I thought about her giving him a child. "Make her get rid of it." When the words left my mouth, I couldn't believe what came out. I wasn't this person, or was I? I just knew I could forgive him for being with her but a baby, I couldn't forgive.

"I can't believe you would say that to me." He was looking at me like he didn't know who I was. "No. If this means you and I are over, so be it. I won't pick you over my child and you're childish for even saying something so stupid."

"You're not picking the child over me. You're picking her over us. It's a difference. What was so fucking special about that bitch?" Everything I was saying was coming from a place of hurt. He didn't understand it. I saw the frustration on his face. "What's so special about her, tell me. What does she have that I don't?"

"My child."

This was like a boxing match, and I was just knocked out. "You're right. It's over." I turned to walk away, and I felt his arms wrap around me. He laid his head on my shoulder, and I felt the tears flowing again. I wanted to accept his comfort. I wanted his warm embrace to swallow me and make me whole again. He was whispering something, but I couldn't hear him.

"I'm so sorry City."

He wasn't sorry. He was like most men; sorry he got caught. He was going to keep this secret until the end of time. Every single time I went out of town he would continue playing house. While I continued to play the fool. "You're right. You're a sorry ass bastard." I turned and started to swing on him. Before I knew it, I jumped up and straddled him still swinging. He didn't hit me back. He just took every punch, every hit, every swing. I was being pulled off him by Ace and Jinx. I was still swinging, but I was crying at the same time and screaming at him. He was just standing there looking at me. He wasn't going to fight back because he knew it was over. He knew deep down he had feelings for her. It wasn't just about the baby. It was her too. He wasn't willing to give her up. I broke free and started hitting him again. "You caught feelings for that cheap, project bitch. I can't believe you King." Ace grabbed me again and locked his arms around my chest.

"Calm down City. Just calm down." He was begging me to stop.

"I can't calm down. He caught feelings for a bitch. You know what King, you deserve the life you get with her. And since you and her want to clock my moves, let her know, I copped my own Range Rover, and I get a new car every year because I got it like that. I don't have to ask you to buy a car for me. Tell her that brownstone is mine, too. I don't need your money. I never needed it. I loved Hakeem, not King. I accepted King and learned to love him too. Don't call me, don't drop by you live out your dream life with that downgraded bitch. Let me go. I'm done."

He let me go and I turned and caught a glimpse of myself in the mirror. My clothes were all messed up, my hair was all over my head and my face looked like a clown with smeared make-up everywhere. All eyes were on me and each one of them was judging me. Some of them had pity in their eyes, but mostly they wore smirks. King had won; he won because here I was willing to go battle over him. He was what most men admired, a player. The damn water works started again. Who was this person? Because this wasn't me. I started walking toward the door trying to fix my clothes and my hair. When I made it the door and I opened it, I didn't bother to look back. I heard it slam, and I was trying to find my phone, so I could request an Uber to get home, but my hands were shaking so bad, I couldn't. I hear the door open and slam again. I could hear someone walking toward me, so I was trying to dig faster in my purse, but I gave up. I was trying to zip my purse, so I could just start walking, but I couldn't get the damn thing to zip. Suddenly, hands were on top of my hands and when I saw them, I knew it was Ace's from the scars.

"Come on, let me take you home."

I wasn't capable of even putting up a fight. He put his arms around my shoulder, and I broke down again. It felt like he was carrying me to his car. When he opened the door, I got in and cried some more. He reached over and snapped my seat belt. He got in and started driving. It was silent except for the radio.

"Can you take me to the airport please?"

"What time is your flight?"

"It's in a few days but I need to leave tonight. I don't want to be home. He'll come there, and I can't look at him right now."

"Why don't I take you home and let you fix—freshen up, book your flight, pack your bags and then I'll drive you to the airport. I'll make sure he doesn't show up."

"Thank you."

At home, I walked in. "Make yourself at home. I won't be long." I walked into my bedroom and sat on the bed trying to make sense of everything that just happened, but I couldn't. I hopped in the shower and changed clothes and packed like I was never coming back. I didn't want to see New York for a while. This home had so many memories of me and King. I didn't want to be surrounded by them. I walked back to the living room, and I didn't see him. I walked to the kitchen, and he was sitting at the counter going through his phone.

"I made you some tea. Drink some, it will help to calm you down."

I sat down beside him and poured me some tea. "I hope you're not trying to kill me for hitting your brother."

"No, I would've just shot you."

"He deserved it."

"Well one thing I know for sure, you've got some hands on you."

"You knew?"

"He's my brother, we don't keep a lot of secrets from each other."

"I just feel so stupid listening to her talk about the man who said he loves me, like I was nothing to him. Like what we had was a joke. I saw her, she was a joke to me. He could've at least upgraded." He laughed. I held up my hand. "Truthfully, as a man and not as his brother, you like her and him together?"

"Thinking as his brother and a man, no. I like you City. You're like this big annoying sister I never had." He smiled and put his phone down and looked me in my face. "You're a better woman for him but you two keep fighting each other for control. You want to control him, and he wants to control you. That's not how a relationship works. I never really got this open thing you both did. But it wasn't for me to understand. I don't like Cola; she's a ghetto hood rat that's using him. I don't get it either. But again, it's not for me to understand. All I can do is give him my advice and make sure I have his back. He's hardheaded you know."

I smiled. "Don't I. I wish he would have told me. To find out like this was crazy."

"He was afraid to tell you. He didn't want to lose you."

"Look how that worked out."

"Give it some time."

"I can't do that. A child is a deal breaker."

"It hurts but just give it some time. I can't promise the hurt will go away, but you learn to put it aside and move on each day."

"I didn't know he wanted kids that bad. I mean, we talked about it but agreed it would come later. I guess I wasn't willing to give him something he wanted. I just like having my freedom."

"I understand. You and him need to talk. Have an actual sit-down conversation about everything once you've calmed down. You have history and history is something you can't erase."

"History is just that, history. He broke the rules, and he broke us."

We sat in silence while I finished my tea. I booked my flight and my hotel. I was going to be in Atlanta in a few hours. I couldn't face Paige yet. I needed some time to myself. I needed to process everything. Who was I kidding? I needed Paige but I'm way to stubborn to admit she was right.

"How is she doing?"

"She says she's good but I planned this trip so I could see for myself. I'll be honest with you. There's something about Kane I just don't trust. Something about the way he moves."

"He gives you those kinds of vibes?"

"Always did from the moment I first met him. You're crazy, but I know you love her."

"Ok, thanks, I think."

"She's truly happy when she's with you. She's herself and I can see the love you guys share. I know she went back to him, and

I don't know why, but don't give up on her just yet. She got the necklace, she loves it." I looked at him and he was smiling a boyish smile.

"I'm glad she likes it."

"Come on, my flight is in two hours. Thank you, Ace. I know I've been trying to keep you away from Paige for all these years but that was at her request. After her trip here, I can't honor that request anymore. You're free to stalk her again." I laughed because I figured he was already doing it.

"Let's go. And you're welcome. But let me correct you, I don't stalk. I watch to make sure she's safe. It's a difference."

"Sure it is. Feel free to stalk away. And tell Hakeem, I'll be out of town. He can come and get his things. If not, I'll burn them when I get it back." He stood and shook his head. I was serious. I wanted nothing of his. I didn't even want to talk with him. I wanted to pretend with everything in me that I no longer loved him. But I knew that was a lie. I walked out, took one last look around and took a deep breath, then I closed and locked the door. I loved this brownstone but just like Hakeem King Mann, it was time to let it go.

Chapter Twenty-Two

Coincidences, Consequences & Circumstances

Paige Turner Daniels

Believe nothing happens by chance. I created the right place, the right time and just the right circumstance.

I was at the office as usual. The past few days with Kane and I had been weird to say the least. I couldn't shake the feeling I had that he was still cheating on me. I just couldn't prove it. He thought I was the stupidest women in the world, but I was far from it. That day I went to his office he smelled like Dove soap. He didn't buy Dove he bought Old Spice. I even checked his gym bag to make sure he didn't change up. Sure enough, it was Old Spice. I went through everything in my head and when I started to rationalize and make excuses for him, I knew I had gone crazy. What woman did that? Who made excuse after excuse for a cheating man? Me, that's who. Instead of facing the truth, I buried myself in my work. This new client was killing me. Every time I got all my stats together on their business, they popped up with two or three more. They were unorganized and sporadic with their finances. It was amazing they were making any money at all and able to stay afloat.

Danni knocked on my door and opened it. "Paige, you have a visitor."

I looked at my calendar to make sure I didn't have anything scheduled. When I was sure I didn't, I asked, "A visitor? Is it a client?"

"No, it's Synplicity."

"City? She's not due for another few days." I stood up and walked around my desk to greet her. "City, you're early, I wasn't expecting you for another few days." When she walked in my office she was wearing shades. She walked around my office like she was inspecting it.

"Look at you, my little Paige Turner, another chapter in your life just as amazing as the last one. This office is huge, no wonder you spend all your time here," City said.

When she spoke, she was turned away from me, but I knew something was wrong. I just felt the coldness in her voice. I walked behind her and reached my arms out to give her a hug. When she turned around and saw me, she hugged me and just held it. It was like we were at the airport again, only this time it wasn't happiness, it was something else. I pulled away and removed her shades. Her eyes were puffy and red. "What happened, what's wrong?" I guided her to take a seat, and I sat on the edge of my desk.

"I know you're busy, but I need you."

"I'm never too busy for you. Now tell me, whose ass are we kicking?"

"Nobody because I already did it. Hakeem broke us. He got some wanna be, watered down, cheap, knock off version of me pregnant."

"Pregnant? Oh hell no! I'm so sorry City. Let me grab my purse and let's go back to my place."

"No, I don't want to look at Kane. No offense. I just don't want him to see me like this. I have a room at the Twelve in Atlantic Station; we can go there."

"Cool, let me grab my purse."

In the hotel room, City told me everything. I'd never seen her cry so hard in my life before. She was a wreck, and I completely understood. As much as they weren't in a relationship, they were in a relationship.

"I know I brought this on myself by not committing to him, but I didn't want to give up myself for a relationship. I didn't want to end up miserable. If I can't take pictures on my terms, then I'm miserable."

"A relationship should be give and take, not giving up everything. You weren't wrong. You just loved yourself above everything else. There's nothing wrong with that at all City."

"I feel like I lost the love of my life. And that shit hurts because she's giving him something I could have given him a long time ago if I hadn't lost it."

"You were pregnant? When? You never told me."

"It was about two years ago. I was about three months, and I went to California to do a beach summer shoot. I slipped on the rocks and fell, and I lost the baby. He and I both agreed it just wasn't the right time. We agreed to wait until we got married. I blamed myself for losing our baby. Deep down, I felt like he blamed me too. It was around that time he started stressing me to slow down and stay in New York more. I did the opposite and look what it did. It broke us up. Now she gets to give what I couldn't. Do you know how that makes me feel?"

"Don't blame yourself. There was no way to predict that would happen. You didn't do it on purpose. I can only imagine what you must be feeling."

"He loves her."

"He loves you. Now don't be fooled. He fucked her it's a difference."

"No really, he has feelings for her. I told him to make her get rid of it."

"You did what? That was low City. The baby is innocent in all of this."

"I know. When I said it, I was so hurt, and I was looking at him and I felt desperate to keep him in my life. I didn't mean it. But the way he said no to me. He's feeling her."

"The feelings are for the child. Did you think about it that way?"

"No, I didn't."

"Give it some time. I know a baby is a deal breaker, but you never know how this will play out."

She laughed. "That's the same thing your boo said."

I was confused as hell. "My boo?"

"Ace, he brought me home after I jumped on Hakeem. He made me some tea, we talked, and he took me to the airport. I didn't see it before, you know, what you saw in him besides looks. He's smart and he made me feel at ease. He's still crazy. But I think he was the right kind of crazy for you. Anyway, he said the same thing you said, give it time."

"He is smart, and I was always in my comfort zone with him. Listen to us both. Give it some time."

"That's what I plan on doing. I took a job in Asia and then Europe and it's Africa after that. I'll be gone for about a year."

"I can't tell you not to disappear but don't walk away until you are absolutely sure it's over. Anything could happen in the next few months."

"I just can't accept the baby. It would remind me so much of the one I lost. I just can't do it."

I wrapped my arms around her and just held and rocked her. "I wish I could take away all your hurt."

"You can't, and neither can he. I just want to be away to clear my mind."

"When do the new adventures start?"

"I leave for Asia tomorrow."

"Wait a minute, tomorrow? I thought you we going to do some clubbing and hanging out."

"I would love to, but this is the first place he'll look. If he's looking for me at all. I'm not taking any chances. I want to be away from him and this situation until I can't think and speak without the hurt controlling me. I don't really feel like being out and around people anyway."

"I get it. I have you for one night so I'm staying. Let's order some comfort food and binge watch tv until we fall asleep."

A Few Days Later

Getting ready for my big meeting with this new client, I was in the conference room preparing to give my analysis of how I was going to fix their financial problems when the door opened, and I saw Danni come in followed by my boss and a few other men. I stood and walked over to the door to greet everyone when I stopped dead in my tracks. I couldn't believe my eyes. There he was dressed in a navy-blue Armani suit complete with a powder blue shirt to accent it. All that chocolate in that suit had to be a crime. Our eyes met, and he smiled. I tripped, but I caught myself on the end of the table. Danni got close to me and whispered. "Girl, he is fine. Get yourself together." Hell, I knew he was fine but why was he here?

My boss Mr. Chambers walked him toward me. "Ace, this is the legendary Paige Turner Daniels. Paige, this is Ace Mann, owner of Realm Enterprises. Take a seat over there and we'll let Paige get started with the presentation."

I smiled and walked away from him, not knowing what he was up to at all. But as they say, the show must go on. I'm going to make this presentation like the professional I am. I wasn't going to focus on me wanting to jump in his arms or me wanting to feel his lips on mine. No, I was going to focus on this presentation.

"As always Paige, that was excellent. Ace, you're in the right place to get all your financial needs meet. I'll let you and Paige meet to discuss everything. Thank you again for choosing us. I look forward to a long-term relationship with you." Mr. Chambers and his associates stood and shook Ace's hand and walked out. The only people left were me, Danni and him.

"You want to tell me what this is about Pharaoh?"

"You look beautiful Paige, the color in your dress complements your hair. I like the way it's pinned up today."

"Thank you, but that's not what I asked." I was blushing, and I couldn't control it. I was trying something new with my hair, pin curls. I had been wearing this style for a few days and Kane didn't say anything about it. I hadn't seen Pharaoh in months and just like that, he knew it was different.

"Well, I was looking for a new accountant and I heard you were the best in the business. As you can see, my businesses are losing money, and I need to figure out how to increase and not decrease my revenue."

"You had your choice of several great accountants in New York. You didn't need to come all the way down here. Pharaoh, I—"

"My choice was you."

Damn, he had my kitty dripping. The way he said it was so sexy and so confident. "It's just, we have history. I don't want that to be a problem." I was trying to focus but I just couldn't anymore.

He started walking toward me and I was stuck just standing there. The closer he got the more I smelled his cologne, and it smelled like heaven. I was trying to force my eyes to look somewhere else, but they were locked with his. When he reached me, he stood in front of me and softly caressed my cheek with his hand.

"I need you." My knees almost gave out on me. "I need you to help me business wise. I'm great at buying and selling and designing, but now I need to maintain my profits. I don't trust a lot of people. I trust you and I know you'll get the job done. I need to make a few calls and then let's order some lunch and get down to it."

He turned to walk away and out the room. "You're not slick Pharaoh. We keep this professional. This is business and we will treat it that way."

"I'll be as professional as you want me to be." He winked and walked out. I let go of the breath I was holding in, and I started fanning myself.

"Well that was intense as hell. I need to go to the bathroom and clean myself up because I feel like I just watched—you know what, I'm not sure what the hell I just witnessed, but it was intense as hell. Spill it, how do you know him?" Danni said.

I had forgotten she was still in the room. "He's an old friend."

"Old friend? Wait, not the necklace old friend?"

"Yeah, that's him."

"Well, this just got interesting. I'll be on time every day to watch you and this friend and all that pent-up sexual frustration you two have going on between you both."

"There's no sexual frustration. He's someone from my past. It's not like that at all."

"It looks like he's trying to be someone in your future. And your lips are saying one thing, but your body and breathing are saying something totally different. Yep, this will be interesting to watch."

"You just order up some food and don't worry about this. I got this."

"Sure, you do. I'll order something from Panera right away. And remember, keep it professional." She laughed and walked out the room.

Why was he here? Why was I reacting this way? I made my choice. Kane was my husband, and we had these vows and he and I were going to make it work as a married couple. I wasn't going to let my feelings for Pharaoh mess that up. I needed to put my feelings aside. I needed to set some rules and boundaries. I needed him to understand that this was a business relationship and nothing else. I watched him walk back in the room, and before he could say anything, I laid out my rules.

"If you want me to help your businesses, I will. Not only because I know you but because they need my help. However, if we do this I have rules."

He took a seat and gave me a smirk. "All business I see. I'm listening, set your rules."

"That's right, this will be all business." I didn't know if I was repeating that for him or myself. "We stick to just business. You don't make any advances toward me, and I don't make any toward you. No flirting or sexual contact. We just work."

"Just work, I got it. No sexual contact at all. Are you sure?" He licked his lips, and I felt my kitty jumping again. At this rate, I was going to need some depends or something to control all this wetness.

I cleared my throat. "That's correct. I'm married you know. Now, do we have an agreement?"

"We do. As long as you control yourself around me."

"Me! Don't worry, I have full control." No, I didn't have full control; that was a damn lie. Just looking at him was bringing back so many memories. Having him this close and in my personal space was going to be hard, but I could do it. I thought I could. I hoped I could. I'd better, or everything I worked so hard for was going to crumble. I didn't want to disappoint Kane. He wanted this DA position so bad. I wasn't going to mess it up for him. Looking at Pharaoh, I knew I was in trouble, big trouble.

Chapter Twenty-Three

Dreams & Nightmares
Pharaoh Ace Mann

My dreams were just as big as yours. But you didn't seem to care. I laid waiting for my turn, but it never came. My dreams were left unfulfilled and turned into a nightmare.

I spent the last few weeks with Paige in conference rooms or her office. I was following all her rules. It was hard as hell. I got to see the smart, accomplished woman she had grown into. All the reports were right; she was top at what she did. I was enjoying getting to know this side of her. She was able to articulate herself in a way that was assertive and convincing. She also had this touch of gentleness and attentiveness to cover every detail and get you to understand her point of view. We didn't always agree. Like right now. But it was fun watching her prove her point and try to get me to change my mind. This was a new sexy side of her to me. I was finding her mind just as beautiful and fuckable as her body. But I always did. This was just on a different level.

"Pharaoh listen, if you cut the wages of your staff this will increase your profit by at least 25% by the end of the year."

Her face was serious, and she was focused on trying to get me to see her point. "I understand the increase, but do you understand the impact that would have on my staff? Stop thinking of them in terms of numbers and think of them as people. They have families and lives just like you and I do. Cutting wages is not an option. Find another way to create an increase for me."

"That's kind of you. You're a great boss and I respect your decision. Most bosses cave when I say increase. I'm impressed you see your employees as people."

"I've impressed you; do I get a gold star?"

She was smiling, and we made eye contact, and she bit her bottom lip like she always did, and I knew she was still fighting this attraction. She didn't understand how much time I was willing to invest in waiting for her.

"No gold star, but I'll find a way to get you that increase. I got some great connections on some investments. In the meantime, let's schedule something for next week. I'm starving."

Her phone went off and she read the text. I saw the look of disappointment on her face. "Is everything ok?"

"Kane and I had plans to meet at this place I've been trying to get to for a minute, and he cancels once again. I know he's busy, but sometimes he's too busy."

"You make time for the things you value. We're done for the night, right?"

"Yes, we are."

"Well let me take you."

"Thank you, but I don't think that would be a good idea."

"What's not a good idea? I need to eat; you need to eat. What's the problem? Don't overthink it. I just hate seeing you disappointed."

"You know what, why not. Let's go, it's this place downtown called City Winery. I've heard it was amazing, and I've been trying to get there for a minute but I'm always super busy and so is he."

Her eyes were all lit up like a kid, so I knew she was excited. Although wine was not my drink of choice, I would do anything for her. She was chatting away, and I was admiring everything about her. The way her curves looked in the high-waisted skirt she wore today. The way her blouse covered just enough of her breasts, but they were still sitting up just right for me to want to lick them. Today her hair was up in a high bun highlighting her beautiful face. Everything about her was simply astounding.

At the restaurant, we sat at a table near the wall. The lights were dim, but it wasn't dark. The music was good, our conversation was flowing, and I was enjoying being out with her. She was finally relaxing around me again. I could see her guards falling, and she was letting me in.

"I'm going to be honest Pharaoh, I didn't see you as a businessman. I know you own the club, but I thought that was it."

"You underestimate me I see."

"Not underestimate. Okay, when I saw you again in New York I should have asked if you were still in the streets. I just assumed you were."

"I don't want to lie to you. I'm not completely removed from anything but I'm moving toward walking away, but I have to make sure my future is secure."

"Thank you for not lying to me. But you've always been honest with me. You just never disclosed what you do or how you do it."

"I don't feel the need to lie. Details aren't important. Just know I'm changing."

We talked and drank for another few hours before she said she needed to get home. I didn't want her to go. I wanted her to leave with me. "Let me walk you to your car."

"Thank you for tonight. This place really lives up to the hype and now I can at least brag to Danni that I've been."

"I enjoyed it too! I thought the view was incredible." She turned around with a look of confusion.

"What view? We were sitting by the wall."

"I know, but I got to look at you all night." I sandwiched her between me and the car. We were so close I felt her heart racing. I was going to take my time. I pushed the little strand of hair that had fallen behind her ear, mimicking a move I'd seen her do a million times. My fingers went from her hair to her neck to the very top of her breast. I smiled because her breathing was increasing. I continued to travel to her nipples. I felt her piercings through the blouse she's wearing. I wanted so bad to bite and kiss them, but I didn't. I circled my arms around her waist and pulled her closer. "I enjoy looking at you and the conversation. Let's do it again. Get home safe. Text me to let me know." I pressed my lips to hers for a quick peck and stepped back. She looked frazzled and dropped her keys. I bent down to pick them up and opened her door.

"Umm. . . yeah, I'll text you when I get home."

I didn't need to follow her. I had hired someone to stay close to her. When City expressed her dislike for Kane, I started to look into him. I checked just surface things. I needed Ronnie to dig deeper but nothing I found was good, and that stressed me. I wanted her safe, but I didn't want to scare her away from me. For now, I'd just sit back and play my part. Not only was she letting her guards down with me again, but she was starting to trust me. I was waiting for the moment she realized she was still in love with me.

A Few Nights Later

It was the night of the Mayor's Ball. I was invited, and I wanted to bring Paige, but I knew her name was already on the guest list. Anybody who was somebody in Atlanta would be in attendance. I planned to do some more networking with the mayor. I had negotiations in the works to get a contract with the city to purchase a few of the vacant buildings around the area they considered urban. I saw them as gold mines. I had checked a few of the properties and I was already drawing up plans on how to redesign them. Many people considered all black areas problem areas. I didn't. When you build quality buildings companies would purchase them and bring not only jobs to the area, but other businesses. I saw the bigger picture in everything.

Out the corner of my eye, I saw Paige walk in looking like a dream. Her hair was down and tonight it was bone straight. She had on a peach-colored dress that was skintight. She turned, and it was backless right up to the top of her ass. I saw Kane walk behind her and place his hand on her arm. It was almost as if he was pulling her instead of walking with her. This dude was a clown. I watched him drag her from person to person making introductions. The way he introduced her and moved her behind was weird. He's not including her in any of his conversations. She looked uncomfortable. I was doing what I did best, standing in the shadows watching.

I could tell from Paige's body language she was bored and uninterested. I couldn't figure out what they had in common but like King said, I thought she felt obligated to him. Like she owed him for something. He walked her toward a group of women and then he walked away. She was fidgety and looked so out of place. I saw her walk over to the bar and order a drink. I peeped her husband whisper in the ear of a woman and then he walked away. She followed right behind him. He was bold, I gave him that.

I walked toward the bar. She's sitting there scrolling through her phone and sipping her drink. I figured this happened often. She seemed all too comfortable with it. That's a part of her I didn't like. She used to demand respect. I've got to get her back to that person.

"That color really looks good on you. It makes your skin glow." I walked up behind her and ran my finger down her spine. She turned and smiled.

"Pharaoh, what are you doing here?" I saw her check me from head to toe and nod her head in approval.

"I was invited. The real question is, what are you doing over here all alone? You're too beautiful to be left unguarded." I took the seat next to her and ordered some water.

Smirking, she shook her head. "I see you're still a cautious man."

"Always. Tell me why you're sitting over here all alone?"

"These events aren't my type of thing." Turning around in her seat to look around the room. "I don't fit in well with the other wives."

"That's because you stand out too much. They're intimated by you."

"That's not it. I think I'm a little too ghetto for them."

"Ghetto? Is that what you really think?" She turned back to the bar and lowered her head. "You've changed a lot shorty. I don't like it."

"Excuse me! It's not for you to like. Just so you know, I haven't changed that much."

"The Paige I knew was comfortable standing out in a crowd. She didn't hide at the bar. She knew she was intelligent, beautiful and ghetto. But that's what made you unique. When you sat alone it was because you chose to sit alone, not because some dumb, ugly Stepford wives forced you out of their circle."

"No one forced me out of anything. I just—"

"You just what? Allowed him to strip you of your confidence. Bring that feisty little shorty back I used to know."

"Don't insult me. I'm still feisty." She stood up and folded her arms.

"No, you're a shark in the business world but a punk in your personal life." I stood right in front of her. "You're allowing these women and that husband of yours who disappeared over thirty minutes ago with some dumb bitch, to walk all over you. Stand up for yourself." She needed to be pushed. Her confidence was gone, and she needed to remember who she was. I wanted her to remember that strong side of herself.

"You got some nerve. I don't care what you think of me. And I trust Kane. He promised we would make this marriage work again. And that's what he's doing."

I laughed. "You can't be serious. You're many things shorty, but dumb is not one. Look around the room. Do you see him?"

She scanned the room, and I saw her eyes start to water. "You were always such an ass. You think I don't know where he is. I know. You think I don't feel like a fool. Well I do. You think I give a fuck about these stuck-up ass women. I don't. I care that I promised to give him a chance to change. That's what I'm trying to do."

Now I understood why she left. He was messing over her. This wasn't new to her. I felt angry he had been hurting her all this time and I didn't know it. "Is this what you call change? Paige, don't stick around playing a fool for him. You're better than that. So much better." I moved closer to her and caressed her face. I heard someone clear their throat behind me.

"What's going on here? Paige, you want to explain to me why your little boyfriend is here feeling you up." He's angry, but I didn't care.

"She doesn't know why I'm here. Ask me why I'm here." I stepped closer to him.

"Listen, this is a formal event. We don't have time for your thuggish games and childish antics."

Before I could respond, I felt a hand on my shoulder. It was Mr. Chambers, Paige's boss, and the Mayor with a few other people. "Ace, I'm so glad you could make it on such short notice. Paige, you look amazing."

"Mr. Chambers and Mayor Anderson, it's great to see you both. I'm glad I was able to make it too." I shook hands with everyone.

"Chambers, is this the beautiful young woman you and Ace were telling me I need as my personal accountant earlier? If so, all you needed to say was she was breathtaking, and I would've been sold. It's nice to meet you, Paige, right?" He extended his hand toward Paige.

"Yes sir, it's a pleasure to meet you Mayor Anderson."

"It's a pleasure for my wife and I to meet you Mayor Anderson. Kane Daniels sir." He made sure he stuck his hand out for the mayor to shake his hand too. I thought it was sad. How did he claim to be such a big man in this city, and he wasn't even close to all the major players? I watched the mayor shake his hand and turn back to me.

"Ace, let me introduce you to some of the council members. I've been talking about your community programs for those empty buildings, and they had some questions."

"No problem Mayor. Paige, why don't you tag along. I want to make sure the mayor is not trying to get me to buy the whole city. You can keep me on budget." I took her by the hand and slid my other hand down the small of her back. I allowed her to walk a little ahead of me. When she and the mayor were out of listening distance, I turned to Kane and said, "Let a real boss show you how to work a room. None of that pony and dance stuff you were doing."

The rest of the night was spent walking around introducing myself to the city council members and talking with the mayor and his wife at their table. I kept Paige by my side and made sure she was included in the conversations. The way she shined when she spoke about budgets and planning was nothing short of amazing. The evening was winding down and Paige and I were walking back to the bar. She said she was thirsty and so was I, but not for a drink, for her.

"I know what you did tonight. You didn't need me."

I looked her directly in her eyes. "You were a great asset tonight. You were more than needed, you were wanted. Do you want me to take you home?"

"She has her husband here to take her home. Paige, if you're done working, some reporters want to ask me some questions. I need you by my side."

"Pharaoh, I'll see you around and thank you." She turned and walked away.

"I guess it wasn't clear to you in New York she chose me. Stay away from my wife." I guess he felt like he was doing something.

"That's going to be hard to do, especially since she and I are doing business together. Don't get your panties in a bunch. Unless you feel threatened. Are you threatened by my presence?" I moved closer to him, and he said nothing. "Don't worry, you don't need to answer. I know you are, and you should be."

"Nothing about you is threatening. You see who she's leaving with again. And she comes home every night to me. She loves me and she's faithful to me. And she'll remain that way."

"You talk about her like she's an animal. She's not. And I'll let you enjoy it for now. I'm a man with patience. But don't press your luck. I can only control the thug in me for so long. And trust, you don't want to meet the real Ace." I walked away. I was a man of few words. And my word limit with him had been reached.

I watched Paige walking toward the mayor and the camera crew. Fame wasn't my thing. I didn't care if people knew me or not. I wanted her to feel special and the way she was smiling, I knew she did. Damn she looked good in that dress. I wish I was the one taking it off tonight.

Chapter Twenty-Four

Peaches and Cream
Paige Turner Daniels

I couldn't hide it if I wanted. It was written all over me. My body was blushing and calling him uncontrollably. My peach was screaming and wouldn't stop until it was creaming.

I was ready to go. We had been taking pictures for over thirty minutes. I kept scanning the room for Pharaoh, but I didn't see him. Kane was sucking it all up. He loved this kind of attention. A few of the people were reporters and he was enjoying answering their questions. Someone asked if I was his wife, and he pulled me close to him.

"Yes, this is my beautiful wife Paige. Doesn't she look gorgeous tonight?" He smiled at me and then back at the reporters and cameras.

I found it funny because that's not what he was saying to me before we left the house. He told me my dress was way too tight, and this was not a club event but a ball. He complained about everything from the color of my dress down to the way I was wearing my hair. I was over him and this head game he was playing with me. I was so deep in thought I didn't hear a reporter ask me a question.

"Paige, how do feel about your husband running for DA?" the reporter questioned.

"I think Kane has the skills and ability to make a wonderful DA. I fully support him."

"Are you sure you can be supportive to him in light of the information that was just released about your family?"

I was trying to see who was asking the questions. But all I heard was her voice. "I'm sorry, what about my family? And what does that have to do with my husband running for DA?" I just knew they were about to bring up my mother. I could feel my whole body tense up.

"Calm down, don't get so defensive. It's just a simple question," Kane whispered to me.

"Well, we know your mother is doing life for murder and your father was killed in a drug deal gone wrong in at a hotel not far from here right after she was locked up. It would seem with Kane being on the prosecuting team that would put you both on different sides of the table. How does that make you feel?" She stepped forward and was trying to push the microphone in my face. I couldn't think. All I heard was my father was dead. And it wasn't long after my mom went to jail. I didn't speak. I was waiting on Kane to say that's enough, but he didn't say anything. I turned and quickly walked to the ladies' room. I couldn't process what she was saying and how did they know he was dead, because I didn't know. My mom didn't know. I wanted to cry or scream but I couldn't, not here at least. I heard Kane knocking on the door and calling my name. I walked out, and he's standing there looking angry.

"You really are messing everything up for me tonight. First, you want to wear that damn dress. Then you spend the whole night prancing around with that thug ass nigga ignoring me. And now when you get asked a simple question, you run. Do you want me to lose?"

"Did you hear what she said to me? She said my father is dead. That's not something I knew. It caught me off guard and shocked me."

"That wasn't my question. Do you want me to lose? Because that's how you're acting. Don't you get it? This is more important to me than your crazy ass, messed up family."

I felt like something was about to snap. And I knew exactly who I wanted it to snap on. "Un-fucking believable! You're lucky as hell I have this dress and shoes on because I would go upside your head. Then you would really lose because they'd catch me on camera beating the fuck out of you. Your problem is you think the world revolves around you, but it doesn't. This coldness may work in the courtroom, but this is real life. I'm not a witness you're cross examining; I'm your wife!" He tried to touch me, and I slapped his hand away. "Be thankful my boss and those cameras are here or all the ghetto you keep talking about I have in me would come right out and kick your ass."

I pushed past him and headed toward the nearest exit. I didn't have my car, so I pulled up my Uber app to request one. When it asked for a destination, I knew I didn't want to go home but there was nowhere else I could go. While I was waiting I tried calling City, but I didn't get an answer. I called the only person I knew would answer. When he picked up, I didn't know what to say.

"Hey, I didn't think I would talk to you until Monday."

"Pharaoh."

"What's wrong? Is everything ok?"

"No, can I come over?"

"Of course, I'll send you the location."

I plugged his location in, and I thought it would be a hotel, but it was a house somewhere out in Sandy Springs. The ride wasn't long, but I kept hearing the words from that reporter; my father was killed. He was dead. It was so unreal to me. I arrived to see Pharaoh waiting at the door.

"I know it's late but—" I couldn't hold it anymore; I just broke down. I felt him wrap his arms around me and I just cried into his chest. He didn't talk, and I didn't need him to, I just needed him to be there. I needed to feel safe. He was always my safety. He let go and guided me inside.

"I saw what happened on the news after you called. I'm sorry you had to find out about your dad that way. Come sit down."

"All this time I've hated my dad for leaving my mom to take the fall for him, and he was dead. Now I know why he didn't go back to get her. And the fucked-up part is she still has hope he'll come back one day and rescue her. Shit, I can't go and tell her he's dead. She would die of heartbreak. She's always defended him, she'll be devastated. I just can't believe it."

"Take your time and process it first before you say anything to her. We can find out the facts first. I have a guy; he can pull any and everything up on anybody. Let me call and talk with him before you do anything."

"Ok." He walked out the room to make the call. I found the restroom. I was looking in the mirror at my face and my make-up was smudged. I needed to wipe all this mess off. I grabbed a few paper towels and started wiping my face. I was leaning over the sink just trying to come to terms with everything when I felt his hand around me.

"I made the call; he's going to get back to me. While we wait, are you hungry? Do you want anything to drink?"

"No, I'm good. I need a hot shower and the bed. I just can't go home because I married an asshole. He treated me like an idiot tonight. Well not just tonight. It was the worst; he acts like I didn't matter at all. How did I let it get this far? When did I become this pathetic person? He's been walking over me, and I've just been taking it."

"You're not pathetic. You thought what most women think. You thought you could change him. Men only change when they want. Not because you want them to change." He turned me toward him and lifted my chin, so I was looking directly at him. "You're far from pathetic. The way you worked that room tonight. You did an amazing job. The way you toss around those numbers is nothing short of amazing."

I was blushing. "I was just doing my job. Besides, Kane didn't think so. To him, it wasn't enough attention on him. He's also pissed that I'm working with you."

"That sounds like a personal problem to me. And he's insecure if he's threatened by us working together."

"Can I be honest?"

"Always."

"I know what you did tonight, and I needed that wake-up call. I feel like I'm always walking behind him. Tonight, was me stepping up and showing that I'm more than just his wife. That felt good. I didn't think I could change him. I just thought when he came and got me from New York he was ready to change, and I felt as his wife I should give him that opportunity. I just feel so smothered by him."

"You shouldn't feel like that in a marriage."

"I know, but I do."

"Let me honest too Paige. You was right, I was trying to keep you in a box. I only knew the artist in you. These past few weeks I've gotten to see this other side of you. You're still as smart and kind as I remember, but you've grown. You've grown into this incredible woman. I also see a gifted accountant. Your financial knowledge can give some of those big shots on Wall Street a run for their money. You don't need to stand behind him in his shadow. You're made to stand out. You have your own accomplishments. Be proud and don't give him that kind of control over you."

I was letting his words sink in when I noticed how he was staring at me. His stare was so intense I felt self-conscious. I started to fix my hair and my dress. He stepped back and looked me up and down. "I know I look a mess."

"You're self-conscious? And you shouldn't be. You look amazing in that dress. That color is perfect on you. The way it shows off every curve." He licked his lips.

"You like it?" I smiled and shook my head. "I was told it was ghetto and the color with my shape made me look like a big, round peach."

"A peach huh?"

"What?"

"I was just thinking tonight, I saw you let yourself go and you worked that room like you owned it. The way you spoke, the way you expressed yourself and corrected those old ass white men turned me on so fucking much. Every step you took in that dress that ass was bouncing just right, and I had to fight with myself to not pull you in one of those bathrooms. I was thinking of you as a peach, but the kind I wanted to taste. I know you have your rules for us but I'm breaking all that right now."

I felt his fingers touch me. He started at my neck and moved down my spine to the top of my ass. He was still talking but I didn't know what he was saying. I was trying to stay strong, but I couldn't. The gentleness of his touch and heat from his breath was driving me insane. Before I knew it, he was unbuttoning the top of my dress. He moved so fast I couldn't object. The top of my dress fell, and my breasts were completely exposed. I was trying to cover them, but he stood in front of me and held my hands at my waist. He stepped back again. He raised his hands and removed the nipple cover ups I'm wearing.

"Don't get shy with me. Take off the rest for me, slowly."

He stood back and just stared at me. I was speechless and turned on all at the same time. I didn't move.

"Let me see them."

I didn't understand. "See them? You're already looking at them."

"No, not them. Let me see my butterflies. They want to be free. Release them. Pull the rest of that dress down. I know you don't have on any draws. Not the way that ass was bouncing."

I smiled. Everything in my mind was saying no. All my moral fibers were saying this was wrong. But the desire in me won and I dropped the rest of the dress. I stood there naked, trying to cover my stomach. His eyes were roaming over every part of my body.

"You shorty, are a masterpiece. Every part of your body is perfect."

"It's not, I've gained some weight and my scar is horrible." I saw the sadness in his eyes and regretted saying that last part.

"I told you the last time the tattoos covering it are beautiful. When I see you, I see nothing but perfection."

He bought me closer to him and kissed me. "Give me permission to make you feel good tonight." His lips were on my lips before I could answer. The way he was kissing me, I couldn't say no even if I was able to speak. He pulled away and took my hand and walked me through the house and up the stairs to another bathroom. He started the water in the shower, and we got in together. He was washing every part of my body, and it felt like heaven. When he was done, he pinned me against the wall and started kissing me again. I knew he wanted to make this about me, but I wanted to make it about him. He made me feel smart, wanted and understood, not to mention strong and powerful. I hadn't felt this way in years. I broke the kiss and got down on my knees. I didn't care my silk press was about to be all messed up. I cared about what was right in front of me. His dick was absolutely beautiful. I knew women said that all the time. But it was. It was the perfect shade of chocolate, the length and girth are just right, and it was always standing at attention for me. I wrapped my hands around it and then I wrapped my lips around it. I was sucking and slurping and deep throating him like we were making a porn movie. I popped him out my mouth and took my tongue and licked him from his head to his balls. I took each ball in my mouth and hummed lightly. Just enough to hear him moan. I spit on his dick and took him back in mouth.

"Damn shorty, suck this dick!"

When I heard him moan again, I looked up and his face was in pure pleasure. The water running down his body splashing on me was turning me on even more. I felt him jerk and his knee buckle, and I knew he was close to giving me my favorite drink. He put his hands on the wall to catch himself, but I didn't stop. I was trying to swallow all of him, even though my jaws were being stretched, and

I felt tears mixed with water rolling down my face. I could feel him in my throat. I just went harder until I felt him loose. I swallowed all of it. When I was done, he helped me out the shower and dried me off. We walked back to what I assumed was his bedroom and he sat me on the bed.

"Stay right here."

He left the room and when he returned, he walked in with a can of whipped cream. He stood in front of me and spread open my legs. "Put your feet on the bed." I did exactly what I was told. I felt his finger glide across my opening and then I felt kisses on my inner thigh. His fingers were replaced with his lips. He kissed me and whispered something. *I think he's talking to my pussy.* "Did you say something?" He didn't answer, he just spread my lips open. I felt his tongue spreading around all my juices. I heard and felt him spray the whipped cream on me. He was back to licking and sucking. I swear this man could teach a class on oral sex; he was a master at it. He knew when to go slow and when to go fast. He knew when to suck on my clit and when to stick his tongue inside of me. I felt my climax coming and I was trying to move him because it was too intense, but he slapped my hand away. It felt like my head was swimming and my body was in another world. My legs locked onto his head, and I felt him flip me over. I was riding his face like it was for my life. I was moaning and scream his name, and I didn't know if he was still breathing, but I felt my climax coming and I couldn't stop to check. I was about to release an ocean; I was so backed up. I was attempting to lift myself off him, but he pulled me back down and continued sucking and licking me. I cum and he continued until I cum all over again. I was out of breath, and I couldn't move.

He lifted me and flipped me on my back. He was kissing my inner thighs again and then he moved up to my stomach. When he got to my breasts, he started playing with my nipples and pulling my nipple rings. The hardness between his legs felt like it grew more as he entered me. I wanted to scream. The pleasure and pain caused me to gush.

"Shorty, you taste just like a peach. But I knew you would. You feel so damn good. You're so damn wet."

He was stroking me so slow and intense. It wasn't what I wanted. I wanted to feel him. I didn't want him to be gentle with me. I wanted him to fuck me tonight. After everything I'd been through these past few months, hell years, and then tonight, I needed it. I wanted him to fuck away the pain of my mother being in jail, my father being dead and the memory of me being unloved. I felt tears coming out my eyes. I just needed to feel tonight. "Fuck me!"

"As you wish."

He pulled himself out of me and I wanted to kick myself for saying anything. He tapped my leg.

"Stand up."

I did exactly what he said, never breaking eye contact. He was stroking himself, staring at me. He walked behind me, grabbed my hands and put them on the dresser. I arched my back a little preparing myself.

Then he bit my earlobe and said, "I'm about to fuck you until you come to your damn senses. Letting him treat you like your nothing. You're fucking amazing. Arched that shit better. Stop playing with me. I told you I would come and get you. Don't run from me again. Not now or ever."

I was so damn wet. It was this shit that turned me on so damn much. I felt him ram himself into me and it took my breath away. He grabbed me by the back of my hair and pulled lightly, but with enough force to make me moan. I looked up in the mirror and the look on his face was intense. Each stroke got stronger, moving me and the dresser.

"You're all mine, Paige!" I felt myself squirt. I didn't squirt but the look in his eyes, the sound of his voice, the fact that his dick was damn near in my chest was just enough to take me there. He pushed my head down and slapped my ass.

"You ain't never going back. This is all mine."

All I could say was, "Yes, yes all yours!"

He fucked me against the dresser, the wall, on the bed, on the floor and in the kitchen. I told him I was thirsty, and he granted me some water and then bent me over the counter. Just when I felt like my body could no longer take it, he brought me back to the shower and washed me again. Now we're in bed and he's caressing my face. I knew I'd be sore in the morning because he twisted me into every position in the world. I didn't even know I was still that flexible.

"Thank you for seeing me." I kissed his lips.

"I'm always here for you."

"No, I mean thank you for seeing me for who I am right now. For seeing my strength, but also my insecurities. For not pressuring me to decide. For respecting me when I made the wrong decision. But thank you most for coming to get me."

"You don't need to thank me. I knew I was the better choice," his cocky ass said and smirked. I let my eyes close, and in the silence a million thoughts came flooding into my mind. Kane, my mom, my dad, and me. I felt him pull me close and I buried my head in his chest, and he held me tighter. Just like that, I felt safe. I was safe. If nothing else, he would keep me safe. He would make everything bad go away. At least that's what I told myself.

Chapter Twenty-Five

The Truth

Ace "Pharaoh" Mann

I was always this person; you just didn't see me in that way. I didn't hide the ugly in me, you just chose not to see. There it is, the truth, the truth was you never really knew me.

I wake up to Paige still laying directly on my chest curled up like a baby. She stayed that way the whole night. If I moved, she moved. I needed to piss but I didn't want to wake her. I moved slowly and stuck a pillow under her arm. I used the bathroom and headed to the kitchen to fix some breakfast. I checked my phone, and I had a text from Ronnie. I called him, so he could tell me what I needed to know.

"Morning Ace. I got everything you need and more. It's not good. It's not good at all." The tone in his voice told me this wasn't about to be pretty.

"Tell me everything."

When Ronnie was done. I was seeing red. I was ready to go on my own killing spree. There were way too many hustles in the world. There was never a need to hustle a woman. Everything Ronnie just ran down to me was beyond crazy. It was unbelievable.

"Ace, you still there?"

"I'm just trying to understand how and why he picked her."

"Seems simple to me, money."

"No, he has money."

"Not her type of money. I don't even know how he's been able to get away with this type of con this long. Unless. . ."

"Unless he was never planning on ending the con. He was planning on ending her life." This was worse than I first thought. "How did he find her?"

"He worked for an insurance company. The Kane Daniels you think you know is not the same person. The real Mr. Daniels was an attorney, but he's been dead for over fifteen years. He didn't have any family, and he had a very large insurance policy which was cashed in by one Kentrell Watts. It just so happens that same insurance company wrote a policy on Paige's dad. He's already making moves to insure she gets that money."

"Wait, run that last part by me again."

"What part?"

"The part where his name isn't even Kane." I'd seen a lot of cons done. A lot of different ways but never something this deep and this shady. He'd been living a lie for years and then had the nerve to run for DA. He really thought he was the shit. He was playing her for a fool and was going to kill my Paige. My Paige! I was already planning how I was going to kill him, slowly, in my mind.

"Ace, I hope she will be ok after finding out this information. If she needs someone—"

"Someone like who? She's got me! Watch yourself Ronnie. Don't make me do to you what I'm going to do to him."

"I knew you really liked her. I'm good Ace. I'm just trying to confirm my hunch."

"Keep your hunches to yourself."

I ended the call and prepared myself to give her this news. But first I sent a text to King and Jinx. If Kane, or Kentrell, wanted to play big boy games, I was going to introduce him to the masters of the game. He ran the wrong con on the wrong woman. Movement from behind me broke my murderous thoughts. I turned and she's walking toward me, wearing one of my shirts. She still had sleep in her eyes. Her hair wasn't straight anymore. It's a mess that's surrounding her face; it's perfect to me. I needed to smile to make sure she didn't sense that there's a problem, but I couldn't. The world was full of fucked up people, but Paige wasn't one of them. She was a good girl, who turned into a good woman. She made the mistake of giving her all to the wrong man. This could've costed her, her life. I spent a few years without her, but I knew where she was. I could put eyes on her anytime I wanted. The thought of not having her on the same earth as me, was tugging at my heart. I couldn't lose her again. I wasn't going to lose her again. I would kill anyone or anything that was gonna be a danger to her. That's a promise.

"What's wrong, Pharaoh?"

"You trust me?"

"Yes, I do."

Her answer was definite; there's no hesitation. I placed her hand in mine, and I guided her to one of the chairs that was right in front the bed. "Good. I needed to be sure because what I'm going to tell you won't be easy, but just know I got you." I broke down everything to her. Her expressions went from sadness to shock back to sadness and stayed at shock. When I was done, her hands were on her chest, and she looked like she was about to faint. "Breathe, please breathe."

"I don't get it. You mean the man I've been with all this time, the man I shared myself with, the man I married has been running a con on me? And for what, MONEY?!!!"

She was standing now and screaming. She was pacing the floor, and her hands were moving everywhere. She was talking, but not to me directly. "From everything Ronnie pulled for me it shows everything Kentrell Watts has done has been for the money."

"Wait, who is Kentrell Watts?"

"That's his real name."

"I know you fucking lying." Her accent wasn't thick and if you didn't know she was from New Orleans, you would miss it. It only came out when she said certain words and in certain moments.

This was one of those moments. "He's even been lying to me about his name? Wait, wait, just wait." Her hands were back on her chest, and she was trying to catch her breath again. "Why? Why would he do that to me? He pretended to love me. He let me tell him everything about me. I shared my life with him. I walked down the aisle with him. We stood in front of God and got married. Does this mean?" There was sadness again on her face and I saw the tears start to fall from her eyes. I walked towards her. But she stopped me. "Give me a laptop or let me use your computer."

"It's on the counter." She turned and headed for it. I was a few steps behind her. She spotted it. "Let me just log in it for you." I logged in and moved out the way. I watched her tapping away on the keys like a mad woman. I didn't know what she was searching for, but I saw her gasp. "What is it?"

"He's been stealing money. I haven't really noticed. I never pay attention to this account. It's our joint account. I got a notice a few weeks ago and I went to talk to him about it, but I put it to the back of my mind. I don't use this account. I only have a tiny bit of my earnings going into it. How could I have been so dumb? Why didn't I see it? How stupid am I?"

"You're not stupid or dumb. He's good. Before the marriage, I researched him and everything about him seemed legit. It was all surface stuff."

"The marriage? It's not real. It's all fake. My whole life for the past few years has been fake. I've been completely oblivious to all the signs he was giving. He's never shared all of himself with me. He's been guarded since I first met him. I just thought that's who he was, you know. City told me she never liked him. And then I let him separate us. I let him control and steer me. I introduced him to so many investors, so many friends, so many co-workers. I was opening the door for him to get money from everyone."

"You can't change what you didn't know." She looked at me and walked toward the patio doors.

"How long was he going to keep this up? Until he took everything?"

I wasn't going to answer. I didn't want to scare her. "Probably."

"He was running for DA. How was he going to pull it off? You can't fake something like that. The government does a background check."

"He wasn't going to run. There's no application. He never completed all the materials to run. I think he did it to increase the money intake from you. He's been paying himself since this announcement. The banquet hall is under his name. So that check he cut went directly to him. The catering company is his too. All under the name Kentrell Watts." I walked closer to her. "Paige, your father had a very large policy on his life. He knew with the announcement of your father's death that would allow you to get the policy. It was all about the money."

"Money. I don't care about money. I don't need the money. I needed my daddy. I needed my mom." She broke down crying. "I can't believe this was all for some damn money. He could have it all. It means nothing to me. I will gladly give everything I have to not feel like I'm a fucking joke right now."

I walked up to her, and I removed her hands from her face. I lifted her chin and looked her in her eyes. "You get to cry right now but no more tears for him. He's not worth your tears. He's a piece of shit. You said you trust me. Trust me to know I will take care of everything." She shook her head up and down and then laid her head on my chest. "You're not going back home to him. Call Danni, tell her you spent the night at a hotel because you had an argument with him, and you need her to ride with you to get some clothes." I felt her hug me tighter. "Don't worry, I'll be right behind you the whole time. Get some clothes and go to the Hilton downtown and check in for a week's stay. I will pick you up."

"Why can't I tell Danni the truth? Is she working with him or something?"

"At this point, I don't know. Let's just be safe."

"Pharaoh, what if he's there? What do I say?"

"He's not there. I had someone to check. Get only what you need, and I'll buy you anything else you require."

"Ok." She turned to walk back upstairs. "Thank you."

"I told you a long time ago I would always protect you no matter what, and I will." She didn't understand how deep my love for her went. She didn't know I would protect her at all cost. She didn't know, but she was about to find out. My phone rang and it was King.

"Ace, your text was brief. What do you need?"

"Full support." Full support was code for guns and shooters. My brother and I handled special cases ourselves. We ran a crew that handled everyone else. When work required it, we all worked together. "Ronnie will send all the info to you. You and Jinx meet me in Atlanta tomorrow and I'll explain everything."

"I got you, say less."

"Where's City? She needs her right now."

"In New Orleans with her mom. I'll send Jinx to get her."

I told that clown he didn't want me to show him Ace, but he didn't listen. He was about to get an introduction to the thugs he kept calling us. And make no mistake about it, it was going to be something he would never forget.

Chapter Twenty-Six

Hakeem "King" Mann

You're carrying my seed. That's just a piece of me. You want all of me and that was never a possibility. I made the mistake of letting you get comfortable next to me. My bad ma, but you only a mistake to me.

When I hung up the phone with Pharaoh, I got up and started putting my clothes on. I sent a text to Jinx to meet me at the spot, so we could discuss details and head on out. I heard the bathroom door open, and Cola came out. I immediately regretted my decision to spend the night with her. She had called me about two in the morning asking me to pick her up something to eat. Once I got here she started telling me how the baby was moving so much, and she couldn't get comfortable. I stayed with her trying to get her to relax. I knew it was a trick to get me to stay over. I hadn't really been fucking with her since everything went down with me and City. I couldn't figure out why she chose to go to that spot way across town to get some food and she knew that was City's hood. I knew she was on that bullshit. Then all the talking she was doing. I killed niggas for less. She knew the rules. When we together, we together. When we not, we not. This wasn't a relationship; we were just fucking. She was lucky she was carrying my seed. That was the only thing saving her life right now.

"Where you going this early in the morning King?"

"I got to make some moves. I won't be here for the appointment tomorrow. I'll put some money in your account to make sure you're good. Text me and let me know what's good with my baby."

"Wait, what? We're supposed to find out the sex tomorrow."

"I know but like I said, I got moves to make."

"It's *her* again isn't it? You're running off to be with her and you promised to not miss any more appointments."

"Don't start Cola."

"Don't start what King? Every single time that bitch City calls you jump."

I was on her fast as hell and my hand was around her throat. Slightly lifted off the ground, she was clawing at my hand. "Watch your fucking mouth. I told you not to call her out her name." I let her down and she was gasping for air. "I told you I have something to fucking handle and you act like you don't understand. You're already skating on thin ice with me Cola. That mouth of yours already has you in trouble. Stop running your fucking mouth!"

"I'm sorry. And I wasn't running my mouth. I was just talking with my friend. Who knew she would be on some creep shit? I didn't even see her."

"You shouldn't have been there in the first place."

"Oh, where she steps foot I can't step foot? I was only trying to get something for you. I know it's your favorite."

"No, her feet are fucking special. You can't step where she steps."

"But I could suck and fuck the same dick she does. I don't get it."

"You know what I mean. This is your side of town, stay on it."

"What happens when I have the baby? What do you want me to do then? Keep hiding in this corner of the world. Make sure we don't pass on the same streets as her? You said you would tell her."

"I planned on telling her, but you fucked that all up by opening your mouth." She sat on the bed and folded her arms. Cola used to be my relief when I was stressed. She was some of the things I wanted in a woman. But she wasn't the woman I wanted. She was pretty to me. What her body didn't have she made up for with her mouth. She damn near sucked my soul out of me the first night I met her. She was attentive when I needed, and she made everything about me, and I ate that shit up. I did all the shit I did for her because I thought she was worth it. She used to talk about getting back in school, opening a hair shop and getting out of the hood. But all that talk stopped when I took her out the club. I told her as long as she had me, I would have her. That was just my mouth talking because City and I were on one of our many breaks. Once we got back together, I told Cola the rules, she knew and said she understood. Everything was gravy until the baby. Once she knew she was having this baby, my baby, she started talking all this family crap. To me, the baby was my family, not her. I'd been ready to call this shit off, but I was staying around because of the baby. My dad raised me to be a man and handle my responsibilities. That's what I was going to do. Not even City was going to change that.

I took a good look around the room. It was dirty as hell in here. Clothes were everywhere and shoes and open containers. I hated to look at this place with sober eyes. It's a reality check for me. She never cleaned unless I complained. My mom was a clean freak that passed on to me and Pharaoh. City was the same way. I never saw her place dirty even when she was in out of town. She would unpack as soon as she got in because she didn't like looking at the suitcases everywhere. The thoughts of my baby growing up in this messy ass room was killing me. I knew I needed to at least move her into a two-bedroom before the baby came. "Why this place so damn dirty all the time?"

"I'm just tired King. I don't have the energy I used to have, you know that. Besides, you keep buying stuff for the baby and there's no place to put it. I thought you were going to get me a two-bedroom. Or maybe we could just move in with you."

"Dead that right now. I already told you, you ain't never moving in with me. Cola, we not together. I ain't trying to move you into nothing else until you learn to keep this place clean."

"So a bigger place for your baby to lay their head is asking too much. But you got that bi—her a whole brownstone and it's just her."

She knew not to call her a bitch again. I was ready and set to jump on her all over again. She lifted her hand and rubbed her neck. I wondered how she knew City lived in a brownstone. I'm not a pillow talker. That was some soft nigga shit. I fucked and went my ass to sleep. In my line of work, a closed mouth was required. I thought back to what City said, *tell her I paid for that brownstone.* I was looking at her different. "How you know so much about her? How she living, and what she drives?"

"I don't know shit about her. And don't be bringing her up in my bedroom. This is my home and the only place I don't have to compete with her."

"Compete? Ma, you'll never be able to compete with her. See, while you clocking her shit, she making moves to get more shit. She ain't waiting on me to upgrade her to a new place or get her a whip, she just goes out and gets it herself. That's the difference between you and her." I watched her eyes start to water.

"You didn't know the difference in us when you was calling and texting me to come over because you need me 'cause she was out making moves to get shit."

"Don't think because I was giving you this dick it meant more than what it was. I slipped up and I'm man enough to take care of my responsibility."

"Be man enough to admit what we been doing for the past couple of years is more than fucking and sucking. We're in a relationship, too. Don't get it twisted like it was your first time going raw in me. I'm the one at the club with you every weekend. I'm the one making sure you have a hot dinner. I'm the one you call when you need your dick sucked. I'm the one you call when you're stressed. You pay my bills. You've slept here more times than I can count. You pulled me out the club so no one else would see this body. She might have more of you, but she don't have all of you. I have it. So you right, I can't compete 'cause this baby makes us a family and that's something her ass will never be able to give you."

I laughed. "Oh you think having that baby makes us family? You think the little pocket change I give you is something? It's nothing. You think I'm paying your rent? I own this fucking building. Again, it's nothing. Your head game is good, and your throat is warm when I'm shooting my load down it. Nothing more, nothing less. You have no clue how little you mean to me. I don't need you to raise a baby." I didn't want to put my hands on her again; that wasn't me at all. But lately she'd been taking me there. I turned to her before I walked out the door. "Now stay your ass away from City. That's my last time saying it to you." I heard her kiss her teeth as I was leaving out the door. I really fucked up on this one. I headed over to the spot to meet Jinx.

When I got to the warehouse, I saw Jinx's car. One thing about him was he stayed ready. We had a few warehouses, but this one was completely for our special business purposes. We used this space to meet and go over plans. Our name wasn't on the building, and we kept the outside gated and well-armed. I walked in and Jinx was chilling watching *First Take*.

"What's up King, you catch that game last night?" He turned and looked at me.

"I saw it. Them calls were bullshit." I sat across from him.

"Yeah it was. But what's good? I didn't know Ace was working with a case solo."

Once in a while we took solo cases if one of us was busy or if something needed to be handled right away. But it was rare. I made sure to run a tight ship. We planned and over-planned if needed. But every client was well researched, and every kill was well planned.

That's how we'd been able to stay in business so long and stay under the radar and out of jail. We didn't take on clients that didn't check out. I had no clue what was going on with this thing. I just knew my brother called and we were going to be there if he needed us. Pharaoh had grown up a lot. He wasn't a hot head anymore. I knew his days were numbered in this business and I didn't mind. He was doing his thing with these buildings, and I wouldn't be the one to stand in his way. "I don't have a clue, but he said meet him in Atlanta." I noticed Jinx looking at me and smiling. "What?"

"I'm glad your eye healed."

"Fuck you!" I raised my hand to feel my eye. City had clocked my ass and had me walking around with a black eye. I swear she hit like a man. Had she been a man, she never would have gotten that hit in, but she caught me off guard.

"I won't lie; I'll take her to fight with me any day."

"Shut up man. She caught me off guard."

"Nah, you saw it coming but she was like Mayweather in there with that one and done."

I just shook my head. "Like I said, she caught me off guard."

"If that's your story and you sticking to it, so be it. Have you talked with her yet?"

"I can't, she changed all her numbers. She's not staying at any of her usual places. Her website is down saying under construction, so I can't contact her that way either. She was trying to ghost me. That's not like her. When I fuck up I send her some flowers and some jewelry, and she calls and says *nigga what I look like, a slow bitch? Come better*. I end up flying out to whatever location she's at and surprise her. We spend a few days making up and everything is all good after that. But I got eyes on her. That's the only reason I'm not tripping. I just don't know what to say to her."

"King, this ain't some you forgot her birthday type of shit. Nigga, you were in a whole other relationship, and she had to hear about it from the streets. You just got to give her some time. Flowers and jewelry won't fix it. You let another bitch one-up her."

"I wasn't in a relationship with Cola. Why does everyone keep saying that shit? We were just fucking." That's all I was doing with her, just fucking.

"If that's your story and you sticking to it, you ain't never getting City back."

"It's not a story. We were just fucking."

"Come on King. You were taking her out on dates and shit. She was cooking dinner for you. She was at the club whenever you were at the club, even if City was there. I would see her lurking in the shadows watching. You took her out the club. You were paying her bills. When you text, she answered. When she text, you answered. She running 'round the city talking about you with them damn loose lips and you letting her live. You're the only one who doesn't know you were in a relationship with her. You're a smart man, figure it out. Either you want her, or you don't. At this point, she's out of pocket and you won't be able to put her back in it. She has something on you, this baby. You need to decide if you're sharing custody or becoming a family." He started to light a blunt and took a toke and passed it to me. "And are you sure the baby is yours before you make any decision? You know once a hoe always a hoe."

I took a pull, and I started thinking on everything Jinx just laid on me. He was right. I was treating Cola like we were in a relationship. That's how I slipped up; I got comfortable with her ass. "She got good sense Jinx. If that baby ain't mine—" I couldn't even complete that last sentence. It was making my stomach turn thinking about the last few months. For years she'd been on that Depo shot birth control and suddenly when I started telling her we needed a break, she came up pregnant. Just the thought that she might be trying to play me had me ready to choke her ass again.

"Just make sure you get that DNA test. At the end of the day men lie, women lie but that test will tell the truth."

"You right, that test will be the truth. I got a package for you to pick up in New Orleans before we get to Atlanta."

"Ah, shit. King, I will hit her ass back if she hits me."

"It's me she hates, not you. You ain't got to worry about with her; it's Mrs. Dana that will be the problem. Let's just say that's big City! And she don't play." I smiled. I couldn't wait to see City. I spoke with her before every job. She would calm my nerves and tell me if I didn't come home she would come and get me. I wanted to hear her voice right now. I didn't need my nerves calmed I just missed our talks and listening to her tell me what new place she discovered. I would see all her pictures before she posted them. She valued my advice, and I valued hers. I just needed to know she's doing ok. I was stupid and selfish, but it was never my goal to hurt her.

Chapter Twenty-Seven

Baby Zaddys
Nikole "Cola" Peterson

This wasn't how it was supposed to go. You were my good trick. My money giving, stayed hard, long zaddy dick. I found I couldn't just walk away, and it wasn't just the money making me stay. I've fallen for you and this baby makes us true. You and I, Zaddy. You and I.

Here I was sitting at another doctor's appointment without King. This shit was for the birds. King promised me he wouldn't miss any more appointments and like a fool, I believed him. I knew he was in the streets, and he needed to take care of things, but I needed him here with me. I hated being pregnant. I didn't even want to have this baby. I only kept it because I saw the look in his eyes when I told him I was expecting. He looked at me different. I was waiting on him to give me the money for an abortion, instead he up and opened up an account for me to take care of all my needs. I just knew I hit the jackpot until the realization of what was really happening started to sink in. I looked around the office and I saw two women with their men. They were rubbing their stomachs and smiling with each other. I saw a few more women and like me, they were alone, but I noticed how their hands seemed to find their way to their stomachs as well. I wasn't like them. I only touched my stomach when King was around. I felt no connection to this baby. He or she was only a means to an end for me. My little golden meal ticket, and then I would be out. This wasn't part of the plan, but I knew how to improvise. I'd always been quick on my feet.

Just like the night I first saw King. I was working at a strip club called Honey. I wasn't a stripper; I didn't have the shape for a dancer. I was a bottle girl. It didn't pay as much as stripping would've, but I made great tips. These breasts were a great asset, and men loved to look. He was in VIP tossing money like it was nothing. I was attracted to him immediately. He was tall and slim, but he was sexy as hell with that smooth, chocolate skin. And when he smiled it was stunning, and that was saying a lot for a man. The thing that turned me on the most was the way he was pulling money out of his pocket like it was nothing. Even the guys in his section were all doing the same. But he was the boss, I could tell. I sat in the cut and watched him the next few hours. I had just started so I wasn't allowed to work VIP. That was fine with me. I never was the type to look thirsty. Instead, I did what I did best. I was reading him and waiting for my opportunity. I was damn good at reading men. It's like playing poker without the cards. See, a man will say anything to get you, it's what he doesn't say and how he moves that gives him away. All men had a tell. I was waiting to see his. I saw him walk away to take a call, and when he returned he sat at the bar for a minute with his head down. I saw him text and trying to call someone, but he kept getting a voicemail. I moved closer to him, and I saw the picture on the screen; it was a woman. I thought to myself, bingo. She was either stressing him or it was something else. I was hoping it was stress because I could take care of that with no problem. He picked up the phone again and I heard him leave a message. *I miss you baby. I know you working but come back soon.* It was the way he said it. I heard the loneliness in his voice. I bumped into him and apologized and asked if I could get him anything. The rest was history. It was that easy. He was like a woman in a vulnerable state, and he just needed someone; I made sure it was me.

I had to keep his attention by doing some crazy shit. Sucking his dick at a club in front of everyone, fighting the other bitches off and trying to be everything he needed. I didn't mind at all. The money he was giving was good, and the dick. I swear I been with a lot of men, but that dick King had was a blessing. He knew my body like no one else. The more time I spent with him the more I started to fall for him. What a cliché! I should have cut my losses a long time ago. But it was the way he cared for me. The way he talked and listened to me and my dreams without judgement. When he told me to dead the club, I did. I told him I was sick of staying with my mom, he got me my own place. He only told me no when that bitch was in town. Although he never lied about being in a relationship, I started to feel like he and I were in one. That was until the night of my birthday one year. I begged him to take me out, but he promised we would celebrate the next weekend. I went out with my girls and there they were together in *our* club. He was so loving and caring with her. It was unreal. She snapped her fingers, and he jumped. He was kissing her neck and holding her hand and dancing and singing with her. Watching them was like watching one of those romance movies. I sent him a text, he ignored it. I watched him put his phone on DND. That hurt my feelings. No way was I going to be ignored. I got ready to walk up there and set him and miss thang straight, but I was stopped by one of his guys, Jinx, and his brother Ace. They told me tonight was not the night. I told them I needed to see him; it was my birthday. When Ace said, *'don't you know your place?'* I felt it in my soul. He never liked me and didn't do anything to hide it. I walked back to my section with my tail between my legs. When King did call he said, *'City will always be number one.'* That hurt me to my core. I decided it was time for me walk away. But he came over and put me in a dick-coma. That was almost two years ago. You think I would've learned. I kept hoping if I was everything he wanted he would see it and leave her. But he didn't.

A few months ago, I noticed his visits were getting less and less. He started complaining about everything I did. The apartment wasn't clean. My cooking was bad. I knew it was only a matter of time before he broke up with me. I had to do something. The baby wasn't to keep him. It was to get more money, so I could finally walk away. I was sick of living in that bitch's shadow. I had looked her up a few times and she was good at what she did. She was interviewed by some show, and I saw her standing in front that big ass brownstone. She was loading one of her new cars up with her equipment. Showing off a day in fabulous life. That shit left me salty. As much money as he was giving me, it was never going to equal to the amount of money he was giving her. I'd be damned if I'd put in this time and walked away empty-handed. The only thing was now I had to go through with it. I'm far from a motherly type. I planned on leaving this baby with my mom just like the other one. I hadn't seen my six-year-old daughter in years. She was well taken care of. I made sure of that. My mom didn't live in the projects like I told him; she was back home in South Carolina.

There were a lot of things I bent the truth on with him, but my feelings weren't one. I cared for him. There was this little bit of hope left that he and I could make it work with the baby, but that was laid to rest after the night she overheard me talking about him. He came over fired up that night, looking like he had gone a few rounds with someone. He told me how it was my fault she left him all because I couldn't keep my mouth shut. He saw me as his problem. He didn't see what he did as a problem. Just like a damn man to never admit what they did was wrong. At least now I knew where I stood. This was going to make it easier to walk away from him. Also, the little guilt I felt quickly disappeared. There might be a 50/50 chance that this wasn't his baby. The thing was, he trusted me, so I knew he wasn't going to test the baby; he already said he wouldn't. I was safe. This better be a boy so I could truly milk him for everything. I needed a car. A Range like that bitch drives. I felt Dante tap me on my leg.

"Come on, the nurse is calling your name."

"Oh, I didn't even hear her." We walked to the back and the same nurse who I couldn't stand was there to take my vitals. She was always eyeing me. I thought maybe her and King had something going on, but he said he didn't know her.

"I see you have your brother again today." She smiled and looked from me to him.

"Yes, Hakeem wasn't able to make it today." I smiled back at her. It was a good thing Dante knew the deal because she would have busted me. I knew that's what she was trying to do. But I was already ahead of her. Dante and I had been on and off for the past ten years. He was the father of my first child. I was lonely one night when King was chasing City around the world. I called, and he came. I told him everything. He knew the deal. He also knew it was a chance this baby wasn't his, and he was ok with that too. Just like me, he wasn't the fatherly type. He was only here for the money. After I push out this baby, he was going to drive me back to my mom's house and get me set up to work in a club out there for a minute. Not long though, just until I could come back to New York. I knew King would try and kill me if this baby ain't his. But I'm two steps ahead. I watched her leave the room to go and get the doctor.

"She got it out for you Cola! Watch and make she don't tell that dumb ass trick before we get this money."

"Don't worry Dante, nothing will stop me from securing this bag."

"That's my girl."

I looked at Dante and I knew he wasn't the same as King. He's a small-time pimp but I'm his ride or die bitch so I didn't have to work as hard. King was rich, handsome and a boss. Dante was only handsome. The thing was, I knew he loved me. I didn't need to come in second to anyone for him. That was all I wanted. I was done trying to make King love me. Now I was going to make him pay for the next 18 years.

Chapter Twenty-Eight

Eyes Wide Open

Paige Turner Daniels

These eyes of mine were closed to how you treated me. They didn't see the reality that you never loved me. These tears won't wash my pain away. I dry them and see you for who you are today. They're red now and stained but they're wide open to your game.

I sat across from Pharaoh. He was holding a conversation with City's mom, my aunt Dana, but his eyes were watching me intensely. We showed up at her door this morning and she insisted on fixing us a huge breakfast. She had shrimp and grits, eggs, sausage and catfish. It was all my favorites, but I couldn't touch my plate. I didn't have an appetite. Who could eat after finding out that they'd been living a lie? The last couple of days had been crazy. Trying to get out of Atlanta without being seen. Driving to New Orleans because we couldn't fly here. Coming to terms with the death of my father and trying to wrap my mind around the fact I'd been living a lie for the past few years. That part right there, the lie part was causing a pain in my heart and making my stomach upset. I cringed every time my mind recalled the fact I'd been living with a man I didn't even know. I was giving my body to someone that was only fooling me. I was trusting and free with every part of me and my body and my money with a man whose name was a fake. Just that fact only had me shaking. How fucking dumb was I? How blind was I? Everyone saw he was no good but me. Pharaoh touched my hand. His touch put me at ease again. I didn't even know how he did that.

"Honey, what's the matter, you been in Atlanta that long you don't recognize good food? You better eat. I made all your favorites. It's a ride up there to Angola; this will hold you." Aunt Dana looked at me and took a seat. "I'm sorry you had to find out about your dad this way, but I knew nothing, but death could keep him from your mom. He loved that heifer." She laughed.

"Everything is so good Mrs. Dana. Eat shorty," Pharaoh said.

I told Pharaoh I wanted to come here so I could tell my mom in person. He agreed. He said he had some people meeting us here, so we would fly back to Atlanta. I didn't know how I could face my mom today. How I could tell her she was never getting out of that place? She and I wrote often, and I swear she believed my dad was going to ride in on some white horse and save her any day. "Do you think she knew? You know, felt like he was dead, somewhere deep down inside." I mean, I thought about it, but I also thought he had just skipped out on her and me.

"Deep down, she knew. I think we all did. It was the hope that he was coming that's been keeping her going in that place. I just wish she would've let us help her instead of saying she would wait. This will be hard for her. But I'll be there so you don't need to bear this burden alone. City can come too as soon as she stops pretending her greedy ass ain't hungry." She was staring behind us. "Bring your ass on in here. It's just Paige and Pharaoh. King ain't found your ass yet!"

"City!!!" I turned around and she was standing there in her robe. "I thought you were out of the country. I tried calling you." I stood up and put my hands on my hips.

"I know. I was scanning my calls. You know I was going to call you back. I just needed some time. So what's going on? And why are you two together?" Looking from me to Pharaoh, she sat down and started fixing her plate. "Mom, you ain't fix all this for me when I came home. I always knew Paige was your favorite."

"Girl, go ahead with that. I never get to see my niece. That crazy ass husband of hers keeps her trapped in Atlanta. Plus, I'm just glad to see her and Pharaoh together again."

City's mom or as I call her, my Tee Dana, never liked Kane. She just said, *if you like it I love it.* If I came home so I could visit her, he never came with me. When I went to see my mom in jail, he never came. Now that I thought about it, he'd never met my mom. But Pharaoh had a few times. He would fly me home anytime I said I was homesick, and I needed my mom. The thoughts of us exploring New Orleans together invaded my mind. I could truly say here, and New York contained no memories of me and Kane. But me and Pharaoh had some everlasting ones.

"Y'all still ain't answer my question. What are you two doing together? Did you finally come to your senses Paige and leave that no good husband of yours?" I looked up to see City stuffing her mouth with food. She and Tee Dana were waiting on me to answer.

I didn't want to admit it. I didn't want them to know. I was mortified, and I knew they both would say they told me so. I gave them half of an answer. "I found out some things I didn't like. Just like you City, I need some time."

"He got a baby too Paige?" City screamed and looked at Pharaoh who put his hands up in a surrender motion.

"Not that I know of. I'll explain everything later. Let me handle things with my mom first." The doorbell rang and Pharaoh was up and ready to get it.

My tee Dana looked at me. "Are you sure everything is ok, Paige?"

"I promise it's fine. And I'm good."

"I know you good. That man walked in here and checked my place out like he was the damn Secret Service, and he hasn't stopped watching you. I know he's going to take care of you. But do I need to call your cousins?"

"No! It's fine really Tee Dana." My cousins were a different type of crazy. I think it was something they put in the water down here. They would start shooting and then ask questions. They were always ready and willing to go to jail for any dumb reason. This was my problem, and I was going to handle it. "That's just Pharaoh, you know that."

"Mom, you know he extra about Paige."

She laughed. "Don't I know it. The first time I met him, when I went to New York to visit you and City, he had his eyes fixed on your every move. Even when no one was looking. It was a little creepy, but you liked it. I would catch your ass blushing and smiling at him. You know he reminds me a lot of your dad. That's how he was with your mom. Real protective of her. It's different this time. There's murder in his eyes. Whatever is going on, you stay close to him. He'll make sure you're good. And you don't have to tell me now. City will just tell me later." She looked at City and laughed hard. "Your ass can't hold water."

She was right, City and Tee Dana were close as hell. She told her everything. Tee Dana had already chewed Pharaoh's ear off about King hurting her daughter. She told him she owed King an ass whipping. Was there murder in Pharaoh's eyes? Was he going to kill Kane or Kentrell or whomever the fuck he was? I wanted to feel sympathy, but I didn't. I wasn't the type of person to wish death on anyone. But the way I started putting things together, the angrier I got. I wanted Kane to suffer, maybe not die, but hurt like I hurt.

"She's right City. You tell all the secrets." I picked up my fork and forced myself to eat. Pharaoh came back in the kitchen and behind him were King and Jinx. I looked at City who hadn't noticed.

"Mrs. Dana, I hope you don't mind feeding a few more. They were supposed to meet us in Atlanta later today. But we had a change of plans."

I saw City turn and her and King's eyes met, and I grabbed her hand. "Before you say anything, let me talk with you and Tee Dana in the other room please."

"Paige, is this a joke? Did you know he was coming?" City was standing, and I could tell she was fighting back tears.

"I promise to explain everything. Just please come into the other room so we can talk."

She agreed and all three of us started walking out the kitchen. I nodded at Jinx and popped King upside the head. Tee Dana did the same thing. City just rolled her eyes. I sat them down in the next room and I told them everything. I told them how Kane wasn't really Kane. How he'd been using me and how my marriage was fake. I explained to City that King was only there to assist Pharaoh in whatever plan he had. And if I would've known she was there, I never would have agreed to him coming. I would have waited until we returned to Atlanta for them to meet up. I told her we would be gone before midnight tonight.

"Go back to Atlanta? What the hell are you going back for?" City asked.

"I'm not running this time. I can't run again. He's made a fool out of me. And I refuse to let him get away with it."

"Paige, you can let Pharaoh handle it. You don't need to be there."

"No, it's not his problem. It's mine. I was dumb enough to fall for this man's act. I was stupid enough to marry him and I gave him access to my accounts. I allowed him to make me feel like I was less than a woman with all his damn affairs. And the first time I was able to walk away, I walked right back into his arms. No, Pharaoh can do what he does, but I'm going to be there. I'm going to make sure he gets what's coming to him. And I want to be there to see it." I was angry now. Every word I spoke was true. I wasn't going to run anymore. I was going to face my problems head on. This was my mess, and I wasn't going to leave it for someone else to clean it up.

"It's about damn time niece! I been waiting on that backbone in you to show up. You picked the perfect time to let it grow."

"Mom, don't encourage her. If Pharaoh called for reinforcements that means the situation is dangerous. I'm always down to fight but we don't know what he's capable of."

"Whatever he's capable of is nothing compared to what I'm capable of. I promise Paige is in good hands." Pharaoh stepped next to me and took my hand. "We should get ready to get on the road to see your mom."

"You're right, we need to go." I entwined my fingers with his. The closer I was to him, the safer I felt. I wasn't going to stay behind without him. I needed to be right next to him. He was giving me my strength and the courage I needed to get this done. Sure, I could do without him. I just didn't want to!

"Well give me a few minutes to pack a bag. It's no way I'm letting you go by your damn self. I can tolerate being in the jackass' presence as long as he doesn't talk to me. But I'll be damn if I miss out on finally getting to kick Kane and Kentrell ass!"

I wanted to correct her and tell her it was just one person, but she was already stumping up the stairs. I looked at Jinx and he was cracking up. King was standing there looking like a lost little boy. I didn't know how this all would play out. I just knew I needed it to be over soon.

Back in Atlanta

The visit with my mom went just as I expected. She was devastated. When she broke it down to me, I realized she wasn't crying because he was dead. She was crying because she knew he never would have abandoned her. His death a few months after she was jailed proved it. My tee Dana opened her mouth and told her what was going on with me and Kane. I swear her and City had the same big mouth. My mom told me to handle my business. She said it was time for me to finally stand up for myself, and I agreed.

We were all at Pharaoh's house back in Atlanta. It was late and I should have been sleep, but I couldn't sleep. I had so many thoughts running through my mind. This plan needed to work. But for it to work I had to prepare myself to walk away from everything I'd known. My job, my friends, my home and maybe even Atlanta. It was going to get ugly. That's that best I could put it.

"Paige, you're still up? Have you heard anything from Pharaoh?"

"He sent me a text about two hours ago, but that was it. I'm not worried. I know he's ok. I was just sitting here thinking if I could really go through with everything. I talked some big game today. Now I need to back it up."

"Yes, the hell you do. Got me out here with the enemy, you better back all that shit up."

I started cracking up. Those two were on the jet just staring at each other. The only thing that kept her from jumping on him was Jinx asking how old Tee Dana was. Talking about she was fine as hell. Tee Dana was a mixture of me and City. My thickness but City's color. And my mom was the exact opposite. City's slim build and my color. I kept telling him she would only break his heart. He said with that body and her cooking skills; she could break anything she wanted. That was the first time I heard Jinx really talk. He reminded me a little of Pharaoh the way he watched his environment. The three of them made sense together. It was a good thing Pharaoh's house was big enough to give everyone their own room or else it would've been world war three in here. Pharaoh and I were sleeping in the same room and that was my choice.

"I just want all of this over soon as possible. After it's done, nothing in my life will be the same. Just like after the accident years ago. I feel like I keep starting over and I hate it. I don't want to keep starting life over and over."

"Don't think of it as starting over. Think of it as a revival of an old love. You and Pharaoh fit. No matter how you try to fight it, you just do. Is it fucked up what Kane did? Yes, but it gives you a free pass to get out of a loveless marriage. You weren't happy with Kane or Kentrell. You were so busy being loyal to some damn vows you couldn't be honest with yourself. That's how you got fooled. It wasn't because you were dumb or stupid. You're one of those people that believes if you give love you get it back in return. That's not always how life goes."

"You're right, it's a free pass. At least I wasn't really married to his lying ass. It makes me feel less guilty about sleeping with Pharaoh."

"Were you two back together before or after you found out he was lying?"

"We're not together, but it was before."

"Don't fool yourself again. Y'all together."

"That was low."

"I didn't mean it that way. You guys are very touchy, feely with each other. You can't sleep right now because he's not here. He's not going to let you leave him again. You're together, just accept it. Finally, Paige you can give love, and someone will return it the right way. Do you feel safe with him? Do you feel loved by him?"

"Yes, yes and yes to all those things. But I don't want to jump from one relationship right into another."

"Too late!"

"Have you talked with King?" I wanted to change the subject. I knew how I felt about Pharaoh and how he felt about me. But I didn't know how we were going to work out everything.

"Nope. I lock the door at night, so he doesn't try to sneak in. And the worst part is he hasn't."

"Wait, I'm confused. Do you want him to come in or not?"

"Yes and no. I want him to fight for us. He just let me walk away and he didn't even chase me. Hell, Pharaoh is about to go to war for your ass. He done brought a whole damn army to take a nigga down. Meanwhile, I can't get King to even acknowledge me when I enter the room."

"Let me be honest. Me and Tee Dana threatened him. We told him to fix this shit. We made him swear he wouldn't get back with you until it was fixed. She may or may not have had a gun. But if you want him to come into your room tonight to dick you down and you wake up in the morning feeling like crap because nothing is resolved, I can give him a key to the door. He gave me his word he would give you some time."

"Bitch, you and my momma cockblocking me."

"Nope, just protecting you from yourself. We know you and him have this long ass history. But this is something you need to talk about."

"I know we need to talk but I'm horny as hell."

"Get you a toy or use them damn fingers. You know once y'all have sex you will end up feeling like crap. City, you got to decide. You can choose to forgive him but if you do, that requires you accepting the baby. Are you ready to do that?"

"You know how to ruin a wet dream. I just miss him, you know. Being this close to him and not being able to talk to him or touch him feels like death."

She laid her head on my shoulder. "I know, but it could be worse."

"How?"

I felt her wipe her eyes. "You could be married to a fake bastard that was trying to steal all your money and leave you dusty." We both started laughing. "Don't laugh so damn hard. That's some real-life Jerry Springer mess that my ass is living in right now."

"I know it's not funny, but he got your ass. With his fake Boris Kodjoe looking ass. Did he get you for everything? You know you can come live with me in New York again. Although I'm considering selling the brownstone."

"I'm good. I haven't thought about moving back to New York again. But I don't even know if Atlanta is the right place for me. I don't know what I'm going to do. I haven't thought that far."

"Whatever you decide, I'm here for you."

"Thank you." We sat silently holding each other until we heard the front door open. The guys walked in and the looks on their faces were unreadable. I wanted to ask was it over, but I knew it wasn't. I knew something else happened, I could feel it in my gut.

"Paige, did you tell your assistant Danni any of our plans?"

Pharaoh was standing over me staring at me and so were King and Jinx. They were all waiting on my answer. "No, I did just what you said. Exactly what you said. I told her Kane, and I had a disagreement, and I wanted to cool off for a few days at the hotel. I needed her to help me get some clothes. Why, what's wrong?"

"Sit down shorty."

"No, I don't want to sit down."

"Did she go to the hotel with you?"

"No, she didn't go back to the hotel with me. Tell me what's going on now!"

"Danni was found dead today."

It felt like my chest was about to cave in. I couldn't breathe. Everyone was talking but I couldn't hear what they were saying. She worked with me for a few years but in the past few months, we had really gotten close. She was kind and caring. She would tell it to you straight with no chaser but in a nasty, nice, roundabout way. She told me several times I was so much better than Kane, and I refused to listen. She was talking about going back to school to get her business degree and I had told her I would totally support it. I told her I would cut her hours but still give her the same pay. I was all for her getting her degree. There was a position opening in HR and she wanted it but was passed up because she didn't have the degree. She only had a few hours to complete, and I promised I would help with all her math classes. "How did she die?"

"She was beaten, and her neck was slit," Jinx said, and Pharaoh started waving him off. "No, she needs to know. Tell her how serious this is. She was trying to leave the house earlier. She needs to know it's not safe."

"That's not your call Jinx." Pharaoh started to walk toward him, but King stepped in between them.

"Calm down man. He's right, they need to know. It's not fun and games. This isn't something she can just walk away from." King turned to both me and City. "You ladies are not to leave the house without one of us. If you want to order food or go the store, we will take care of it. But for now, no one can leave."

"You can't tell us what to do, King." City stood with her hands on her hips.

"City, this is not the damn time for it. I don't want to fuss with your ass. We are just trying to protect you. Do you want to end up dead too?" He walked toward her, and the look in his eyes was serious.

"No." She sat back down.

My mind was racing. Was he saying what I think he was saying? "Did Kane kill her? Did she die because of me?"

"Let's go and talk in the room Paige."

Pharaoh had his hand on my arm. I wasn't going anywhere. I wanted to know exactly what was going on. "No, tell me right now. She was my friend. And I don't have many of those. She was a good person, and she trusted me. If I put her in danger, you tell me."

"He killed her looking for you. He was never going to let you just leave him. He was planning on killing you. That was the end game Paige. Take all your money and kill you and collect on your policy. He has a very large life insurance policy on you, and you're worth more to him dead than alive."

When the words left Pharaoh's mouth, I was speechless. Not only was I sleeping with a fraud, but he wanted me dead too. Did he really hate me that much? What did I do to him to deserve death? I loved him. I cooked, cleaned and took care of everything he needed. I made sure the house ran smoothly. Even in the midst of him cheating on me, I was still good to him. He never loved me. This was all just a game. A game where I was going to end up dead. I was scared. All this time I was hating Pharaoh for putting me in harm's way, and here I was sleeping with the enemy. My mind was completely blown. "I'm sorry, this is all my fault. I got her killed and I'm going to end up dead. All of this for some damn money." I broke down and started crying for Danni and for me. I felt Pharaoh wrap his arms around me and I started to cry harder.

"Look at me shorty." He cupped my chin and lifted my face until our eyes met. "I won't let nothing happen to you. You said you trust me. Trust he'll die a painful death before he harms one hair on your head."

I just nodded my head. And when he brought his lips to meet mine, it was a soft, gentle peck, but it quieted my crying. He walked me into the room and laid me in the bed. I curled up like a baby. I watched him take his shoes off then he walked out of eyesight. The bed dipped and he was behind me. I felt the tears rolling down my face again. His arm was around me and he was pulling me close to him. But I turned so I could face him. "I'm so sorry. I made you the bad guy in my life and here I was sleeping with the bad guy every night. I'm sorry because I was a fool to not give you a chance again when I gave him chance after chance. Here you are trying to protect me, and I don't deserve it. I don't deserve you loving me."

He caressed my cheek. "Deserve? Hmmm. . . interesting. I felt the same with you our whole relationship. And when I lost you I felt like I deserved it. You know we don't get to tell our hearts to stop loving someone. Even with you absent from my life for so many years, my heart would still skip a beat at the mention of your name. I knew you were hurt. I knew my lifestyle did that to you. You almost died. You lost pieces of you I can't ever replace. But that never changed my love for you. Even though I told my heart many times to let you go, it didn't listen. And when I finally got to see you again, it felt like I could breathe again. Everything with you feels so right." He took my hands and placed them on his heart. "My heart will never stop loving you. I will never stop loving you. You don't ever need to question me loving you and you deserving it. You gave me purpose and direction when chicks only saw a meal ticket. They didn't understand me or get my weird ass ways. You do."

"I missed you so fucking much! I didn't want you back in my life like this. I didn't want you coming to rescue me after a fuck up."

"I missed you too shorty. It doesn't matter how I came back into your life. Just know I came back. And now I'm never letting you go again."

"Thank you!" I ran my fingers up his arm, and I landed on his face. His goatee was still cut the same way and still looked good on him. I ran my fingertips underneath and through the hair. He closed his eyes. I caressed his jawline. It's strong and masculine like him. I traced his lips. I kissed his eyes one by one. Then, I kissed each cheek until I traced his lips again, but this time with my tongue. I kissed him slowly and our kiss intensified to the point I was on top of him. "I'm scared Pharaoh." He flipped me over and his eyes were open and gazing into mine.

"On my life, I will never let him hurt you. I'll protect you with everything in me."

I believed him. I let him back into my heart again. I was safe in his arms. I did deserve love. Did I deserve the type of love Pharaoh was giving me? I didn't know, I just knew I wanted it. I wanted all he was going to give me. And right now, he was giving me life. And I wanted it! When he entered me I knew there was no going back. He was making love to me, and I couldn't help my tears. He kissed my tears and my eyes. His strokes were slow and deep, and I felt each one in my soul. I knew he loved me. I felt it. "I love you Pharaoh!"

"It's about damn time you realize it."

When I thought he couldn't go deeper, he did, and I couldn't hold it. My orgasm washed over me like a wave that was carrying every emotion I'd denied over the past few years. I released my fear, my doubt, my pain and my hurt. I smiled and he kissed me again. He was still inside me collecting more feelings and I was happy to let him do it. I was in heaven. This felt right. This was right.

Chapter Twenty-Nine

All My Cards on The Table
Synplicity "City" Walker

This isn't chess, it's poker, and my face hasn't changed. But my heart is bleeding for you driving me insane. I want to bluff with the cards I'm holding but not with you. All my cards are on the table, the bet's up to you.

It was three a.m., and I was lying in bed still thinking about everything going on with Paige. This thing with her and Kane was crazy. I knew something about him was fake. I felt it when I first met him. He was trying too hard to impress me. I saw the controlling side of him when she didn't. When I saw how happy she was I stepped back, and I put my hunches to the side. Now I was lying here regretting not going with my first mind. I was jumpy. Every small sound made me mute the tv and listen. I really wanted to go crawl in bed with her and Pharaoh because I knew he was protecting her ass. King didn't even ask me if I was ok. At this point, I might as well be invisible to him. I needed comfort food to get me to fall asleep. I was about to Netflix and chill with my damn self. I walked downstairs to the kitchen and turned on the light and I jumped when I see a man moving. "Damn, King you scared the shit out of me."

"I didn't mean to! You should be sleep anyway."

"Well you shouldn't be sitting here in the dark guarding the snacks in the kitchen." He smiled, licked his lips, stood and started walking toward me. His walk was so damn sexy, I felt the wetness in my draws, and I was trying to control myself. *Remember he has someone else City. Just don't make eye contact with him.* Too late, I looked directly in his eyes.

"I know you're not fucking with me right now but if you need me, I'm here."

"I'm good." He was next to me now and I could smell his cologne. It was intoxicating. He reached for me, but I stepped back.

"I'm sorry, I won't touch you. I just know when you start snacking it's because you can't sleep and you're nervous about something. I'm here if you need me City."

He started to walk out of the kitchen, and I felt like an ass. "I'm sorry King. I wasn't trying to be mean to you or run you away. You were in here first. Let me just grab my snack and I'll turn the light out, so you can continue to do your Batman thing."

"You got jokes, I was only thinking that's all. Your favorite chips are in the pantry."

"Thank you." I loved those Dill Pickle chips. Now all I needed was a Coke.

"There's Cokes in the fridge."

"Yes! I can't eat these without a Coke."

"I know."

"This is strange. I mean it feels weird."

"It does."

"King, I'm scared, and I always felt safe with you. But right now, with us not being us, I feel like crawling in the bed with Pharaoh and Paige to feel safe."

"I'm still right here. I know things are not the same with us, but I would never let anything happen to you. And you know they nasty; they probably fucking." He walked back toward me and closed the space between us. "All these years and you pick now to think I wouldn't make sure you're safe."

I didn't know the right words to say or any words to say. "Well, I'm about to watch some Netflix if you want to watch with me since you're still up?" I knew I was going to regret him coming upstairs with me. I thought about what Paige said. But I just needed someone close to me tonight.

"I don't think that's a good idea. But just know I'm here for you."

"You really do love her?"

"What, love who? No City, let's not do this right now. I just know me coming upstairs will lead to something else and I don't think that's a good idea right now."

"Why is not a good idea? Because you're fully committed to her now?"

"Come on man, you got it all wrong."

I grabbed my snacks and headed out the kitchen. My pride was hurt. He would protect me but from a distance. He was really trying to be faithful to her. "Goodnight."

"City, please don't walk away like this again."

I turned around and slammed the snacks down on the counter. The tears I was already fighting were streaming down my face. "What do you want from me? Do want me to beg you to be with me? Do you want me to say I miss you so much it hurts? Do you want me to say I'm terrified of being in that room alone? Because I am. Do you want me to say I need you? Because I do. Do you want me to say I'll accept the baby? Because I can't say it right now."

"No, don't say it because I know you won't mean it." He put his hands behind his head in frustration. "Come sit down."

I walked toward the table he pointed to, and I sat. He handed me some tissue and I wiped my eyes. "I'm sitting, now what?"

He sat across from me. "I'm going to do something I should have done a long time ago. I'm going to put all my cards on the table. I don't want you to keep doubting my feelings for you or thinking something that's not true. I just need you to be woman enough to understand. Can you do that?"

"Yes."

"No City. I'm going to be completely honest and I need for you listen without reacting."

"I can't promise you I won't react. I can say I will listen. I think this is long overdue."

"Ok good. This relationship or non-relationship thing we've been doing stopped working for me a long time ago."

"Why didn't you say anything?"

"I was afraid of losing you. You and I are the same. I like being in charge and so do you. I didn't want to take you away from your work, but I wanted you with me. I got lonely. The texts, calls and Facetime just wasn't working for me anymore. I met Cola and it was supposed to be the usual hit it and move on like we agreed to do. Something happened where it didn't go as planned. I started spending time with her. It became more and more time together. Soon we were acting like a couple. I knew she didn't have shit, so I moved her into one of the buildings I own."

"So you don't pay her rent?"

"Really City, is that all you heard?"

"No. I'm listening." I wanted to smile but I didn't. She thought he was doing something. It was costing him nothing.

"Stop interrupting. That's one of your biggest problems. You don't listen to me. I'm telling you how I feel, and you're just worried about if I provided for a bitch or not."

That part was like a gut punch. Have I not been listening to him? Is this what happened to us? "I'm sorry. I'm listening, I promise."

"I was getting ready to cut everything off with her when you told me you were expecting. I was so damn excited. But you, you were treating it like it was just another thing in your life you had to work into your schedule. I was angry at you for losing our child. You just kept working like it was nothing. I didn't know how to feel about it."

He put his head in his hands. I didn't know what to say. I was speechless. I grieved so hard for the loss of the baby. I didn't know how to tell him the truth. "King."

"Let me finish. I called you so many times and you didn't answer. I needed you. That's when she and I got closer. I got careless one night and slipped up. It's not an excuse. I should have been more careful. I can't change the situation. I can't make it go away."

"I know you can't. It was wrong of me to say make her get rid of it. I need to know do you love her?" I needed conformation before I opened up all the way. I didn't want to look like a fool.

"No. Do I like her? Yes. I know she's using me but it's nice to have someone there that cares about me. That asks me how my day was and do I need anything."

"You think I don't care King? After all this time."

"Your actions. Your actions, say something different. You're so self-absorbed and selfish and self-centered. It's hard to tell if you love anyone else but yourself. Even after the accident with Paige, you went off on some job assignment and left her there. She needed you. She needed your guidance. Look at the mess she's gotten herself into now. She's in real danger and so are you."

"Wow! So all of this is my fault?"

"I didn't say that—"

"Pretty much, that's what you just said. I'm all the things you've said I am, but you forgot to mention caring and loving. I love Paige but she's a grown ass woman. I've taken care of her for as long as I could, but I couldn't heal her heart. She's fragile yes, but she wants to stand on her own and I wasn't going to get in her way. I couldn't keep guiding her in the direction I wanted her to take. She needed to find her own way in the world. I'm sorry her direction brought her to Kane. I warned her about him many times. But again, she's grown. I knew I wasn't there back then like I should have been, but I'm here now." I stood up from the table. And I saw him getting ready to talk again but I held my hands up. "You think I'm that selfish that the death of my baby didn't touch me. It did. While you were coming around judging me, your eyes didn't notice that I wasn't eating. You didn't see the darkness that filled my eyes. I tried to kill myself one day and one of my workers found me. I was rushed to a hospital where they pumped my stomach. I entered a 120-day in-patient treatment program to help me with my depression. I couldn't answer your calls because phones weren't allowed. So, while my selfish ass was trying to get better, you were falling into some pussy. We are the same. Except I know who I am. You don't know who you are because you're just as self-centered as me."

I walked out the kitchen. I didn't even want the snacks anymore. My plan now was to get under the covers and cry myself to sleep. I knew I put up a front like I was so strong, but I had feelings too. I knew Paige was fragile. She'd been that way since watching her father kill that man. I knew she felt some kind of way toward her father, but he saved her that night. One of her dad's workers was trying to rape her and her father found him and killed him right there. In order for him to stay out of jail, her mother took the charge. She blamed herself for not knowing what was going on under her own roof. The therapist said Paige blocked it out and didn't remember. Said she turned to the next page in her life and kept going. Something in her remembered because it was a stormy night, and she still hated storms. I made sure she never slept alone on those nights when we were kids, all the way until we were teenagers. I tried many times to get her to remember but she would just freak out whenever we talked. King thought it was weird that a grown woman hated storms until I told him the story. I told him we all kept a close eye on her because she never spoke about things, and we were afraid when she did remember she wasn't going to handle it well. When she started to paint that became her outlet. After the accident, she promised me she was fine. She told me to stop babysitting her and live my life. That's what I did.

No one knew about me trying to kill myself. Not even my mom, and I shared everything with her. It was a moment of weakness for me. In that moment of weakness King ran to someone else, when it was me who needed him. I laid across the bed and pulled the covers over my head. I felt so alone. His words were running through my mind creating doubt in who I was and who I am. I watched my mom pass up her dream to take care of everyone else, including my dad. Who up and left the first chance he got. When Paige came to live with us my mom worked two jobs to make sure we were well taken care of. I didn't want to be like her. Giving up something I really wanted and trying to take care of everyone else was not going to be in my cards. I wanted my cake, and I wanted to be able to eat it too! King was that wild card in my plans. When I fell in love with him, I fell hard. He was and still is everything I ever wanted. I just wasn't ready to give up my career and he didn't want to compromise. That's not true. I would have given it for the baby and him. But I lost them both. My career was all I had now. I couldn't even focus on it because my heart was broken. I couldn't find my passion anymore. I closed everything down and went home to my mom to get my head together. Now this had to happen.

The door to my room opened and closed. I felt the bed dip and I smelled him before he touched me. My body responded to him before I did. It relaxed when he touched me. A cry escaped my lips. One that I didn't want him to hear, but it came out.

"City, I didn't know. I'm so fucking sorry. I would have been there for you. Bae, I'm sorry. I never want to lose you."

"Don't King. Just let me be. You got what you want." I jerked my body away from him, but he was strong, and he pulled me closer.

"I want you and only you. Don't fight me on this. Let me hold you. Let your guard down. Let me love you."

I felt vulnerable and that was new to me. I didn't want to let my guard down, but I was exhausted trying to play superwoman. I let him hold me and rock me like I was child. I let the tears flow from my eyes for my baby, for me and for him. I blocked out the outside world. It was only me and him right now. That felt good to say.

Tomorrow it may change but right now, I needed him. I needed him to make me feel good. I needed him to make me feel loved. I needed him now and always. Right now, we were starting with tonight. He was open and honest with me. He put all his cards on the table, and I saw now it wasn't just him running, but me running from him. I just couldn't run anymore.

Chapter Thirty

Hide and Seek
Kane Daniels

You think you can hide from me. I'm the master at finding people you see. Hide and seek is a child's game to me, I'm a grown ass man. When I find you we will end this little game.

"What do you mean you can't find her? The bitch is staying at the hotel. That's what her assistant said." I was talking on the phone with Mundy, my partner in crime I sent to take care of Paige. I couldn't find this bitch for nothing. Shit was starting to piss me off. Since the night of the Mayor's Ball, I had only seen her once and that was on video only. I had security cameras installed all around the house to always watch her. Her and Danni came in the next day and packed some of her clothes and she was gone. I tried to track her phone with no luck; it was off. I thought maybe she went back to New York, but I had checked the airports.

She was really smart. She had all the money moved from our joint account and she had a freeze on our investment accounts. I knew she was blocking me from getting to the money. I just wasn't sure how much she knew about me. Or if she knew anything. If she did, I needed to put an end to her quick before she messed up my other deals.

"I know what her assistant said but she's not there. In fact, her bags aren't even there," Mundy said.

"She's playing games with me."

"Man listen; I did some checking on my own. This Ace guy you mentioned is Ace Mann. Do you know who that is?"

"Some half ass, square, wanna be thug nigga that's her ex. What does it matter?" I heard him chuckle.

"You don't know. The Mann brothers are the best in the business. They work for the Cartel and freelance. They're damn good at what they do. I've heard stories about Ace and King. They say King is outright crazy, but Ace is a different kind of crazy."

"I don't give a fuck if they were the Cartel themselves. I want her found and I want her dead. I put in too much time for this shit not to work."

"I told you this was too much. You went way over on this one. Cut your losses and let's move on. It's over. Let her go."

"Nah, she gone give me everything she owes me. I want that money from her dad's policy, and I want the money from her policy."

"The connects she gave will get us paid for years. We have an endless well of money."

"I want all the money."

"I think it's more than more money. Your ass was feeling her; that's why it took this damn long. I ain't never seen it take this long to work a woman. I got to admit, her ass was beautiful."

"I wasn't feeling her. I was finessing her. It's a difference. She's a gold mine. As long as I kept digging, she kept giving."

"Well pack up your tools, it's over."

"It's not over until I say it's over."

"I get it, you got something to prove because it's the first one to walk away from you. But get this, playing with those brothers is like playing with fire. So that's on you. Hit me up when you got something solid."

I couldn't believe Mundy was willing to walk away without getting all the money. That wasn't him at all. We'd been doing this for years and now he wanted to get cold feet. Claiming I fell for Paige. I didn't fall for her ass. Maybe a little. She was different from all the other women we finessed. She was downright beautiful, and the sex was amazing. Her body did things you only see on porn videos. I found myself enjoying time with her. Our conversations were good. She wasn't one-dimensional like most women. You know the ones so into their looks they couldn't discuss real world events. Or the ones so into keeping up with the Kardashians they forgot to take care of home. Paige was smart, and she knew about politics and music. She would work all day but still come home and cook dinner. Although she wasn't super submissive, she was submissive enough. She made sure my clothes were dry cleaned, she served me my plates at the dinner table, and she would get in the shower and wash me when I had a long day. That often led to her sucking my dick. Just thinking about it was getting my dick hard. Together, we were a real power couple. She and I walked through doors together and put most couples to shame.

The reality check came when she started talking about a family. It was a year into our relationship, and we had been fake married for five months. I saw her looking at baby clothes on a trip to the mall. I asked her was she pregnant. She said no, she was just thinking about our future and the way we were fucking, she was sure it would happen soon. I smiled and agreed. Just for a moment, I thought of a little Kane or Paige. But who was I kidding, Kane doesn't exist. There was no future. There would be no kids. I had a vasectomy years ago so nothing or no one could tie me down. This was a job just like any other. I treated it as such.

I got myself together and worked her like we planned. Mundy and I had been running these types of games for years. Each time it only got bigger and better, and we ended up richer and richer. This was no different. Every time I thought about wrapping it up with her and disappearing, she moved up in her company and the door opened to more money opportunities. I stayed and passed the information on to Mundy. Either we invested or found a way to get money out of everyone she introduced us to.

Just like I figured, I started getting bored with Paige. Don't get me wrong, she was amazing and all, but she started doing what women always did; she started nagging and pointing out my faults. She wanted me home more. She wanted to spend time with me. She was getting clingy. I knew it was time to move on. I started a few new out-of-state schemes. I had something big planned next. But Paige wasn't dumb. She noticed I wasn't coming home, and she noticed I was spending more time out of state. My plan was to disappear within the next year, but when she up and left for New York I couldn't believe it. I knew she was running back to him. As a man, that hurt my pride. I didn't care if this was real or not; she was my wife. She belonged to me. I changed the plan. I came up with the plan to fake run for DA. I wanted to milk her for everything. I was never going to take the money from her dad's policy but when I saw her look at Ace, I knew she was in love with him. We were together for a while, and she never looked at me that way. When we flew back from New York and had sex, her body felt different, and she was responding to me different. I knew she fucked him. That was just disrespectful. That's when I knew she had to die. I don't care what I did to her; it didn't give her the right to do anything to me. She didn't know how good she had it. I could have taken everything beforehand, but I was trying to spare her because of how I felt for her. I put her above the others I dealt with before. She was my good, faithful girl. She turned out to be just another bitch.

I logged on to my laptop and watched the video of her and Danielle, her assistant, again. I needed to see if I missed something. When I caught Danielle in the garage last night, she didn't want to tell me anything about Paige. She was loyal to her until I broke her. I had her confessing like she was a little Catholic schoolgirl. She said Paige only told her she needed a few days off to get herself together. She was angry with me about the way I treated her. She said Paige was going to check into the hotel and that was it. I thanked her and then slit her throat. I never liked her anyway. She was always rolling her eyes at me when I would visit Paige. I knew she was filling her head with those, *'girl you can do better'*, quotes.

I watched Paige move calmly around the room throwing crap in a few bags. I was trying to see if she was on to me if she knew anything. But from the looks of it, she didn't. She was her usual self. Packing but stopping to fuss at the same time. She bent over and I pictured me behind her just one more time. I just wanted to feel her again before I choked the life out of her. She could run but she couldn't hide forever. I called the PI I used in New York to put him on to finding her for me. Although she didn't show up there, she was bound to show up soon. I'd wait. I'd waited this long. I could wait a little longer. I had all the time in the world to play this little game of hide and seek with her. In the meantime, I was going to keep playing attorney to all these dirty ass drug dealers. They kept me busy and my pockets fat.

Chapter Thirty-One

Chapter Thirty-One

Meet Ace
Ace "Pharaoh" Mann

My mom told me don't love too hard or it would be the death of me. But if there's no Paige, there's no me. Death would be kind enough to take me.

It'd been three weeks, and I had been watching Kane, or Kentrell. My plan was to just kill him on sight, but Paige spared his life. She was still grieving Danni's death. It hurt her even more when I told her she couldn't go the funeral. I knew he would look for her there. She begged me not to shed more blood because she would only feel responsible, and she wouldn't be able to live with herself. I somewhat agreed. If he moved wrong, that agreement was going out the window. For the most part he kept to his schedule on the surface. He went to work, fucked a bitch or two and went home. This told me two things about him; he had no clue Paige was on to him, and he didn't know I was on to him. He contacted the same PI he used in New York who in turn called me to let me know he was looking for Paige. I had her write him a letter. He thought she was out of the country with City getting her head together and she would be back at the end of the month, which would be next week. These past few weeks gave me enough time to get everything in place. Ronnie had a trace on all his accounts. I knew he was busy moving money. I'm guessing he was sitting up to move on to his next victim.

I'd been having my ear to the streets just in case he had a hit out on Paige. I heard a few whispers that someone was trying to meet up with us. I had Jinx to set up a meeting between the person and King. I was doing what I did best, sitting in the shadows watching and listening. Some guy by the name of Mundy introduced himself to King and Jinx.

"Listen, I just want to say thanks for seeing me on such short notice. I was hoping I could speak with you and Ace," Mundy said.

He looked nervous and he had every right to be. When King was serious he was mean as fuck and right now, he was serious. He was stressing about staying here and missing doctor's appointments with Cola. She was calling him daily asking when he would return. He didn't think I noticed this baby situation was weighing him down. Jinx told me he was having some doubts. I didn't know if City was putting those doubts in his mind, or if he was finally realizing that Cola wasn't shit. Either way, time would reveal the truth. When it did, I would be there for him just like he was here for me.

"Ace couldn't make it. He had some business in New York," Jinx answered.

"I thought he was here in Atlanta," Mundy said looking around.

"You keeping tabs on my brother? Like Jinx said, business. What can I do for you Mundy? You said this was important," King spoke.

"I just assumed he was here. What I have to say is important. I was asking about Ace because I have information on Paige."

My ears perked up. What the fuck did he know about my Paige? I moved closer to make sure I didn't miss a word.

"Paige? I thought this was different type of meeting." King always played it cool. If you looked like you were eager for the information, the informant would use that to their advantage. If you pretended like it wasn't your concern, they would become desperate, and the information started to flow like a river.

"I know Paige and Ace have history. I figured he would want to know her life is in danger. I thought maybe that would be worth something to him."

"There is it again. You mention my brother. Jinx, he said that like he knows Ace or Paige." Jinx didn't laugh or break his stare from Mundy. "You know my brother? Or you know Paige? Which one?"

"I don't know him. But I know the reputation you both have. I know Paige in a roundabout type of way."

"Jinx, you remember Paige? I thought she was married to some attorney or something. And you don't look like the marrying type, and you don't look like an attorney."

"I'm neither one. But then again, neither is her husband. I figured Ace would want to know that Kane is not really who he claims to be."

"And what does that have to do with you?"

"I need a resolution to a problem. Again, I'm completely aware of you and Ace's reputation in the business. Up until now, I haven't had any problem with you or the people who hire you. I want to keep it that way. I see a problem arising and I need it nipped in the bud."

"I'm listening."

"Paige's marriage is a fake. Her husband isn't a real attorney. He and I were partners but like I said, he's screwing me out of my cut."

Jinx moved forward. "What you saying is, he's playing her and now he's playing you? You need us to take care of your problem."

"That's it. See this thing with Paige has gone too far and run too long. I told him to cut ties with her a long time ago, but he didn't. When I heard that Ace was her ex-boyfriend, I really wanted to wash my hands of the whole situation. I don't want no problems. I told him to end it once and for all. I told him who Ace was. What you both do. He started thinking with his ego and said he couldn't let go of her now. I think he's planning on killing her now."

"You're not prepared to take it that far."

"That was never part of the plan. I'm many things but not a killer. Like I said before, I didn't want no problems with you or him. I just want my cut."

"With the information you just laid on me, I don't know if your partner will be around to give you your cut."

"I don't need him to get it. I know where it's hidden. I just need access to it."

"And what do we get? Other than breaking Paige's heart."

"I can pay your regular fee of $200,000. But I thought Ace would like this information for free."

"That's not our fee. That's for the ones under us."

"I can get you more. I just need access to all the money."

"Sounds good because it will require more. I'll let my brother know everything. We'll get back in touch with you in a few."

"Thank you, King for taking this meeting."

Jinx stopped him. "Does it usually take this long to complete one of your jobs as you call it?"

"Not really. I think he started falling for her. But who wouldn't? She's beautiful and what she did in that bedroom, man! He was lucky. Just those piercings and tattoos alone were sexy as hell. But seeing her on that sex tape, I completely understood why he couldn't walk away."

He smiled and turned to walk away. I was moving faster than my mind could think and before I knew it, I hit him with a right to the face. It caught him off guard.

"What sex tape?"

"Wait a minute."

"Nah, no wait a minute now. You been watching him trick her for years. Let's not wait anymore. What fucking tape?" I hit him a few more times to show him I wasn't playing. I saw the blood flowing from his lip and his eye was swelling.

"He made some tapes of him and her. He showed it to a few of us a couple of times."

"Where are they?"

"I don't know." He was trying to wipe his mouth and get up. I kicked him and started hitting him again.

"Where are the fucking tapes?" I pulled out my gun and stuck it in his mouth. "Keep playing with me. You said you heard about me and King. Guess what all the shit you heard is true times ten. This could go the easy way, or I can take you somewhere and give you an on-the-job tutorial of what we do. One way or another, I will get what I need."

"They're in a safe at their home," he mumbled with the gun in his mouth.

"See, the easy way wasn't so hard. And the money? Is it there too?"

"Come on man. I need that money."

I pulled the gun out of his mouth, and I shot him in the leg. He didn't say anything, so I shoot him in the other leg. "The way I see it, by the time you get to that money someone will be wheeling you in there."

"Ok, ok, he has it spread out all over the Atlanta area and surrounding cities. All the houses have security cameras. They all have safes containing stuff we use to blackmail people."

I pointed my gun at his head and pulled the trigger. I turned and looked at King and Jinx. "Put a call in to the clean-up crew. I'll hit the team to grab him. This game ends tonight."

"They already on the way. We're ready," King said and stepped over the body toward the door, and Jinx was right behind.

"Say King, does City have any piercings?"

"Jinx, you really asking me this shit?"

"Hell, yeah. I been trying to figure out why y'all so crazy over them. But I get it now. You think Mrs. Dana got some?"

"I'm two seconds from letting Ace loose on you."

Jinx turned to me, and I just looked at him.

"Y'all so damn selfish. Keeping secrets and shit. A nigga like me wanna be crazy in love too!"

That was Jinx's way of cooling me down. Killing Mundy wasn't in the plan, but plans changed. I didn't want to go on a rampage, but I felt like it was needed. It wasn't enough he conned Paige, lowered her self-esteem, stole her money and cheated on her every chance he got. He had to humiliate her by showing a tape of her. That was my body he was showing the world. We were headed to a spot we found over the past few weeks that was quiet and perfect for what I was planning.

"Ace, don't even think about looking at any of those tapes when we get them."

"I wasn't planning on it, King. I just want them destroyed. And not a word of this to her."

"How will we know we got the right tapes?" Jinx asked.

"It doesn't matter; we destroy it all."

I received a text from Paige on the way.

Paige: It's late, are you ok?

Pharaoh: Yes, go back to sleep. I'll be there soon.

Paige: Make sure you come back to me. I love you.

Pharaoh: Always! Love you, too! Go to sleep.

I had a few members of my team watching the house. I knew she was safe. She and I had grown closer over the past few weeks. She didn't like being in the house all day, but I had a big, fenced-in yard, so she would often sit out there. She was in her head about everything. She was sad one moment and tried her best to pretend she was the okay the next moment. I hated watching her battle herself while she walked in the yard. I would watch her until I couldn't stand the distance between us anymore. I was seeing red just thinking about the hurt this man did to her. If he thought he meet Ace before, he was mistaken. He was dealing with Pharaoh but tonight, he'd meet Ace.

I walked into the spot, and I saw him tied to a chair. He looked at me and I saw his eyes grow big. "From the look in your eyes, you weren't ready to see me again. Let me make the proper introductions. This is Jinx and my brother King and me, I'm Ace."

"I know who the fuck you are. What do you want with me? If it's Paige, you can have that bitch. I'm done with her anyway."

I punched him in the face hitting his jaw, drawing blood. "Call her a bitch again. I'm a man of few words so we can keep this short. You picked the wrong one to finesse this time. You should have done what Mundy said and moved on."

"I couldn't leave her; her pussy was too good." He spit blood in my direction and smiled. "Boy, the things she and I used to do together. She was fucking amazing in bed. One of the best I ever had. I know you missed that shit."

I was seeing red, but I was going to keep my cool. I was about to enjoy every moment. I kicked the chair from under him, and he hit the ground hard. I followed up with a kick to his stomach. "Don't worry, I don't miss it anymore. She's in my bed waiting on me." I motioned for King to string him up. Sitting was too good for him. I walked over, and I opened my suitcase of tools. I was going to make sure he felt the same hurt she felt. When I turned around, he was hanging from the meat factory hook that we installed in the ceiling.

"Before you get to work Ace, I got to get a few in for City. She been wanted me to kill this nigga."

King and Jinx took turns punching and kicking him. I started selecting the first tool I wanted to use. I wanted to start with his fingernails. Then I'd work my way to his ears. I think I'd save his tongue for last because I wanted to hear every single scream that came out. I turned and watched them work. Each blow they gave him brought me great pleasure. When they were done, his eyes were barely open, and his face was unrecognizable. Now it was my turn.

It was five thirty in the morning and I was standing here watching Paige sleep. I had gotten home and taken a shower. I sat outside and smoked with King to calm ourselves. I climbed in bed with her and pulled her close to me. She smelled like vanilla and peaches tonight. I closed my eyes and her smell and the way her body felt next to mine took away all the things I did tonight. When I was done, there was nothing but a pool of blood and pieces of his skin on the floor. I cut him up and burned what was left. I made it over to the home they shared and got that safe open and destroyed the tapes before she could see them. She didn't need any more drama in her life. Usually, I would need a few days to wind myself down but tonight, all I needed was her. I felt her move.

"Pharaoh?"

"Go back to sleep."

"It's finally over?"

I didn't answer her; I just buried my face in the crook of her neck and allowed her scent to put me to sleep.

Chapter Thirty-Two

Babies, Lies and Growth

Hakeem 'King' Mann

With each heartbeat I grew more and more excited. To think, a little me. I couldn't wait to hold you in my hands. I couldn't wait to watch you grow. Just the thought of a mini me created growth in me.

I was at the doctor's office with Cola. She was about ready to bring my son into the world. I couldn't wait to see his face. I wondered if he'd look like me.

"Can we stop and get something to eat?"

"Let's grab some chicken up here." I stopped at a chicken place right up the street. Since coming back from Atlanta, I hadn't really been spending a lot of time with Cola. I wasn't spending a lot of time with City either. I was mainly working. The last time City and I were together was to go to some movie she wanted to see. It was a double date with Paige and Pharaoh. City said she didn't want to be the third wheel, hence her invitation to me. At dinner I watched Pharaoh, he was so happy. I admired my baby brother. He was younger, but he was more grounded then me. He knew exactly what he wanted. I was proud of him. He was a better man than me. He saw what he wanted, and he went out and got it. I knew us doing business together was over. He didn't need to say it. I just knew it. He was ready to settle down and start a family. I saw it written all over his face.

The next day I went and had a sit-down conversation with my pops in jail. We talked about Pharaoh and how happy he was to be back with Paige. I told him about Cola and the baby. He wasn't surprised or upset. He knew City and I were having some problems.

He just said the same thing Jinx and Pharaoh said, to get a test. He told me when I was ready to settle down, I would know. He cautioned me to not be like him. Losing the one person he truly loved chasing behind someone who got him caught up. I took his words to heart. I knew what he was saying to me. What he didn't know was I was already on it.

Sitting across from Cola, I studied her for a minute. I was trying to figure out who she was and if she could lie to me. After the situation with Paige and her marriage, everyone was suspect. She was smiling but there was something behind the smile. She was squirming in her seat. Her body language told me she was uneasy with me. "I know I haven't been around much lately, but business has been booming."

"It's cool. I get it."

"Is there a problem, Cola?"

"No, why?"

"You've been quiet. You're never quiet. I guess as the due date starts to get closer it gets real."

"King, I need to tell you something."

"Say what you need to say."

"You said it was over between you and City. I saw you two together. Well not me, but a friend sent me a photo of you and her at the movies. I know that's where you've spending all your time."

"Your friends are watching me now?"

"No. But with you disappearing for almost three months, they were looking out for me. You think you can share time with me, her and the baby. You can't."

"I wasn't planning on sharing my time with you, her and the baby. It was always gonna be the baby and her."

"I knew you didn't give a shit about me. I was just there filling a damn void for you when she wasn't here. This is my baby, not hers, and I'll be damn if she gets anywhere near it."

"IF, it's my baby, she will be there. You just got to get used to it."

"Did you just say if? Are you seriously doubting me at this point? I could have this baby any day now and now you have doubts! What gives you the right to doubt me now? Or should I say who?"

"The fact that your brother goes to every doctor's appointment I miss. Or the fact that you've been slowly moving your things out the apartment."

The look of shock on her face was priceless. She didn't think I knew. I got a call from one of the nurses at the doctor's office when I was out of town. Ace and I helped her out of a situation a few years back. When I told Cola I didn't know her, I lied. But I never tell business. She said she just thought I should know how cozy Cola and her brother looked together. As far as I knew, she didn't have any other family here except her mom. I had Ronnie pull up everything on her. She'd been lying to me this whole time. This wasn't even her first child. Her mom didn't live in the projects; she was living somewhere out of state with Cola's other child. I wanted to wrap my hands around her neck. But for the baby's sake, I didn't. Instead, I was just going to wait for her to drop the baby, get the DNA and then maybe choke her ass to death. I couldn't blame this all on her. I was trying to have my cake and eat it too, but I ended up almost losing City, and for what? Someone who was only looking for a come up.

"King, please, it's not what you think."

"Enlighten me. Tell me what it is."

"It started out as something else but the more time we spent together, the more I fell for you. I thought maybe you and I could be something, but you wouldn't leave her alone. Even when it was just us you had her picture on your phone. You would text her or she would call you and you'd spend most of our time talking with her. Even when we were fucking you would close your eyes and whisper her name. I heard it."

"I didn't mean to hurt you. But don't be fooled, you always knew what this was."

"But you did hurt me. You made me feel worthless and insecure and stupid. Running around catering to your every need. I couldn't even be myself because I was never gonna be as perfect as her."

"Like I said, Cola, I didn't mean to hurt you. I can only say if this is my child, he will be well taken care of. We both got what we wanted. You got the pleasure of being taken care of. You got a little money out of me. And I got my needs met. We equal."

"Is that how you feel? Like, that's it?"

"That's it. It's over for us."

One Week Later

I was sitting at my home watching TV. I had been inside for a few days. I didn't feel like being around the rest of the world. In the last 72 hours, everything had changed. Cola had the baby, but it wasn't my baby. I sent Jinx to make sure she was out of that damn apartment. Her baby daddy could provide for her and the child. I was done. Pharaoh offered to take her out, but I told him no. I had made my bed so now I had to lay in it. This was just as much my fault as it was hers. Although for the past few months I had been preparing myself for this moment, I still wasn't prepared. I was looking forward to having a baby, being a father. For the second time, it didn't happen. I was thinking this was my karma for all the things I'd done. All the women I'd hurt. All the people I'd killed. The sound of the doorbell broke me out of my thoughts. I went to answer it, and City was standing there. She was wearing her hair in braids today; she was dressed in some jeans and a pullover with some UGGS on her feet. It was simple but on her, it looked sophisticated. She had some bags in her hand that she pushed into my chest forcing me to grab them.

"Let me guess, you were in my neighborhood."

"Now you know I rarely come to this side of town. I hate the long ass drive. Move out the way, let me in." She brushed past me.

"Well come on in."

"I was." She walked right to the kitchen. "It's a mess in here King. Your cleaning lady on vacation?"

"Pretty much. Don't come in here judging my place."

"Well I can't cook in no dirty kitchen. Give me a few, let me clean this up."

I put the bags on the counter, and I sat back down to continue watching tv. I could hear her slamming stuff and banging pots. Then I heard music. I wasn't sure what she was doing, but it didn't matter. She was welcomed. It was too quiet in here anyway. I must have drifted off because she was tapping me on my shoulder and pushing a plate in my face.

"What's this City?"

"Just some smothered chops, mashed potatoes and corn. I know you're hungry."

I couldn't lie, everything on the plate was looking good, and I was hungry. I couldn't remember the last time I ate something. I dug right in. "This is good. I didn't even realize how hungry I was."

"Move over so I can sit down. I know it's good, my mama taught me well."

She squeezed next to me on the sofa and blew on her nails as she talked about her cooking. We sat in silence for a few minutes watching *Black Panther*. "Who told you?"

"Pharaoh. He told me you needed me. I figured the rest out on my own. You know he be tight lipped about you and your business."

"Just like that, you came."

"Yes, I know what it's like to be in a dark place. I know the feeling of not wanting to leave the house or talk to anyone. We don't have to talk about it. I can just sit here so you know you're not alone."

There it was the reason I stayed with her all these years. The reason I never walked away. I sat my plate down and noticed she had picked up everything around the room. I didn't even hear her moving around. I didn't answer her; I just took her legs and laid them across mine. I took a deep breath. We needed to talk about a lot of things. I wanted her back but this time, in a real relationship not an open one. I wouldn't block her career. Maybe it was time I started seeing the world. Not chasing her or anything, just riding with her. I wanted to tell her I wanted kids, but I didn't want to rush her. Instead of saying these things, I laid my head on her shoulder. "I love you."

"You fucking better." She took my hand and entwined her fingers with mine. "I love you too King. I always will."

We both sat back and continued watching the movie. I was ready to settle down with her. It wasn't going to be easy because she wasn't easy. She was fire. But I liked playing with fire. This right here, right now, felt good. I wanted it to continue feeling this way.

Chapter Thirty-Three

Endings and Beginnings

Paige Turner ~~Daniels~~

I reached for you in my dreams. But I don't need to dream anymore. I get to live out my dreams each time you walk through the door.

It'd been four months since the night Pharaoh came home and laid next to me and slept soundly. He hadn't had a good night's sleep any night since we had been together. But that night, he came in and went right to sleep. I knew it was over. I knew the person I knew as Kane was dead. I didn't shed not one damn tear. Nothing in me felt sorrow for him. He deserved what he got. I was glad it was over and done. I didn't need to see him any more to be reminded of my mistake. I went to the police with the information I had on Kane, well Kentrell. I said he disappeared with more than half of my money. They were currently searching for him for fraud. The people at his job were distraught to learn their golden boy was a nothing but a fake. They discovered he had stolen from them and some of their clients. He had even stolen from that slut Leslie. I guess no one was exempt from his shady ass.

I made the decision to take some time off from work. I told my boss the death of Danni and everything with Kane and I was overwhelming for me. Only half of that was true. I missed Danni; she was a great person, a good assistant and a great friend. The office was darkness to me without her there. In my mind, I knew I wasn't planning on returning. I continued to stay at Pharaoh's place until I cleared out all my stuff from my home. I donated or sold almost everything out of that place. I only kept most of my clothes and shoes. That was the only thing of value to me. Imagine after three years of building a life with him, it only took two months to make it disappear like it never happened.

I came back to New York with Pharaoh and City. She was by my side for every moment, every tear and every time I needed her. It was only right I was here to see her through the birth of King's baby. Although I watched them get closer in Atlanta, I saw the hurt in City's eyes when she realized it was all going to end the moment they stepped back in New York. She knew she would need to share him with the other woman once again. And possibly would be sharing him with the other woman and a baby. I didn't know how she would react, but I was going to be right here for her. I was so glad that didn't happen. Pharaoh completely understood and didn't pressure me to stay at his place. He was busy completing construction on a new place he was opening tonight.

I was putting the finishing touches on my make-up when City walked in and sat on the bed. "You look cute."

"Thanks girl. I was trying to find the right outfit, but I have no clue what kind of place this will be. Do you know?" She was wearing some wide-leg pants that made her legs look like they were a mile long. She had it paired with a lace top and a sports jacket over it.

"He said it was a café or bistro. I'm keeping it casual." I had a little black cocktail dress on. It stopped mid-thigh displaying a part of my tattoo and my scarred leg. Today, I wasn't self-conscious about it. It was a part of me. A part of my past I couldn't change. I was finally healed from it. I was wearing my butterfly necklace. I could finally wear it guilt free. "Is King meeting you there?"

"Yeah, he is." I noticed how she smiled when she answered.

"I see you over there cheesing. Are y'all back together again?"

"We're just taking it slow. Well he is, I'm trying to get my back blown out tonight."

"Nasty ass."

"Whatever, I want to be nasty tonight. It's been a minute. Do you know how hard it was to not sleep with him in Atlanta? We were lying in bed together and my kitty was purring and burning up for him. I had to take cold showers just to calm her ass down. But tonight, I'mma be all on that dick. Please believe it."

"Your ass about to rape that man. You do know no means no, right?"

"His ass ain't saying no. I know he wants it just as bad as me. Plus, I got on his favorite tonight, lace. He won't be able to keep his hands off me."

I gave her a high five. "Yes, you better get your man back."

"Paige after everything, you are sitting up in here glowing. I can see the love on you. But it's something else. Hold on." She hopped up and dashed out the room and came back with a box in her hand.

"What is that?"

"You know what it is. Go take a piss on it. That glow is more than love. I think you might have a little one in there."

"Now you know I can't have any kids. Me and that fool tried many times over the past few years and nothing. Thank God I dodged a bullet with that one."

"Girl, yes you did. You could have a little fake baby running around here not knowing it's real name." We both laughed. "Just take it. Whether you are or not, it's only five minutes of our lives." She handed me the box and I took it into the bathroom with me.

We both sat on the bed staring at nothing. I heard the timer go off on my phone and we both jumped. "Damn, you got me a nervous wreck in here. You look, I can't."

"Before I look, remember this is just something we did to pass time."

"No, it's something you made me do because you came in talking about me glowing. Go check it." I swear, I could choke her ass. Got me all nervous and shit.

She came out the bathroom smiling. "You 'bout to have a little Pharaoh or Paige. I'm about to be an auntie. Paige you're going to a mommy."

I didn't know what to say. I was trying to think of the last time I had a cycle. Hell, I was trying to think of when it happened. Pharaoh and I weren't using condoms. All this time, I thought I was broken. I thought the loss of the baby years ago had left my body broken. I touched my stomach and wondered how long. "I can't believe it. Do you think he'll be excited? This is a lot you know. We just got back together. I don't even know if we're together. I mean, we never discussed it. This may be too soon. What if he doesn't want kids, or me?" She placed her hand on top of mine.

"Doesn't want you? That man came to a whole different state, purchased a home there just to get closer to you. He saved your life. And you still think he doesn't want you? My little Paige Turner, you're about to be in the best chapter of your life. Throw all that doubt away and enjoy it."

She was right. He did do all those things for me. Yep, for me. This was a new chapter. It was about to be a good chapter. "You're right. A new chapter and a better one."

"Yep, let's go because I want to feed Auntie baby. He better have some good ass food at this place, like he does at Ace's."

We were standing outside Pharaoh's new place and from the outside, it looked amazing. We walked in and my mouth dropped. The place was incredible. The décor, the style, the music. It reminded me of this café I used to visit in Paris. The details were almost the same right down to the booths and tables. Did he remember? I saw him standing across the room looking like a boss. Even though this was a private event and not a regular opening night, he was on top of everything. I walked around for a minute, watching him do his thing. He was dressed in slacks and a button-down shirt. It was causal, but he made it look sexy. I watched him give orders to his staff. I saw all the things I fell in love with. His chocolate, smooth skin, that goatee that complemented his strong, handsome face, and that smile. He was everything I could want and more. I noticed a few women glancing at him, and I was jealous for a moment. He was mine and I wasn't sharing.

The night had been perfect. The food, the music, the whole ambience was perfect. I was watching City and King standing by the bar whispering in each other's ears. I knew they would survive this baby situation. They were drawn to each other, and nothing could pull them apart. They were just being tested. The lights started to dim, and the DJ stopped the music. I saw Pharaoh stand in the middle of everyone. He'd been busy all night, so we hadn't spent much time together, but he did pass by me a few times to steal some kisses. I was blushing just thinking about it.

"I'm a man of few words but tonight, I want to do something I've been wanting to do for a long time. I met a shorty a while ago, she was simply mesmerizing to me. She was a great influence on my life. I don't think she knows just how much. She let me be me and she accepted it. While we were dating, she went to France, and she told me about this beautiful café she fell in love with. It was my inspiration for this spot. See I lost her for a minute, and I wanted a place where I could go and still feel her. The whole vibe in here tonight is her. From the food to the music and the atmosphere. I walked around, and I saw everyone enjoying the food, dancing to the music and smiling. The mood is good, right? That's how she makes me feel all the time. Paige, come here for a minute."

I was sitting at the table trying to hold back tears. I got up and walked toward him. He grabbed my hands, hugged and kissed me.

"Paige, thank you for coming back into my life. I never want to be without you again." He got down on one knee and pulled out a ring box. "Will you marry me?"

My hands flew up to mouth in shock. I didn't see this coming. "Yes!" He sled the ring on my finger, and we embraced again. He whispered in my ear, '*I love you!*' "I love you too Pharaoh. This is unbelievable. The café, this ring, you! You're full of surprises."

"Always, you have to expect the unexpected with me, future Mrs. Mann."

"Well, you're not the only one full of surprises. I'm glad you asked me to marry you. I wouldn't want to have this baby out of wedlock." The expression on his face was one of shock. He looked at me and then placed his hand on my belly. His arms were around me again and he lifted me up and placed a kiss on my belly. City and King came over to congratulate us. I felt full on life.

"I'm so excited baby. Do you know how far along you are?"

"No, I just took the test right before coming here. Do you think this is moving too fast? Are you ready to be a dad? I mean, I don't want to rush anything."

"Shorty, you still doubt me. No, we not rushing anything. If it was up to me, we'd be on our third or fourth child by now. I'm ready to be a dad and a husband."

"Good, because that fake marriage shit wasn't working for me." We both laughed.

"There's nothing fake about this right here."

I felt his hardness against me and needed to feel him inside me. I glanced around the room and people were no longer watching us. I grabbed his hand and headed toward the restroom. I looked back and caught City's eyes. I saw her mouth '*nasty ass.*' I shrugged my shoulders and continued to walk. I felt free and I felt loved. My life had been changed for the better.

Epilogue

2 years later

It was an average Sunday. Pharaoh and I were grilling at the house. Well, he was grilling, I was sitting on the side of our indoor pool with my feet in the water relaxing. I was big, pregnant and lazy as hell. I was ready to pop this baby out of me. I was fat, my feet were swollen, and I couldn't fit any of my clothes. I wasn't complaining because I was enjoying carrying this baby. Every moment, every minute brought me joy just like carrying little AP Jr. did. Speaking of my baby boy, he was sitting on top of King's shoulders in the pool, looking just like his dad. I was hoping my baby girl would look like me. After all, it was me doing all the work.

City came over to join me, bouncing little Kingdom and little Knight. City had two miscarriages before she finally had a successful pregnancy. Imagine her surprise when it was twins. The losses only made her, and King grow closer. Kingdom was so beautiful just like City. She was fussing trying to grab for King. She had him wrapped around her tiny finger. She was going to give them hell once she started walking. I could tell she liked being the center of attention just like her mom and dad. King came right over to get her. She was a daddy's girl for sure. Little Knight was quiet and was a mama's boy, so he was laying on her chest smiling.

Little AP Jr. was now standing behind a chair just watching his dad grill. He was a mini stalker like his dad. He ran over and wrapped his arms around Pharaoh's leg. It warmed my heart watching them together. He mimicked his dad every chance he got. Pharaoh picked him up and told him something then kissed him on the cheek. He came running over by me and hugged me then rubbed my belly and kissed it. He turned, looked at his dad, nodded and gave him a thumbs up. Those two had their own language.

I heard my tee Dana and Jinx walking in, fussing as usual. They'd been having an on again, off again relationship for a while now. She moved to New York after my mom passed last year in jail. I wish she could have gotten to meet my kids. But she was finally free. I was getting a little misty just thinking of it and I felt AP Jr. kiss my cheek.

I looked around and smiled at my family. When I felt Pharaoh's arms wrap around me, I realized how truly blessed I was. None of us were perfect. Neither were our relationships, but we kept trying. We kept loving each other. We kept moving forward.

"What are you over here thinking about Mrs. Mann?"

"Thinking I'm ready for this baby to get out my belly."

"My baby girl will be here soon enough."

"You know this is the last one." He kissed my cheek, then my lips and ran his fingers through my hair. "Well, maybe one more. But my boss won't keep giving maternity leave you know." I worked for him and King, doing the books for all their businesses. I knew Pharaoh was done in the streets, but I didn't know about King. I knew he and City traveled together when she did photoshoots away. But lately, she'd been focused on the kids. She took pictures of them in various parts of the city, and it was the cutest thing.

"As much money as you make me, yes I will. You know I'll do anything for you Mrs. Paige Mann."

"You better, Mr. Ace Pharaoh Mann. Now feed us Daddy." I smiled. My life wasn't perfect, we had our ups and downs, but I was finally loved exactly how I wanted to be loved, and I was free to be me. I guess that's what happens *when a boss loves you.*

About the Author

Nola Jewels, is a New Orleans native who currently resides in Georgia. Growing up in New Orleans, reading became an escape from the reality surrounding her. A love of reading lead to her developing a passion for writing short stories, poetry and works of fiction. Writing and developing her own stories became not only an outlet but a gift. A gift that has grown into an amazing ability to create unique, Urban Tales. Her ability to fill her stories with drama, twisted with romance and suspense, topped with erotica creates a perfect gumbo that leaves readers filled up and wanting more. Nola plans to continue writing and sharing her gift of sensual, loving, honest and unapologetic stories.

Stay in contact:

TikTok: AuthorNolaJewels - https://TikTok.com/authornolajewels
Facebook: Nola Jewels - https://www.facebook.com/nola.jewels.35
IG: Nolajewels_author - https://instagram.com/nolajewels_author
Good Reads: Nola Jewels -
https://www.goodreads.com/author/show/18825874.Nola_Jewels
Amazon Author Page: https://www.amazon.com/~/e/B087TLCS2X

More books by Nola Jewels

A Savage Set My Soul On Fire 1-2
CEO And Hustlers Business Matters 1-2

Available on Paperback via Amazon
E-book Amazon Kindle and Amazon Kindle Unlimited

The Black Agreement – Coming 2025